IGNATIUS
AND
THE SWORDS OF NOSTAW

IGNATIUS
AND
THE SWORDS OF NOSTAW

BOOK 1 OF THE IGNATIUS SERIES

D. A. MUCCI

ST BARTS
PUBLISHING

ACKNOWLEDGEMENTS

Finishing this book would have not been possible without the encouragement of my wife, Jeanne, whose positive feedback and unconditional support helped me persevere to the end of the writing process. I cannot express the thanks and love I have for her patience with me as I wrote, and the multiple times she read and reread the manuscript while providing frank feedback all along the way. And then she led the effort to coordinate website development, illustration, and publicity. That is true love.

Theodora Bryant from Book Editing Associates was the best developmental editor I could have asked for. She could always understand what I was thinking but struggling to put down on paper. Her guidance on writing and plot structure was invaluable, always urging me to put a bit more into the story, making it richer and deeper.

To my focus group crew: Ben, Elisa, Edith, John, Barbara, Pat, Gary, Tammy, Jacques, Ed, Nina, Carl, Grace, Julie, John, Laurie, Joe, TJ, Huong, Tom, Lorie, Alyson, Dave. Thank you all for your feedback on elements of the book.

Note to Reader

Want to know what some of the creatures and castles in this story look like as imagined by the author? View the QR code at the beginning of some chapters using the camera app on your smartphone. A link will pop up that takes you to an illustration of a creature or castle introduced in the upcoming chapter. These illustrations, as well as a color interactive map, can also be found on www.DAMucci.com.

Ignatius and The Swords of Noslaw

1

The towering stone Castle Maol, the unrivaled seat of power in the Kingdom of Skye, sat inland almost bereft of life.

Once known for its inspirational beauty, Skye's forests and meadows were more barren than green now, enveloped by stillness instead of bustling wildlife. Lakes and waterways once teeming with marine life lay stagnant. Most of those who lived here survived under gray clouds of despair.

Several of the eldest knew of the prophecy that would return the land to its prior golden age and quietly hoped it was true.

Only a handful knew the secret that would allow the prophecy to come true. They refused to speak of it.

G etting up off the dirt floor of his prison cell deep in the bowels of Castle Maol, Kylian shuffled his feet forward to the far wall and picked up a small piece of stone. The ear-piercing sound it made as he scratched another line into the stone wall had once made him wince. But after so many years, the intensity of it now filled his ears and invigorated him, as it broke up his mundane routine of prison life.

With no sunlight to guide him, only his internal clock informed him another day had begun. He stared at the wall vaguely visible with light from the stairs above. If it could stare back, it would see a man, once carrying hard-toned muscles on his body, now reduced to skeletal frailty. The clothes on his back, the same ones he wore the day he was thrown in there, were blackened with grime and hung loosely on him. His deep-green eyes, though sunken from malnourishment, still held the spark of fire that rested in his soul, a spark that years of confinement had not extinguished.

Looking at the wall, he counted the lines and nodded.

"That makes fourteen years, as of today. Ah, my brother, your time is running short. It will begin soon."

Footsteps approached. A guard stopped at his iron-barred cell door, stared at him for a moment, then opened it. "The emperor demands your presence."

"The emperor," Kylian said in a quiet, raspy whisper. "My, my, my, so now he calls himself the emperor. Will wonders never cease? How far will that twit of a brother of mine go to stroke his ego? Lead on, ye guard of the emperor."

The climb up the steps was long and hard for Kylian. Malnourishment had long ago robbed him of much of his strength. Nonetheless, he took one step after another and kept his head held high, hiding his delight at soon seeing the light of day once again. It had been at least twelve years since he was last out of the depths of the castle.

The guard unlocked and swung open a heavy barred iron gate at the top of the steps. It led into a walled corridor that kept those enjoying a stroll in the lavish courtyard from viewing the wretched prisoners being dragged to the dungeon.

With a sigh, Kylian turned left to go down the corridor.

The guard grabbed his arm. "Today we take the shorter route." He led him to a small door embedded in the corridor wall.

Sunlight streamed in and splashed across Kylian's face when the door swung open. Kylian instinctively shut his eyes. "One moment, please. I have to let my eyes adjust to the light."

The guard, who had always been kind to Kylian, did not object.

Kylian stood in the doorway, eyes shut, and let the sun wash over his body. As the warmth uplifted his body and soul, his mind went to another time in this place years ago. This courtyard was the special visitors' entrance to the mighty Castle Maol, three hundred feet long by one hundred feet wide. Dignitaries entering had always been delighted with its lush flowers and closely cropped green grass. Kylian and his friends had run and played here in their younger years. Men and ladies of the court strolled the length, entertained by jesters who served at the pleasure of the king. These thoughts brought a smile to his face.

Kylian finally opened his eyes and stifled a gasp as the shocking view of the courtyard came into focus. It was now just dirt and clumps of dead brown grass.

Kylian turned to the guard. "Does it not rain here anymore?"

"It rains."

"Then why does nothing grow here?"

"Too much evil in this place for anything to grow." The guard tugged Kylian's arm. "We have to go now."

Eventually, Kylian and the guard made it to the once-lavish dining hall at the southwest end of the castle. A banquet table intricately carved with artful designs had stood there in a bygone era at the center of a room big enough to seat twenty people on each side. It had been replaced by a bland wooden table that sat four on either side.

Once elegant, this grand dining room only whispered of the regal effect it had once had. The lustrous walls and intricate floor patterns that had adorned it were now dulled with grime.

Kylian shook his head, saddened by the dining hall's decline. "This is not much better than my cell," he said softly.

Fifteen feet beyond the table's end was an open archway that led to an open-air veranda showcasing the aerial view of Lake Peduncular, one of the deepest and widest lakes in the Kingdom of Skye. The lake was surrounded by ancient oak trees. The grandeur of the view was diminished by water the color of acorns produced by trees.

On the veranda stood a figure with his back to Kylian.

Kylian stopped and looked around in mock marvel, shaking his head. In his strained voice, he said, "Ah, Mallak, my brother... or emperor... or whatever you want to be called. I see you have really let the place go since you killed the king and queen," Barely audibly, he added, "along with your pregnant wife."

Kylian stood for a moment in the dining room and ran his fingers through his long matted white hair intertwined with his salt-and-pepper beard. "I guess I should attempt to look more presentable for you." The sarcasm dripped off his words; nonetheless, they fell on deaf ears as Mallak remained on the veranda, his back to him.

A warm, putrid breeze rose off the lifeless lake below and wafted through the tall arched dining room windows designed for two abreast to enjoy the view. The threadbare curtains stirred slightly, weighed down by layers of mildew.

Mallak turned around and walked into the dining room. He was a cruel-looking man, his narrow black eyes devoid of any kindness. He had a twisted hooked nose and thick, straight black hair hanging down to just below the middle of his back. His broad-shouldered build and wide stance contrasted starkly with his weak chin and pockmarked skin. He wore a robe adorned with bizarre swirling patterns that glowed with pulsating violet and silver sparks of energy shooting through the cloth. His walk was jerky and quick, matching his speech pattern.

He pointed to the table in the center of the room. "Sit."

Kylian shuffled over to the middle of the banquet table. The aroma of the food sent a shiver through Kylian. After seating himself, he reached for the bowl of lamb in the center of the table, took two pieces, and placed them on his plate. Next, he scooped up some potatoes and green peas with the palm of his filthy hands and dropped them onto his plate. Last, he filled his glass with dark-red wine. Raising the glass with a shaky hand, he swirled the wine around and took a mouthful.

"I assume you didn't bring me here to poison me. So, I will enjoy your hospitality."

"Why are you so sure?"

"Because you are my brother. You would not have wasted this good wine and food just to kill me. Shall we eat?" Kylian didn't hesitate to use his grimy hands to fill his mouth with lamb; he quickly chewed and swallowed it, then as quickly took another mouthful. He wanted to maximize his intake, not knowing how long his brother would let him eat.

"So, Brother, after so many years of keeping me locked away, with only one other visit… what was it—twelve years ago? Which, I am happy to remind you, did not go very well for you. Why have you sent for me?" Kylian kept eating while he waited for a reply. He was so thin, he could almost feel the food course through him.

"I demand you pledge fealty to me." Mallak stared at Kylian, whose return gaze didn't waver.

Kylian swallowed his food and after calmly wiping his mouth with his cloth napkin said, "No. Same answer as twelve years ago."

"Your arrogance, Brother, keeps you in that cell." Mallak filled his own plate. "Fourteen years in a cell, and you have learned nothing."

"Ah, my brother," Kylian whispered, "don't think I have languished in that cell. Like you, I have developed my own powers these past years. Oh, I cannot control people—if controlling them through fear is real control—or manipulate objects spawned by the powers of your magic robe, but I have gained the power of knowledge. And that is much more powerful than your black magic."

"So, tell me what you think you know," Mallak demanded as he shoved a piece of meat into his mouth and chewed.

Kylian took a sip of wine to wash down his own mouthful of food. He again savored the sensation of good food and drink—the taste, the smell of it. He paused before answering. "You don't have long until the curse that hangs over your head is fulfilled, and that terrifies you. I still have not been able to figure out what you were thinking when you killed our father's mage. What *were* you thinking? Did you forget how powerful his magic was?"

Kylian smirked at Mallak. "Oh, I can understand killing Mother and Father so you could ascend to the throne. But did you really think the mage would go so gently? That he would not put a curse on you with his last dying breath? What was it he said? Oh, yes… he said, 'In your son's eighteenth year, he and his three brothers will rise up and smite you.' Your time is winding down."

Mallak stared at Kylian for a moment before he spoke with a chuckle. "I have no sons."

Kylian met Mallak's stare and smirk with his own. "So you say. Yes, you killed your pregnant wife and all your bastard sons. Then why are you so afraid?"

Kylian was met with a silent, deadly stare.

He shrugged his shoulders and went on. "About your powers—I know you've raised a Death Knight who's pledged fealty to you. Although, you question how strong that fealty bond is, and that terrifies you." Kylian looked around the hall, then sadly stared out the open window for a moment. "I know the landscape now lies barren and structures are crumbling—like this castle. Our people of the kingdom have either moved elsewhere or are withering like their farms and gardens. I know there is a powerful energy in this land you cannot control. And, lastly, I know you doubt your powers. Yes, a lot of the power of that magical robe you wear can be transferred to you, but you are concerned you cannot always control the robe's magic successfully. You are foolish and do not understand why. All of this terrifies you."

"Enough!" Mallak screeched, jumping out of his seat, his mood and demeanor suddenly turning dark and dangerous. "*Guards*! Take this miserable excuse of a brother back to his cell!"

Mallak turned his back on Kylian, then just as quickly turned back. "I would have thought after fourteen years you would show me the respect I deserve. Since that obviously isn't the case, you can languish back in that cell. You say the curse is coming soon? Well, I will see you in another twelve years! And we will see who is terrified then. I do not fear this curse; I do not fear *any*thing." He spun away from Kylian and strode out onto the veranda.

"Oh, I think you will be seeing me a lot sooner than that," Kylian said in a quiet voice as he slipped some food under his worn clothes. He then stood and allowed himself to be led away by the guard.

2

The air hung thick and hot over the suburban town of Susquehanna, Pennsylvania. What little breeze there was wafted a hint of sulfur through the town, emitted from mountainous piles of cast-off coal surrounding the area from long-abandoned coal mines that once fueled the Industrial Revolution. The hot, sticky breezeless day had rolled into another night of uncomfortable, fitful sleep for those who lived in this downcast area.

Air-conditioning was a luxury that most residents in this once thriving coal-mining town had to live without. So nearly all the windows on the endless row of houses were propped open.

Ignatius—who preferred being called Iggy and his brother, John, struggled to sleep on the second floor of their nondescript home indistinguishable from every other house on the street. The air hung heavy in the room despite the open window. The heat was trapped inside, which raised the temperature and mugginess in the small bedroom to an almost unbearable level.

Iggy lay on his bed, struggling for comfort on top of the sheets. He was young-looking for his age. Just fifteen, he was uncoordinated and clumsy, and could pass for twelve with his small frame. He had a shy manner and rarely made eye contact with anyone, not helped by a constant downward gaze and a curtain of dirty-blond hair that prevented people from seeing his sensitive, gentle smile, or his deep brown eyes—eyes that resembled tiger's-eye stone that turned more golden as the light and his mood changed.

Iggy rolled over and stared at John, who, after tossing and turning and despite the heat, had finally drifted off to sleep. Everything Iggy was not, his brother John was: sixteen years old, athletic but wiry, tightly cropped brown hair. To the dismay and envy of the other boys in John's class, the girls liked him. John had learned long ago that if you smiled and made eye contact with them, they would respond to you. When he walked, he carried his five-foot, ten inches' frame with confidence and he wasn't shy about flashing his deep-green eyes and magnetic smile.

In time, sleep finally came to Iggy too. He dreamed he was standing in a dark corner at the end of an outdoor patio. As Iggy looked around, he saw that the patio overlooked dirty lake water about thirty feet below that lapped against the base of a sheer stone cliff. On each side of this patio, there were castle walls, their majesty diminished by a layer of soot clinging to the stone.

An array of twenty soldiers stood around the perimeter of the patio. Iggy could just see the other end of the veranda as he peered between two of those soldiers to decipher what they were guarding. The soldiers were fierce and solemn. Though, on closer inspection, Iggy thought they were nervous, maybe scared.

A tall man with his chin held abnormally high and arms crossed stood at the center of the veranda, staring down his twisted, hooked nose at everyone. His expression vacillated between anger and delight. His long unbrushed black hair fell onto a knee-length robe hanging loosely around his shoulders. The robe had a life of its own as it fed off the wearer's emotions with pulsating violet swirls and chaotic silver sparks that shot across the back. Every now and then the man would tug at the collar of the robe, pulling it back in place onto his shoulders. At first, it looked like he was just readjusting it, but after several tugs, Iggy believed he was afraid the robe would fall off and into the dirt.

A prisoner standing erect with pride stood in front of the robed man, hands tied and feet chained. He was speaking.

"So, Mallak, this is what you have come to," the man said.

His voice was filled with disdain as he practically spit the words at the swirling colors on Mallak's cloak. The man towered a full head above Mallak, his intent eyes never blinking or wavering. His eyes bored so steadily into Mallak's that Iggy wondered if he was delving into his thoughts, reading his mind.

Iggy wasn't sure how but he knew that "Rielick" was the speaker's name.

Rielick seemed to Iggy to be half human and half god with his fair, smooth skin and golden eyes. Just looking at him calmed Iggy's anxiety, which confused him. Why did he feel such a sense of well-being staring at Rielick but fear when looking at Mallak? Then Iggy saw it: there was a fine golden aura that shimmered around Rielick, soothing him; the darkness permeating Mallak had the opposite effect.

Five paces behind Rielick stood three figures who gave Iggy the chills. They stood, equidistant, one leg forward, the other in back, their swords in hand ready to thrust, if necessary. They differed from the guards on the veranda: taller, their armor darker and shinier. The expressions on their faces were focused and hardened as they stared unwavering at the prisoner. They exuded fierceness.

A fourth person stood closer to Rielick. He reminded Iggy of a medieval knight from his history books. He was tall, with broad shoulders covered with tarnished, rusted armor. A black cape flowed down his back, and a blood-red hood covered his head. Iggy was horror-stuck when this knight turned sideways. The red hood hid the dried dead flesh that clung to his skeletal face and eyes that were black but somehow glowed as if there was a lit candle deep inside his eye sockets. The odor was horrific, the wretched smell the essence of death. Iggy almost gagged at the fetid wafts of air.

Iggy was startled by the olfactory sensations and his gagging reaction. Then he reassured himself: *I'm in a dream. I'm safe.*

Mallak walked to Rielick, clearly in a rage, and looked him up and down. He held out his hand, palm open. One guard near him placed a sword in it. Mallak had to quickly use both hands to grasp it, but even this wasn't enough to keep the sword aloft. This was like no sword Iggy had seen before. It was obviously heavy and made of metal of a deep, burnished red hue, with edges that looked razor-sharp.

Mallak finally stated, "So, Rielick, you see you could not outrun me forever. I caught you."

"You did not catch me. I gave myself up. Unlike you, my race deeply values the lives of the innocent. I could have escaped, but I took to heart your threat to kill all those in the village if I did." Rielick continued to stand tall, his voice unwavering.

"Your foolish conviction. That was your downfall," Mallak said with a smirk.

"And your arrogance will be yours. You think you have rid yourself of the Wiate race. You have not; we have gone into deep hiding. You will never be rid of us."

Mallak looked down at his hands. "A fine blade. But I will make it invincible. Celestine blood flows through your veins. Why? I am not sure. There is nothing magical, nothing godlike, nothing special about you and those of your race. Nonetheless, if just one drop of your species' blood touches this blade, think of the power the sword would have. And who holds it."

"There is much more to it than you can comprehend. The power of my race comes from our goodness, from our willingness to place the needs of others over our own. Something you will never understand. Yes, as a Wiate I have Celestine blood coursing through my veins. Some like yourself would call it magical. But its power is nothing compared to the collective power Wiates wield by working in concert to help one another and others.

"You have your sights set on an invincible, magical sword. Be forewarned: spilling my blood will curse you from ever using it, and it will not save you from the future, from *your* future. From the prophecy that hangs over your head. For in his eighteenth year, your son and his three brothers will rise and smite you with that sword."

Mallak looked puzzled. "Rielick, have you lost your power? Can you not see the future? I have no sons. My pregnant wife died. So did my mother and father, fourteen years ago. I lit their funeral pyres."

"Yes. And from what I hear, you were the one who personally killed them, along with the king's mage. You were cursed from that moment on."

"Enough of this!" Mallak's robe glowed and pulsated, transferring power to him. Now with the strength he needed, Mallak lifted the sword and took a mighty swing with the blade.

Iggy's eyes widened, and he trembled as he watched Rielick's head come cleanly off and roll across the floor. Iggy stood frozen, unable to look away but not wanting to watch the vivid gore exploding in front of him. He focused by force of will on the sword as it moved through the arc of its swing; halfway through its curved trajectory it changed into a blazing hot torch. Iggy watched as it scorched Mallak's hands, who released it.

The momentum of the sizzling blade carried it upward behind Mallak toward the vestibule opening, spinning end over end. Gravity took hold, and the sword's weight dropped it straight down, blade first onto the patio, melting the stone it landed on until half the sword's length disappeared into the molten hole it created. In moments, the glow subsided, returning the fiery blade to its normal reddish hue. The liquid stone around quickly hardened, engulfing the blade.

Mallak, doubled over in pain from the burns on his hands, yelled, "Get me that sword!"

One of the many guards who stood on the periphery ran over to do his bidding, but the moment he touched the handle, the blade turned fiery red and hot once more, and he jumped back, yelling in pain as the burning sword branded a scar on his palm.

"The sword is cursed!" he yelled, backing away in fear and pain.

Iggy's heart pounded in his chest, watching all this.

Suddenly, Mallak looked up, eyes red with rage as they drilled into Iggy, who was instantly blinded in a hot flash of yellow.

Iggy fell, his hands grasping at the dirt in the dark corner of the stone floor where he had been standing.

∽

A high-pitched scream poured out of Iggy's open mouth as he bolted upright to a sitting position in his bed.

"Iggy? Are you okay?" John rolled over in his bed, staring at him.

Sweat poured down Iggy's face as he tried to control his breathing. After a deep breath, he nodded. "Yeah, I guess so," he said, a tremor in his voice. "I just... had a bad dream. It was hot, and there was a blinding light in my face. I couldn't see."

"Look at your pillow. The sun's on it. That was the heat and blinding light you saw." John glanced at the clock. Realizing it was time to get up for school he hopped out of bed.

Ignatius sat on the edge of his bed, still shaken, fists clenched tight. When he opened them, dirt poured onto the floor. He stared at his filthy palms and the small scattering of dirt at his feet. *What the heck?*

What kind of dream was that?

Iggy shivered, thinking, he *had* been dreaming, hadn't he?

3

Iggy sat at the edge of his bed, dazed. He wanted to show John the dirt but hesitated. What would he say? "Hey, John, come look at the dirt in my hands. It's from someplace in my dreams"? John would think he'd lost his mind.

Iggy looked at the dirt again. It was senseless.

John bounced around the hot room, preparing for the day, whistling, mind already miles ahead, his thoughts elsewhere.

No, Iggy would keep this to himself. This was his secret to somehow figure out. He sighed and shivered. The room was hot; he was freezing cold.

John put a hand on his shoulder. "Hey, you're awake now; forget the dream." John studied him. "I don't know, Iggy; I worry about you sometimes. You've been having some nasty dreams lately. What's going on? You okay?"

"Yeah, I'm okay. Don't know why all my dreams have been so strange."

"So, maybe you can remember them and write a cool story for your English class."

Iggy looked up at John and shook his head, touching the dirt on his hands and wondering how it got there. "It's like my dreams are warning me." Maybe he was losing his grip.

"Listen, it's most likely nerves about starting high school. Which, I remind you, is today. Let's get some breakfast and start our first day of the school year with a bang. See you downstairs." John took one last look at his reflection in the mirror. "I call the bathroom first." He bolted out the door and into the hall bathroom.

Iggy stayed at the edge of the bed for the next minute, alone in thought. He got up, looked at the dirt on the floor, and shook his head. He walked across the braided throw rug that covered the old wide-planked wooden floor to his dresser and rubbed the sleep out of his eyes with the back of his hands and looked in the mirror at his reflection.

His typically deep-brown eyes had that golden glow this morning. *Geez, could I possibly look weirder on my first day of high school?* He ran his fingers through his mess of hair and scrunched up the part that had gotten flat from sleeping. He had to let it grow long because kids kept teasing him about his bushy eyebrows, which stood out several shades darker than his hair against his fair skin.

He flexed his muscles and chuckled as he examined his biceps. "Bigger than last year. Look out, John, maybe my growth spurt has started."

The first day of high school. This should be interesting.

He grabbed a blue shirt and pulled it over his head, messing his hair up again, just in time to hear the toilet flush and the door open down the hallway. His turn.

He picked up a necklace on the dresser; it was a simple silver chain with a locket attached to it. The outside had a stone that flickered with a kaleidoscope of colors ranging from yellow to bright blue and a vibrant red, depending on the angle of the light. Kids teased him, telling him he wore a girl's necklace. Some even called him *Girly Iggy*, but Iggy's most valuable possession was inside that locket—a picture of him and his mom—so he paid them no attention.

She was killed in a car accident a year after the picture was taken; Iggy had survived it. He never knew his father. Nor had his mother ever talked about him. It had always just been him and his mother.

His mother's best friend, Gwen, not wanting him to be sent to a foster home, had taken him in and raised him as her own. Aunt Gwen had passed the locket on to him. She said it was his mother's and that she'd always worn it around her neck, and she was sure his mother would have wanted him to have it.

Iggy loved Gwen but didn't want to call her "Mom," so they'd settled on Aunt Gwen. Gwen's son, John, though, was and always would be his brother; there was more to brotherhood than having the same parents.

Iggy thought back to the day he'd been wandering around downtown and stopped in a jewelry store. He asked the man behind the counter to look at the stone. The man examined it with a magnifying glass attached to his glasses. He spun it this way and that way. He twisted it in every conceivable angle, shaking his head. After twenty minutes he returned it to Iggy, who was surprised when the jeweler told him he had no idea what kind of stone it was. It was radiant with a rainbow of colors and alive with moving patterns when he looked at it with his jeweler's loop. It had the hardness of a diamond and it reflected light without refracting it like the clearest glass, but they both knew it wasn't either of those things.

Iggy snapped the locket shut and dropped it around his neck. The moment it touched his chest the crystal sparkled, giving off intense warmth that penetrated throughout his body. Shocked and scared, he jerked the locket off his skin, only to have his hand grow warm. It wasn't hot or burning, just warm, which gave him an unexpected feeling of fullness and content. He had never felt anything like it, but just as quickly as the warmth had started, it stopped.

Iggy stared at the necklace wide-eyed, thinking he had imagined the moment. Slowly, he let it fall back against his chest, hoping to experience that radiating warmth once more, but this time he felt nothing except the coolness of the metal and stone.

This is one strange morning.

Breakfast smelled of bacon and eggs, and he heard chatter from Aunt Gwen; she was asking John how he thought their first day would go.

Iggy was also curious how it would go as he entered the kitchen and sat.

"Iggy, first day of high school. You ready for it?" she asked, placing a plate of bacon and eggs, arranged like a smiley face, in front of him.

Iggy chuckled, and Aunt Gwen smiled and gave him a wink. Aunt Gwen believed a morning should start with a family-style breakfast. On the weekends, she insisted they eat dinner together at the table. "You never know," she'd say, "if this is your last meal as a family. Only God knows what's around the next corner."

"Remember the first impression is the one the teachers will carry of you for the entire year."

"Yeah, and so will the girls," John said.

"Oh, John."

"He's got to start out on the right foot. If the girls think he's a wimp, then he'll never get a date, and he'll be a target for the other guys to pick on him," proclaimed the wisdom-laden sixteen-year-old.

"Iggy will do just fine with the girls—and his friends." She poured Iggy more orange juice. "He's far ahead of most high school seniors in science and physics. He should be teaching the classes not taking them. And he speaks three languages fluently. He has a gift. His classmates will envy him."

"Hardly, Mom. With envy, comes a whoopin'. People won't get why he learns languages so easily. I've never understood it either." John stared at Iggy.

"I don't know. I just kind of map it out in my mind and remember it."

"You're weird, you know."

"Yeah, I know."

"Enough, you two. Eat up and get to school. You don't want to be late."

⤲

Heading toward the high school, John asked, "You ready for this, bro? You let yourself get pushed around or bullied, that'll be your destiny. For *all* of high school—you know that, right?" He threw his arm around Iggy and gave him a noogie. Iggy shoved him away with both hands.

"There you go." John laughed. "You've taken your first step to standing up for yourself."

"The thing is, most of the time, it's easier for me to find a clever way to walk away."

"My feeling is hit and get hit back. Short-term pain but long-term gain. It's been working for me."

Iggy winced as John continued teasing him about the horrors that awaited. Two blocks from school, Iggy's best friend, Leonard, joined them. Leonard was only a couple of inches taller than Iggy, but his weight was easily double.

"*Hola*, Iggy, *qwue pasa?*" Leonard asked. He walked with a bounce to his step. "*Hola*, John."

"It's qué pasa, not qwue pasa. There's no w in qué," Iggy said.

"You sure?"

"Positive."

"You're doubting the language genius? Leonard, you have big ones." John snickered.

"I guess you're right. Anyway, Iggy, you ready for the first day of high school? This should be fun."

"We'll see," Iggy said. "I've been warned: 'don't get pushed around.'"

"I'm not worried," Leonard said.

"Given your size, they'd need a bulldozer to push you around," John chimed in lightheartedly.

"Why do you think I bulked up over the summer? For my health?" Leonard laughed and flexed both arms.

"Leonard, I worry about you too. You *and* Iggy. Don't you get tired of being teased about your weight?"

Leonard gave a big smile that showed off his pearly-white teeth and allowed his deep-blue eyes to shine below his wavy dark hair. "How can anyone give this face a hard time? If they do…" He shrugged. "Anyway, it's a lot easier to ignore the jerks that tease you. But the bullies, well, that's another story. Kids our age can be so mean. Why do you think our little buddy here is so mild-mannered?"

"Let's just say I try and I try. Iggy's still a work in progress. Been tryin' to get him to toughen up for years."

"Hey, you two know I'm here and can hear you," Iggy said indignantly. "I am not mild-mannered. I just avoid the bullies. Trust me, underneath this façade you call mild-mannered is a mind always planning and scheming."

"I hope you put your master plan into action before we're both old and walking with canes." Leonard laughed.

John saw some of his friends across the street. "Hey, I'm gonna join them. Listen, Iggy, I'm serious. If you get pushed around today, it'll follow you 'til you graduate. Stand up for yourself and give a little back to them."

John trotted across the street. Leonard gave Iggy a light pat on the back. "You'll do okay. Just remember, you won the summer physics science fair."

"Thanks."

"You are my little genius friend."

When they got a block from school, the number of kids increased with every step. Most everyone lived within walking distance. As Iggy and Leonard got close, they stopped. They stood in front of the two-story brick building with a long semicircle driveway and a small asphalt parking lot. Utilitarian cement steps led to double-wide metal doors and an overhead marquee. Big, bright letters announced, "First Day of School!"

Iggy stopped and took a breath. "Okay, let's do this." He straightened his shoulders and followed Leonard through the front door.

As they entered, teachers instructed ninth graders to go to the right, into the auditorium. When Iggy and Leonard picked their seats, they made sure they weren't up front where the suck-ups sat, not in the back where the bad kids sat, and not dead center where all the popular kids sat. They finally settled on the left side aisle, where the others sat. Iggy scanned the room, careful not to make eye contact with anyone for too long.

Leonard elbowed Iggy in the side. "Look! There's Sandy."

Iggy stared at her as she walked down the aisle and took her spot in the center. His heart fluttered in his chest as it had every time he saw her since the second grade. He'd recognized her pure beauty even back then. Kids said her family were descendants of the Comanche Indian tribe. She had a complexion that the summer sun brought to its fullness, and she had strong shoulders from being a gymnast.

Unfortunately, no one told him in second grade how to win a girl's heart was not to pin her against the side of the school building, kiss her, and tell her how much he loved her and wanted to marry her. All that got Iggy was a fat lip and a black eye from her older brother, who promised that if he ever saw him even talking to Sandy again, he'd break every bone in his body.

The threat worked then and continued to work today. Sandy was off limits. He had yet to say hello to her again, smile at her, or even make eye contact with her since that fateful day.

After the obligatory speeches by the principal and staff, the freshmen were dismissed to their homerooms. As everyone filed out, Iggy mistakenly stepped into the aisle in front of the popular crowd as they passed by. Suddenly he fell back into a seat as a football player shoulder-butted him.

"Gee, did you want to go first?" The football player sneered.

Looking up, Iggy caught a smirk on Sandy's face as she passed.

"Iggy!" Leonard exclaimed. "What were you thinking? That was no way to stay"—he waved his hands in front of his face— "invisible."

"I know. My mind was elsewhere."

"Yeah, your mind was on Sandy. Why don't you just say hello and talk to her?"

"I tried that once. It didn't go well."

"So, for the entire time in high school you're gonna stare at her from across the room and drool?"

"Yep, something like that. Let's get to homeroom before we're late."

~§~

Iggy's homeroom and his first two classes were uneventful. Third period English class proved to be a game changer. The teacher, Ms. Hanson, assigned the seats. This relieved some of Iggy's anxiety of having to pick who he'd sit next to.

Ms. Hanson was a severe-looking older woman with deep-set wrinkles. Today, she wore a polyester knit dress emblazoned with a floral print of multicolor daisies that Iggy swore he had once seen as wallpaper, sporting buttons from neck to knees, surely fashionable decades ago. Her bifocal glasses were either perched on the end of her nose or hanging around her neck on a pearl rhinestone-bedazzled chain. Despite her petite, frail stature, she was a no-nonsense woman.

"Julie," Ms. Hanson started, "you will not be passing any notes back and forth in this classroom. Sam, if you ignore me when I am talking, you will be staring at the wall in the corner. All of you, listen up." She paused and looked around the room. "You may think you are new to me as well as to this school. Let me inform you I have spoken with your middle school teachers about each and every one of you. There is nothing you can do to surprise me. You get out of line with me and you will be dealt with. It is my way or the highway. Those who don't listen will be given detention. Lastly, you will have homework every night that you will turn in at the start of the next class, and there will be daily five-minute quizzes."

Iggy glanced around the room. Most students had fear written all over their faces. But Iggy was relaxed and felt safe. With Ms. Hanson as the teacher, he could let his guard down and enjoy learning in the class without being hassled by those around him.

A girl sat to his left he'd never seen before. Not a surprise. With two middle schools in town, half of the students would be new to him. A momentary glance revealed a haughty-looking girl with a hint of mischief in her eyes and shoulder-length brown hair. This made for an attractive view as he pretended to glance out the window.

What Iggy hadn't expected was that the next time he casually glanced her way, she had strategically repositioned her chair toward him. His eyes widened as she slowly widened her legs, giving him a direct line of sight at her white cotton panties. Flushed hot with total embarrassment, he quickly faced forward. Over the remainder of the class, every time he turned to look out the window, she flashed him. After what seemed to have been the longest, slowest class hour in the history of classes, the bell rang.

Leaving her seat, she turned and smiled at Iggy, saying, "See you tomorrow."

"I look forward to it," Iggy retorted, surprised he'd said that aloud.

She strutted out of the room with a smirk on her face.

Iggy walked out of English class with a smile on his face and his mind preoccupied. Thus, he was not watching where he was going. He walked directly in front of Sandy and bumped into her, sending her books flying to the floor. Before he could recover, a football player pushed him out of the way to come to Sandy's rescue, picking up her books and carrying them for her as they made their way down the hallway.

Iggy made a dispirited trek to the lunchroom, found Leonard, and sat at an empty cafeteria table, unpacking his brown paper bag.

"Hey, bro, how's your day going?" Leonard asked jovially.

"Well, it's going."

"Whoa! Bad start?"

"Yes and no. My first day of high school is only half over, and so far, I've been flashed by a girl for the sole purpose of embarrassing me.

But that worked out much better for me than her. I at least got to enjoy the view. Then, on my way out of class, I made an idiot of myself on an epic level."

"What you're saying is you're having a normal Iggy day?"

Iggy smiled and laughed. "I guess you're right. It has been a normal start to the school year for me. Hard to tell what's going to happen next."

"I'm what's gonna happen next," a voice said from behind him.

Iggy turned to find Tyson standing over him. Tyson was Iggy's age but eight inches taller and easily thirty pounds heavier.

Tyson swaggered closer, sporting black hair slicked back with an attitude that just screamed "Pick a fight!" He stepped forward and leaned into Iggy's personal space, staring down at him. "I understand," Tyson said menacingly, "that you spent your English class staring up my girl's dress."

Iggy reflexively stood and stepped back from Tyson. Leonard looked on wide-eyed in disbelief as Iggy shook his head and exhaled with a heavy sigh.

"Well, you see, actually, that's not true."

"Are you calling my girl a liar?" Tyson matched Iggy's backward step with a forward step, staying in his face.

"No."

"Then you admit you were staring up her dress."

Iggy crinkled up his face and pondered for a moment. "Well, I guess, not exactly. You see, every time I turned her way, she'd open up her legs."

"You calling my girl a slut?"

"More of an exhibitionist."

"You saying she let you look up her dress on purpose?" Tyson barked with saliva spewing just past Iggy's face.

"Uhm. Yeah."

"So, you are calling her a slut?" Tyson finished.

"No."

"But I am," John said from behind Tyson.

Tyson snapped around; his fists clenched. "No one calls my girl a slut!"

He stepped forward, swinging wildly with his right hand to land a blow, but before his fist was halfway around, he tripped over Iggy's foot that had been quickly and strategically placed. As Tyson fell forward, Leonard jumped out of his chair, which slid it into Tyson's path. Tyson smashed into the chair face-first with a cracking sound, instantly drawing blood from his nose.

Tyson let out a yelp and fell to one knee, cupping his bleeding nose. "I tink you broke by dose!"

"I didn't break it; your own clumsiness did. Better head to the nurse and see about that nose. And tell your girlfriend to keep her filthy legs closed." John grabbed Tyson by the shoulder and dragged him to his feet. "Go on, now."

Tyson scurried away. The cafeteria—dead quiet just a moment ago—started up with the buzz of excited conversation.

"You okay, Iggy?"

"Yeah." Iggy did his best to ignore all the necks craning their way.

"Nice footwork."

"I thought you'd appreciate it. Simple physics. Gravity wins all the time."

"Wow. Kind of aggressive of you. What's gotten into you?"

"Just taking to heart your pep talks."

"But don't get yourself killed in the first week of high school. I gotta ask, were you really looking up her dress?"

"Every time I looked toward her, she purposely opened up her legs and showed me her crotch. Maybe she wanted to bait Tyson into starting a fight. I don't know."

John slapped Iggy on the back. "Sweet, I could think of worse ways to spend my English class." He laughed. "Stay out of trouble, you two," he added, turning and walking away.

Iggy looked at Leonard. "Thanks, bro."

"Great minds think alike. Once he fell, I planned to sit on him for you. But you had it under control. And the chair. Actually, that wasn't planned. It just ended there… in his path."

"Yeah, right, Leonard. Let's eat."

⊱

Later that day, Leonard was in high spirits as he and Iggy walked home from school.

"I had a good day today. My teachers were nice. The kids that sit around me are decent. And I even talked with a few girls," Leonard said. "I think the foundation I set bodes well for how the rest of the year will go."

"It was one day, and in high school, circumstances can change fast." Then he told Leonard about running into Sandy. Literally.

Leonard couldn't stop laughing. "You have to get over your fear of her. Just start talking to her."

"Not in this world or lifetime."

"I hate to break it to you, but this is the only world there is, and this is the only life you have."

Thinking of his nightmares, Iggy mumbled, "Thank God for that."

4

Iggy entered school the next day wondering what this day would bring. He was again exposed to panties this time, pink, in English class. Tyson's girlfriend was obviously trying to get a reaction out of him, wanting to make him feel uncomfortable. In a decisive move he turned the tables. He turned pointedly in her direction and stared at her eyes, refusing to look down, with a "Look, I can do this all day" expression on his face.

After a minute, she looked confused and, faltering, turned away, crossing her legs. Iggy plastered a wide grin on his face: Victorious! Though he mused that he would miss the view.

Between classes, Leonard strode up to Iggy in a flurry of agitation. "Hey, Iggy! You and John are in deep shit." Leonard's eyes were wide. "I heard Tyson's brother, Wayne, is really pissed. He blames you for breaking Tyson's nose. You know, Wayne, the leader of the local bully-boys."

Iggy squinted at Leonard. "Bully-boys?"

"Yeah. You know—they're not a full-on gang that, like, sell drugs. They're just bullies. And they're boys. So, bully-boys. Anyway, the word is that after school today he intends to give you and John a little payback."

As he spoke, Iggy saw John at the end of the hallway. He flagged him over and relayed the news.

John stood and thought for a moment. "Okay, Iggy, listen to me. First, you know I won't let anything happen to you. And second, if you let them scare you, then they've already won. Just meet me after school, and we'll walk home together."

"I thought you had football practice," Iggy said.

"I did, but I forgot to have Mom sign the football permission form. I can't practice until I get it turned in." John smiled at Iggy. "Relax. Even if they show up, you think I'm just gonna stand there and let them hit you? Most of the time they win by intimidation. No one hits back because they're too scared. One good punch in the nose, and they'll run."

"But there may be a lot of them." He felt his newfound boldness dwindling fast.

"I have friends too, Iggy. I have friends too."

Much too soon for Iggy's liking, the final school bell rang. Iggy and Leonard met John at his locker, and together they walked out one of the side doors.

"I heard they're gonna jump us in the field at the end of the path," John said, looking untroubled.

"So why are we going that way?" Iggy asked, bewildered.

John put his hand on Iggy's shoulder. "You should never run from bullies, Iggy. I have some friends meeting us there to make sure it's a fair fight."

"No fight is fair to me if I'm the one getting hit."

John kept walking, his hand resting on Iggy's shoulder. Iggy couldn't tell if this was to give him some peace of mind or to make sure he didn't turn and run away. They walked down the path. When they rounded the bend, Iggy stopped. There were at least thirty kids from all the grades clustered on one side of the field. His heart sank when he saw that one of them was Sandy.

Tyson stood on the other side of the field, his nose taped, along with his brother, Wayne, and eight of Wayne's crew. They stood there opening and closing their fists.

Iggy's knees weakened, and he faltered.

John felt the hesitation and squeezed Iggy's shoulder tighter. "It will be all right, Iggy. Today you take the first step in changing your reputation."

"Yeah, I'm gonna change it from alive to dead."

Leonard stopped on the edge of the field. "I think I'll watch from here." He veered off to observe from a safe distance.

John and Iggy walked onto the field and stopped.

"Wayne." John addressed the greasy-haired, pasty-faced boy standing next to Tyson who wore a dirty red sleeveless shirt and old worn jeans that hung well below his waist. "What happens now?"

Wayne walked across the field and stopped in front of John. "Let me 'splain to you what we gonna do. You broke my brother's nose, so I should do the same to your brother."

He looked at Iggy, whose eyes were wide with fear.

John smiled. "First, the word is 'explain,' not '*splain.*' Second, that's not happening while I'm here."

Wayne shook his head. "I see you brought some of your friends."

"That's right," John said.

"Well, they gonna go against my boys?"

John looked around. All Wayne's gang members pulled a hand out of their pocket in unison and flicked their wrists locking their switch-blades in place.

Iggy stared at the shiny metal. Without a second thought, without waiting for John's slick reply, he ran, that flash enough to fully activate his flight response. He was small, but he could run fast. He'd had a lot of practice growing up. Before Wayne or any of his gang members could react, Iggy was past them and down the path leading away from the school.

His lungs burned from his sprint, his heart pounded, and weirdly there was intense heat coming from the locket. His chest felt on fire, and the glow coming from the necklace blinded him. Then, suddenly, a kaleidoscope of color shot out of it and enveloped him.

Iggy didn't stop to wonder about the blinding light. He just kept running.

He rounded the next bend, thinking, *Wayne's gang must be way far behind.* With his arms pumping and his legs churning, he was suddenly lifted off the ground by an iron grip. A hand clamped over his mouth. In one swift motion, he was dropped face down on his belly in a deft maneuver. Then he felt someone on top of him, pinning him down.

"Shh," came a soft whisper in his ear. "Don't move, don't make a sound or we, too, will die. Do you understand?"

Iggy tried in vain to spin his head around. He couldn't see his attacker; the hold on him was fierce, though the man wasn't hurting him. Meanwhile, his pendant burned against his chest. He did his best to nod from beneath the man's grip to show he understood. Although, he didn't understand what "we, too, will die" meant.

While Iggy lay there pinned and perplexed, this man's strength comforted him. Iggy finally gave him a nod, then felt the pressure on his head ease up some. He moved his head slightly and looked ahead, and what he saw in the field in front of him terrified him far more than Wayne's gang members and their knives.

5

Camouflaged by bushes and underbrush, Iggy stared out over an open field.

A creature lay there on its back, at least seven feet long. Its feet had five digits with webbing between the middle three toes, which ended in curved claws. The upper appendages had human hands. Its bulldog head had dark-red eyes and menacing fangs. Loose shaggy doglike fur covered its legs and upper torso. Dark-brown feathers covered the remainder of its body. The creature lay motionless on its back, except it rocked slightly from side to side, its mouth opening and closing to inhale and fill its lungs, which Iggy could tell it was having difficulty doing.

Standing over this dog-bird creature was something even more frightening. Iggy stared at what he instantly named a "zombie soldier" because it reminded him of a character in a video game he'd once played. It stood erect on two legs. The cloth that covered its legs was old tattered loose strings of thread that vaguely resembled pants, dangling from mid-thigh downward. The flesh covering the legs were black leathery ribbons stretched over exposed bone. Its torso was covered with a

worn leather vest with rusted chain mail. Its chin and face consisted of exposed blackened bone with strips of dried flesh hanging off in thin strips. Its head was covered with an old open-faced soldier's helmet that exposed unblinking eyes that were solid black with a glow from deep inside.

Those eyes! Iggy realized they were the eyes of that putrid-smelling creature in his dream.

On its hands were rusted, cracked armor-plated gloves that exposed near-skeleton fingers. It gripped a sword tightly in its right hand.

Iggy stared at the sword and shivered. The hilt was made of wrapped deep-red leather with a similar wrap on the handguard separating the hand grip from the blade. The blade itself was of a deep-black metal that pulsed with different shades of blackness. The sword's razor-fine edge ended with a serrated tip dripping with fresh blood.

Iggy watched the zombie soldier kneel and place its left hand on the chest of the dog-bird creature. Instantly, the creature opened its mouth, and a horrible screech bellowed from the depths of its being. A moment later, the spasm and the screech stopped, and the dog-bird creature lay motionless.

The zombie soldier stood and paused for a moment, pondering something. It turned its whole body and stared directly at Iggy.

Iggy opened his eyes so wide with fright he thought they'd pop out of their sockets. The hand tightened over his mouth.

The zombie soldier stood still for a long time. Then it turned, mounted a satin-black horse that waited twenty feet away, and with a light flick of the reins rode off.

The horse was at least twenty hands high, and each stride carried its rider four times farther than any horse Iggy had ever seen run. The zombie soldier traversed the long wide-open meadow and quickly disappeared over a knoll.

The hand clamped over Iggy's mouth relaxed and pulled away. The crushing weight that had pinned him released him. Iggy lay there motionless for a moment, fearing what he would see. Childishly, he hoped that if he just stayed still, the person would leave him as he muttered to himself, "Wake up. Wake up. This is just a bad dream."

Finally, Iggy risked a look up. Standing over him was a tall man with broad shoulders and soft blue eyes framed by flowing red hair. He wore a tan woven pullover shirt with pants the same color that stopped mid-calf. A strap wrapped over his left shoulder with a handle protruding from an attached sheath that Iggy assumed was the top of a sharp knife.

To Iggy's dismay, as the figure looming over him drew it from its sheath and held it ready to strike, he realized it was an exceptionally long knife.

"Who and what are you? Tell me before I slay you."

Terrified, Iggy sputtered, "I'm-I'm Iggy."

"What is an Iggy?" He lifted the long knife.

"Me, I'm Iggy! That's my name! Please don't kill me!"

"Are you a sorcerer? Speak!"

"*No!*" Iggy screamed. "I'm just Iggy! I'm just a boy!"

After a long pause, the man lowered the knife. "You are clearly not a sorcerer, for you would have attempted to defend yourself. I do not know who or what you are, but one quick move, and it will be your last."

Tears ran down Iggy's face. "Please, don't kill me! I'm just a fifteen-year-old boy." Iggy rolled over and vomited. When he stopped, he rolled into a fetal position and whimpered.

The man reached his hand down to Iggy, and with great hesitation, Iggy grasped hold of it and was effortlessly hoisted to his feet. Iggy stood there frozen with only his eyes moving. They darted from left to right, then focused on the creature left in the field.

"Wh-what was th-that thing that rode off?"

"That was a rumor I fear is now true."

"Okay... but what was it?"

"It was death. Walking death. A Death Knight."

Iggy nodded as if that made sense. At least it aligned with his zombie soldier impression. Iggy pointed to the dog-bird creature. "And what is that?"

"That is a Nostaw. By his size, he looks to be a young Nostaw. Which is very strange. They have never been known to venture this far south from Cambria, their homeland." The stranger looked Iggy over from the top down with distrust. "You are a strange-looking boy. What is that you are wearing?"

"A Polo shirt."

"And that?"

"Jeans."

He pointed to Iggy's feet.

"Converse."

"Who are you?"

"My name is Lecque."

"Lac... Lacue?"

"That is correct. And who are you?"

"Ignatius. But everyone calls me Iggy."

Lecque turned and motioned they were going into the field toward the Nostaw. "You walk in front of me. One wrong move and you will see the tip of my blade coming out of your chest."

Iggy's head snapped in fright. "You want me to go with you to that thing?"

"Yes."

"I-I don't think so. I'll, um, just go back the way I came." Iggy turned and, before the man could stop him, bolted. He sprinted back up the path, rounded the bend, expecting to see John in full-blown combat with Tyson and his gang but stopped dead in his tracks.

In front of him wasn't the school field. Instead, he stared over a massive meadow that stretched before him at least a mile running into a forest's edge at the far side. No one was there, just the rustle of a gentle breeze through the knee-high grass.

Iggy opened his mouth, but no sound came out except his gasping, shallow breathing. He bent over, hands on his knees, trying to slow his breathing, to think, but he could process none of this. He sprinted back to Lecque. The man needed to explain this to him—to give him answers.

He stopped behind the brush where they'd hidden, as close as Iggy dared be to the danger zone. Lecque was kneeling to talk to the Nostaw.

"Is it dead?" Iggy called out.

Lecque looked up. "Nostaws are a race of mighty warriors. Even this one, who is young and on his quest to become a full-fledged warrior, is mightier than you will ever hope to be. You must show him respect for who he is and humble yourself for what you are not. He is not an *it*. He is a Nostaw." Lecque's voice was filled with acid. "And, no, he is not dead. Not yet, though I fear his wounds are beyond anything I can help with. Stand over there where I can see you."

Iggy moved a trembling step from behind the bushes. "Why was that dead thing able to kill him if he's such a mighty warrior?"

"A Death Knight can kill anything it wants to."

With obvious difficulty, the Nostaw turned his head and gazed upon Iggy, his eyes centering on the amulet that had fallen out from under Iggy's shirt, which was dangling freely around his neck.

In that moment, the amulet glowed.

The Nostaw turned to Lecque and motioned him to come closer. Iggy quickly tucked the amulet back under his shirt and watched from his safe distance as Lecque bent down and placed his ear next to the Nostaw's mouth. Lecque jerked back and shook his head with disbelief. The Nostaw reached up and grabbed Lecque, pulling him closer, and spoke to him again.

Lecque nodded slowly and stood. He turned to Iggy. "Come here."

"Er, I don't think so," Iggy said, shaking his head vehemently.

Lecque walked over to Iggy and grabbed him by his arm. "That was not a request, you little whit packer." He dragged Iggy to the Nostaw and pressed down on his shoulders with both hands. "Kneel!"

Iggy collapsed to his knees, so close he could hear the Nostaw's raspy breathing, surprised by the creature's sweet orange scent, subtle and comforting. *A dangerous creature*, he thought, *would not smell so nice.* As their eyes met, Iggy knew he was staring into the eyes of a dying creature.

"Are you sure?" Lecque asked, looking at the Nostaw.

The Nostaw nodded to Lecque.

"Bow your head," Lecque said, disgust in his voice.

"What?"

Without answering, Lecque grabbed Iggy's head with one hand and bent it forward, pushing his chin into his chest until he was only inches from the Nostaw's mouth.

Iggy tried to struggle but could not move. Lecque's grip on him was too tight, too strong. Out of the corner of his eye, he saw the Nostaw slowly lift its head. Its fangs were pointed and sharp and now only a hair's breadth from his face.

Iggy whimpered and moaned, "Nooo! Please!" A tip of one fang touched his ear. Iggy froze, catatonic with fear, not knowing if this ungodly creature would crush his skull with one mighty bite or puncture it with its fangs and suck out his brain.

But there was no pain when he felt a fine movement of the creature's mouth. Then from far away he heard the humming of a song, a gentle song that grew louder in his head. It wasn't long, and it repeated. Mesmerized, the song filled his mind, and he followed the tune and flowed with it. Iggy relaxed, and his breathing returned to normal.

The song stopped, replaced by a soft but strong voice that came from the creature. "That is my song," the Nostaw intoned, its voice soothing, "which is now our song. Keep it safely in your heart. You will know when to use it. It will keep you safe. I am Tilead, a Nostaw Warrior. Through this Blinak Ritual, I pass my rights on to you. You are now Tilead. Become what I was and not what I am now."

"I-I don't understand. I would like to go home," Iggy whimpered.

The Nostaw took in a slow breath before continuing in a raspy whisper, "When I was younger, I was taught that you must finish your journey before you can find your way home. My journey is over. But I am blessed. My journey will not end with me here. I have passed it on to you. By completing it, you can find your way home."

"B-but why me? Why not him?" Iggy glanced at Lecque.

"Our lore tells us of your arrival."

"My arrival? What lore? I don't know what you're talking about."

"I have seen in you what others have already, but you have not. It shines near your heart."

"What does that mean?"

"That is also part of your journey. My elders did not tell me what my journey was. I had to find it on my own. So must you. I can give you a pathway, but you must find that path."

"Wh-what do I have to do?"

"You must take my swords and bond them with your heart and soul, then with Liquid Fire. The swords must taste the Liquid Fire. Only then will they and you be elevated to warrior status."

"Then can I go home?"

"That is a question I am too young to answer."

"I just want to go home."

The Nostaw's mouth pulled away from Iggy. With quick movements, its hands produced two highly polished, curved short swords that ended in a hilt that started with a figure-of-eight guard and a grip inlaid with gold and silver. The Nostaw encircled them around Iggy's neck, one at the back, the other in front, so they formed a complete oval.

Iggy could only imagine how close they were to his neck, but he couldn't feel either cutting his skin.

The Nostaw pulled them away from Iggy's neck and spun them so the handles faced Iggy.

Iggy stared at the blades, unmoving, unblinking, scared to move.

A deep guttural voice rolled out of the Nostaw. "Take them." The tone made it clear Iggy had no choice.

Slowly Iggy raised his hands and grasped the handle of each blade. In the instant that Iggy and the Nostaw both had their hands wrapped around the hilts, the blades glowed purple. In that moment, Iggy felt a gentle warmth radiating from the hilts into his palms and rolling up his arms into his chest. Then the blades returned to their metal sheen.

"It is done" were the Nostaw's last words before releasing his hold on the blades and falling back to the ground where he exhaled one last long breath and died.

Lecque released his grip on Iggy's shoulders, and an instant later Iggy jumped up, taking three steps back. He paced, mumbling, "No, no, no, no, no! This isn't real!" He stopped and faced Lecque. "What just happened?"

"That's what I would like to know. This makes no sense. The Nostaw just performed the Blinak Ritual on you. He made you a Nostaw Warrior."

"No, he said I had to finish his quest to become a Nostaw Warrior. B-but, I can turn it down, right? I mean, this is some kind of mistake. I need to get out of here, to get home. John's waiting; he'll be mad because I ran away."

Lecque shook his head. "Stop talking! Shite! You do not understand. He passed his *soul* to you. Never in history that I've ever heard of has a Nostaw Warrior passed his soul to anyone other than the worthiest Nostaw. He gave you his sacred swords. I do not understand any of this. Are you a powerful wizard that has fooled that Nostaw Warrior instead of a sniveling coward? It is confounding to me. But know this: I do not trust or believe anything you have told me. Give me a reason, any reason, and I will dispatch your head to the dirt. Do you understand me?"

Iggy backed away from the angry stranger then looked at the swords in his hands. "Here." He held them out to Lecque. "You want them? You can have them. I don't want any of this."

In a quick burst of anger, Lecque grabbed Iggy by the throat. "Listen, you worthless coward. I do not know why, but that Nostaw bestowed his greatest honor on you. When a Nostaw Warrior dies, he either lets his soul die or performs the Blinak Ritual. He only does so if he is with someone strong and worthy. He did not pick me! He picked you! When you accepted those swords, you accepted that responsibility. If the swords are not passed on, they fuse to the Nostaw's hands, impossible to remove. A Nostaw will die protecting those swords. If the receiver of the swords willfully gives them up, all Nostaws are bound to hunt down and kill the traitorous receiver. If you ever disrespect those swords or the Blinak Ritual, I promise you I will kill you before any Nostaw gets close enough." Lecque shook his head in disgust. "You clearly are not a wizard. You are nothing but a witless child of no courage."

Lecque released his grip on Iggy and walked back to the tall brush. He led out a beautiful chestnut horse and climbed into the saddle. He walked the horse over to Iggy and reached out a hand. "Get on."

Iggy hesitated. He looked around. "Where are we going?"

"Nilewood. That is where I live."

"Where are we?"

"Did someone hit you on the head? We are in Skye, the Kingdom of Skye. Now, are you getting on? Or am I leaving you here?"

Iggy cautiously held the swords with one hand and took Lecque's outstretched hand with the other. Lecque effortlessly pulled him up behind the saddle. Iggy sat dazed, one hand cradling the swords in his lap, the other wrapped tightly around Lecque's rope belt as they galloped across the field.

Neither spoke.

⚶

Iggy's thoughts were a jumble of back and forth between the terror he felt as he knelt before that creature called a Nostaw and the fear he felt on the field surrounded by Tyson and his gang. One was the fear of the known: Tyson and his gang would beat him up, and it would hurt. The other was the sheer terror of the unknown. What did that Nostaw want him to do? Where am I? Where is this guy taking me? What is Liquid Fire?

Lecque mused over what a Nostaw was doing this far south; they never came this far south. Was he on a quest to become a full-fledged warrior? But why here? And the Death Knight. He had just seen the monster that children hear of in ghost tales from the village storytellers. What he saw was no myth or legend. And who was this strange child who called himself Iggy? Is he the weak coward he presents himself to be? Or is he a clever, deadly magician who needs to have a sword run through him?

After twenty minutes of galloping across the meadows, Lecque slowed the horse to a lope. Iggy shifted back and forth as best he could. His buttocks ached from the bouncing, and his inner thighs burned and were chafed from rubbing against the saddle. Still shaken from what they had seen, Iggy stayed silent, withdrawn into his own world of insecurity and fear. Occasionally, he looked up and glanced around at the rolling green meadows. But mostly he stared down at the two curved swords in his left hand.

As they continued the lope, Iggy tried multiple different positions attempting to ease the pain he was enduring. He finally tensed his legs, finding the rubbing in the saddle was less, but the burn in his thigh muscles was worse. After another twenty to thirty minutes of torture, Iggy tapped Lecque on the back. "You need to slow down. I can't hang on like this much longer."

Lecque slowed the horse to a walk. "What is wrong?"

"My butt is broken, and the skin on my thighs is rubbed raw."

"What is a butt?"

"It's what you sit on."

Lecque pulled on the reins and brought the horse to a stop. "You mean your sit-bone. Get off!"

"What?"

"Get off now!"

Lecque reached around, grabbed Iggy by the arm, and pulled him off the horse. He then dismounted himself. For a moment Lecque scratched his head then turned to Iggy standing there, eyes wide with concern.

"I need answers from you or I will leave you here."

His stare alone intimated Iggy, whose shoulders sank with dismay.

"Where are you from?"

"I-I am from Susquehanna."

"I do not know of any place in the Kingdom of Skye by that name."

"I never heard of any place on Earth called the Kingdom of Skye either. I've never ridden a horse to go anywhere or seen a Nostaw. And I don't want to see another one. Lastly, I'd really like you to take me home."

"Tell me how you arrived back there. Your strange clothes. How have you survived out here alone? You have no supplies. I have many questions."

"I have a lot of questions too." Iggy looked him straight in the eyes and sighed. "I don't know how I got here. I was being chased. There was a hot feeling in my chest, then flashing, blinding lights. The next thing I know, you grabbed me."

"Who was chasing you?"

"I was at school and Wayne's gang was chasing me right before you grabbed me."

"There was no one else there. You are not making sense. Do you think I am a fool?"

"No! No, it doesn't make any sense to me either. I just want to go home." Iggy broke eye contact and looked around at the wide-open fields. Had he been hit on the head? Was he unconscious back in the field with Wayne's gang hovering over him? Was this a dream?

"Tell me why the Nostaw Warrior gave you his swords."

"How would I know? I don't know anything about these swords. I don't know how I got here. I don't even know where *here* is! Please, you have to believe me."

"How old are you?"

"I just turned fifteen."

"You are quite small for fifteen. Not what I would expect from a Nostaw Warrior."

"I am *not* a Nostaw Warrior. I'm just a teenager."

"A teenager? Is that the name for a wizard in that land you come from?"

"No." Iggy's frustration and insecurity were increasing exponentially. "I'm just fifteen, and I want to go home! And my butt aches and my legs are on fire from sitting on that horse!"

Lecque shook his head and muttered to himself, "A smart wizard, a great actor, or a simple whit packer. Which one are you?"

Without saying another word, Lecque climbed back into the saddle. After a moment's hesitation he extended his arm to Iggy and pulled him back up, where Iggy settled behind him. Lecque reached down and adjusted the stirrups.

"Place your feet into these. It will stop you from bouncing so much."

Iggy slid his feet into the stirrups and instantly felt more secure. "Thank you. Back there you said we were going to a place called Nilewood. How far of a ride?"

"Two days."

"My ass is going to ache after that long a ride."

"What is an ass?"

"Your sit-bone."

"Butt, ass. Just call it a sit-bone."

Iggy tried not to groan.

Lecque let the horse walk for the next half hour. Then after three hours of intervals of galloping and walking breaks to rest the horse, Lecque slowed the animal. "I think we are far enough away from danger to let the horse walk until we reach the Fairy Pool."

"I thought you said it was two days."

"Two days to Nilewood. The Fairy Pool is midway."

Iggy sighed and didn't respond. Instead, he watched the countryside go slowly by. Never had he seen such a diverse landscape. To his right, a field of low grass spread before him for miles, only to be dwarfed by a towering range of mountains that ascended into the sky, reaching an unimaginable height. This mountain range was unique to Iggy. Nowhere on its slopes did he see any growth of plant life; there were no trees or greenery, only sheer rock pushed from ground level straight up into the skies. The entire range comprised unforgiving sharp, jagged black stone. A cloudy mist swirled around the peaks, some hidden from view.

Lecque sensed Iggy staring at the mountain range and finally broke their silence. "Those are the Black Cairn Mountains."

"They're enormous."

"They are. They run north to south over fifty leagues."

Iggy wrinkled his eyebrows. "How long is a league?"

"A league is how far a man can walk in one hour. What kind of a place do you come from where you do not know what a league is? What did you call that place again?"

"Susquehanna, Pennsylvania." Iggy gazed at the monstrous black mountains off in the distance again. "So, what's on the other side of the mountains?"

"The land of dark shadows. It is where Scathach lives."

"What's a Scathach?" Iggy asked, wondering if he wanted to know.

"Scathach is not a what but a who. To be exact, she is the most powerful warrior ever to live. It is impossible to get over the Cairns, so, to get around them, you have to travel through the Valley of the Fog." Lecque paused, waiting for a response from Iggy. None came, so he continued. "No one has ever made it through the Valley of the Fog. Or, if they have, they have not returned to tell about it."

"Why?"

"It is said that, if one was able to get through the valley, it is doubtful they would make it to Scathach's fortress. So, the only other way is to scale the Cairns, and no one has ever done that, either. It is said her fortress sits on top of a sheer smooth cliff, as smooth as glass and also unclimbable. At the top of the cliff is Scathach's fortress, guarded by an immense dog that will devour all who approach without Scathach's permission."

Iggy said, "Saying this is all true, though no one has ever made it over the Cairns or up that sheer cliff to verify it, why would anyone want to go through all that trouble to get to Scathach's fortress?"

"She will train anyone who makes it to her fortress to become an unbeatable warrior. For she is unbeatable herself."

They rode on in a slow walk for some time after that, again in silence, each having doubts about the other.

Iggy occasionally stared at the forbidding black cliffs thinking about this Scathach warrior that lived on the other side, hoping he never had a reason to go looking for her.

6

The sun was hanging low on the horizon when Lecque pulled to a stop and dismounted. "We will walk from here to where we will camp so the horse can cool down. Stay alert for danger."

Iggy slid clumsily out of the saddle and fell to the ground awkwardly, holding on tightly to the swords, trying not to drop them. He stood and looked around with great concern. "I hope you don't mean that the creature, the Death Knight, will return."

"No. This area is mostly safe. But after what happened to the Nostaw, we should be cautious."

"Wow, that really makes me feel safe," Iggy mumbled. As they walked, Iggy purposely walked a half pace behind Lecque.

"You should walk next to me," Lecque said. "That way I can keep an eye on you."

"No, that's okay."

"What does okay mean? I have not heard this word," Lecque asked.

"Okay, uh, well, it means different things. 'Okay' means I agree with you. 'I'm okay' means I am fine. 'That's okay' can mean 'I don't think so.'"

Lecque stopped walking and stared at Iggy. "So, you were twisting words to say you do not trust me?"

"No! I only meant it makes me feel better to know that whatever happens will happen to the first in line, and that's you. I learned a long time ago never to volunteer to go first. That can be painful."

Lecque scowled. "You little whit packer. That answer is not any better. Sard it all. Once again, I say get up here. I want you walking where I can see you."

Reluctantly Iggy moved up beside him.

They walked through a small stand of trees. Five minutes later they exited into a rolling meadow. The stark Black Cairns mountain range towered into the clouds in the distance, with no visual end to its lofty reach. They rose without foothills, which highlighted their enormous scale. It appeared as if a hand had pushed them straight up the way a wall looks when placed on flat land. Their sheerness would defy anyone who gave thought to climbing them.

Iggy turned his attention to the land before him. There were clumps of wild herbs in the tall meadow grass that released a sweet aroma as the horse plodded alongside. These scents the horse kicked up into the air triggered a memory. He stopped and stared blankly ahead thinking of a time when he and Aunt Gwen were baking in the kitchen.

"Iggy," Aunt Gwen said, laughing, *"you're getting more flour on you and the floor than into the mixing bowl."* John walked into the kitchen. *"Iggy, you look like a snowman."*

"Hey!" Lecque whispered, "Why did you stop? Did you hear or see something?" Lecque had his hand on the hilt of his sword.

"My aunt Gwen and my brother, John—they'll be worried about me. You have to help me get back to them."

"We are out in the middle of nowhere. I do not even know how you got here. So I have no idea how to get you back there. Unless you are going to turn around and start walking back to Suck Your Hanna Pencil Place on your own, you are stuck with me. Or, more accurately, I am stuck with you."

"I wonder who would know how to help me get home." Iggy's voice trailed off as he looked down at his feet.

"Up here. I want you walking next to me, where I can see you." Lecque waited until Iggy was beside him before he started off again.

They stopped on top of the next rise. It overlooked a small rolling valley. Looking off in the distance, Iggy saw a sheer cliff with several cascading waterfalls pouring its transparent elixir into another pool below. An expansive rolling meadow of green peat sat above the falls that extended to the base of the Black Cairn Mountains at least a mile away. The valley's floor below them had a pool of water that Iggy guessed was as big as a baseball field, filled by a meandering stream. The water danced with colors of topaz and fire red, intermixed with multiple shades of green and blue. At first Iggy thought the water was colored. But as they rode closer, he realized it was the most crystal clear he had ever seen, and the colors came from the rocks lining its bottom.

They rode down an incline until they were level with the pool. Lecque dismounted, and Iggy slid down. "We will stop here and spend the night." Lecque released his horse; it trotted to the edge of the pool to drink.

Their camp was set up in a short time. There wasn't much for Iggy to do other than collect firewood. He let Lecque do most of the scavenging; he stuck close to the camp area trying to sort things out in his mind.

Lecque started to build a fire. "Unless one of us stays awake to feed the fire, it will go out. You will get cold before the sun comes up."

Iggy, who had been sitting on the ground, got up. "Let me do this." He pulled the wood that Lecque had piled up for the fire and placed it off to one side. Lecque stood back without saying a word, a look of cautious curiosity in his eyes.

Iggy gathered several bowling-ball-sized rocks and piled them in the center of where the fire was to be. Then he placed the firewood over them.

"Now you can light the fire."

"What is this? I do not understand the rocks."

"As the fire burns, the rocks will absorb heat. When the fire dies down, or goes out, the rocks will give off the heat, keeping us warm longer."

"You are a wizard, then. You know how to transfer heat to rocks."

"No, not a wizard. I just know things."

Lecque soon had a nice fire going.

Sitting by its edge, Iggy withdrew into himself.

"How was your first day of high school?" Aunt Gwen asked. *"Was it what you expected?"*

"Yes, and then some things I never would have guessed." Iggy smiled at her.

"Do you want to cook with me?"

"Oh, yes." Iggy grabbed his apron and put it on.

"Here," Lecque said.

Iggy snapped out of his daydream.

Lecque held his hand out, passing Iggy a blanket. "Wrap this around you. I do not have an extra bedroll, but the blanket should also help keep you warm through the night."

"Thanks."

"Here are a few dry biscuits." Lecque unceremoniously handed him the food. "Grab that pan, fill it with water, and put it on the fire. At least we can have some warm water."

Iggy got up, took the pan over to the pool of water, and filled it. He stared into the water, and the red sparkling rocks brought back his memory of the sword Mallak had in his hand when he killed Rielick. He returned to the fire and handed the pan of water to Lecque, who grabbed it and put it on the fire to heat.

Lecque sat on the opposite side of the fire and stared at Iggy for some time. Finally, he shook his head and muttered to himself, "That Nostaw must have been delirious. This child is no warrior. He could have picked me, but nooo, he picked him." He rolled over and shut his eyes.

❧

Iggy screamed during the night and woke up with a start, sitting upright. Lecque jumped to his feet, his sword instantly in hand, turning to find any source of danger. Seeing none, he looked toward Iggy. "What is wrong?"

"I-I just had a bad dream."

Lecque sheathed his sword and sat down. "Tell me what caused you such fright."

"I keep having this dream about a Wiate being killed. You are not a Wiate, are you?"

"There are no Wiates left. They were all killed many years ago. *Never* ask a person if he is a Wiate; it can get you killed. Tell me about this dream."

"I keep seeing a Wiate being killed by a sword."

"Are you a mystic?"

"No, no. It's just a dream I keep having."

"When you are asleep or when you are awake also?"

"No, only when I sleep. My brother says I yell out loud in my sleep during bad dreams."

Lecque pointed a finger at Iggy. "You keep that dream to yourself. I do not know what game you're playing. And never ask anyone if they are a Wiate."

"Why?"

"Mallak kills anyone he thinks is a Wiate. That is why." Lecque went to tend the fire.

"Who *is* Mallak? He was in my dream too."

Lecque stared at him. "He is someone you never want to meet, never want to cross. You never want him to even know your name. He calls himself Emperor Mallak, the ruler of Skye. But, in reality, he's a murdering butcher. He will kill at the snap of a finger. Sometimes just for the fun of it. He's evil through and through."

Iggy asked nothing more; he'd heard enough for the moment. "This has to be an extended dream or nightmare," he heard himself say. "I mean, soon I'll wake up and open my eyes and be in my bedroom with John, right?" He tried to believe the words, but it didn't work. Eventually, he was back asleep.

Iggy's sleep didn't last long. He was startled awake when Lecque clamped his hand over Iggy's mouth. His eyes met Lecque's. He nodded his understanding that he needed to stay quiet.

Lecque relaxed his hand and unsheathed his sword. Off in the distance but close enough for concern, Iggy heard an ear-piercing howl that quickly got louder.

Lecque took a defensive stand with his sword held in both hands, ready to strike. He looked at Iggy. "Grab your swords. If you have any knowledge of how to use them, I would advise you to get them at the ready."

Iggy jumped to his feet; the swords fell into the dirt. He quickly retrieved them and fiddled with them to get a firm grip, holding them awkwardly in front of him, his eyes wide with terror. "What is it? Is that Death thing back?" He jerked his head back and forth, trying to gauge where the sound was coming from. He only knew it was getting louder, which he understood meant whatever it was was getting closer.

"No. But I fear it may be just as bad. Fight hard. There will only be winners in this battle."

Iggy felt as if he would throw up. While running was his first instinct, he surprised himself and did not. Suddenly the howling stopped. Dead silence washed over them.

Two sets of glowing eyes appeared at the edge of their camp. One circled to the right, the other to the left.

"When they attack, do not relent."

Iggy hyperventilated with short, fast breaths. He took a deep breath, held it briefly, then finally exhaled. "Okay," he muttered, "let's do this."

A deep chest-thumping growl rang out as both creatures appeared. They were the size of Great Danes, and their faces resembled wild boars', with a horn like a unicorn's centered on their foreheads. They had long fangs that instantly reminded Iggy of saber-toothed tigers'. Their tongues were split like a snake's and flicked in and out of their mouths.

"I will take the one on the right. You take the one on the left," Lecque said.

In that instant, they attacked. The roar was deafening. They pounced. Lecque sidestepped and brought his sword down across the neck of the monster. It clanged. His sword had no effect.

"Sard! The fur is hard as metal!" Lecque exclaimed.

Iggy swung his swords back and forth and up and down in a spastic manner. There was no rhyme or reason to his motions. He felt if he just kept them moving, they might protect him.

The creature reared up and lunged at him. Iggy was so intent on keeping the swords swinging he hardly felt the warmth in his chest or saw the glow under his shirt. The creature's lunge brought it into contact with the sword. Instantly, the swords glowed, and the creature fell to the dirt, dead. Iggy, though stunned, turned to see Lecque struggling with the other creature, his sword bouncing off the metal fur.

In that moment, Iggy surprised himself. He charged the creature and slammed both swords onto its back. That creature also fell to the dirt, dead.

Iggy spun around and around. "Are there any more? Are there any more?"

Lecque looked at the creature and at Iggy, who was jumping around, swinging his swords. "I do not think so. You can rest your swords now. Clearly you have no idea how to fight with swords… but the beast is dead. Maybe you are not such a whit packer.

"What are they?"

Lecque walked to the closest one. "They are Baisd Bheulachs, protectors of the Odal Pass. They are shapeshifting demons. They should not be here." As he spoke, both creatures' bodies shifted to cats then rats, then they disintegrated to dust.

"How do you know, if they change shapes?"

"We are taught their howl as children, so we know to hide if we hear it."

"What kind of place is this? Death Knights, Nostaws, these shapeshifting things!"

"None of them have ever been seen. They are stories we teach our children."

"Well, you have a twisted sense of cheerful bedtime stories you tell your children."

Lecque looked suspiciously at Iggy. "It is strange that they and you have shown up at the same time."

"Yeah, tell me about it! How do you think I feel? I've never killed anything! Never seen anything die! This place is crazy, insane!"

Lecque sheathed his sword, thought about his answer, but only replied, "Thank you. You saved my life."

The sun's rays rolled over the hill and eventually washed over them. Iggy had sat up the rest of the night, unaware he'd fallen asleep from sheer exhaustion. He opened his eyes with a startled, wide-eyed stare and jumped to his feet.

He'd wanted so badly for it all to be a dream.

Lecque was saddling the horse. "I see you are awake. There is another dried biscuit there for you. We'll leave shortly; I want to get home by midday."

"Listen," Iggy all but shouted, "I have no intention of staying here. There are dead soldier things walking around killing other things you call Nostaw, then giant whatever-those-things-were that can turn into... who knows? Whatever they want to turn into. Also, may I add, trying to kill us. And riding horses! No, I need to get back to my brother. To my family. I-I don't know how I got here or why, but I have to get back."

He thought with a pang of Aunt Gwen; she'd probably stayed up all night with worry. He imagined everyone in his town getting ready for school and work.

"As I said yesterday, start walking back that way. But if you leave me, you are on your own, because I am going that way," Lecque said brusquely, pointing with his hand in the opposite direction.

"Not much of a choice. I'll go with you."

"Before we go, we need to do something about those swords. Which

I must say you used… strangely, but efficiently, against the Baisd Bheu-lachs. I do not want you accidently dropping them and not telling me. I have some rope. We will lash them around your waist behind you."

As Lecque dug out some rope from his saddlebag, Iggy grabbed the swords from the ground beside him and stood. He held them behind him, one in each hand, wondering how they'd fit. The instant the swords touched his back, he felt a deep warmth in his hands and down his spine. Shocked, he brought his hands out front.

"They're gone!"

Lecque spun around. "What is gone?"

"The swords! They're gone!"

Lecque stormed over, rage in his voice. "What did you do with them?"

"I didn't do anything!" There was panic in Iggy's voice. "All I did was hold them behind me like this and they disappeared."

Iggy showed Lecque what he did, and in that instant the same warmth surrounded his back and hands. When he pulled his hands from behind him, the swords were in his hands.

"What the…? You *are* a wizard. I just surely have no idea what kind."

"Nooo! I don't know how this happened. I am not filled with any magic!" Iggy put his hands behind him again, and the swords were gone. "See, they're gone. I'll leave them there."

They rode through the morning in silence and suspicion of each other's motives. Iggy was withdrawn, overwhelmed with all the new things in his life and his own bravery last night. *Magic*, he thought, *I have no magic, but maybe these swords do?*

7

Lecque was consumed by his own thoughts as they rode. What was a Nostaw doing so far from his home? Why was there a Death Knight stalking the Nostaw? And, most of all, why did the Nostaw give up his soul and his name of Tilead to Iggy? Having no answers to his questions, he pondered Iggy. Who and what was he? He had heard of wizards and demons taking over human bodies, presenting themselves as meek, only to come out of their shells and slay everyone. He could be a spy for Mallak.

Grateful as he was to Iggy for saving his life the night before, he would still watch him closely… but he couldn't call him a coward anymore.

The long morning took them through many meadows and eventually onto a worn dirt path through woods. Finally, their horse walked into a clearing on a rise overlooking a village and stopped.

"This is the village of Nilewood. I live here." Lecque waited a moment for a reply. After a long silence, he shook his head, clicked his heels into his horse's side, and they walked on.

Thank goodness, Iggy thought. His thighs, legs, and back ached. How did people ride horses for so long? He sighed as the horse kept walking.

They skirted the edge of the village. Eventually they came to a small house constructed of layers of stones with windows of glass and a woven thatched roof; a chimney stuck up out of the center. There was a wooden fence off to the left side, enclosing a pig rolling around in the dirt and snorting, its snout in the air. Off in a larger fenced-in meadow were three cows. There was a chicken coop next to the pigsty. A barn for a couple of horses had been built fifty feet to the right of the house, and a well had been dug between the two structures. He could see a creek far behind the house, and he spotted a plowed field between it and the house.

As Lecque dismounted, the door to the cottage opened, and a girl around Iggy's age came out.

Iggy, who'd been looking around cautiously, suddenly fixated on this girl.

She was gorgeous, with shoulder-length auburn hair that sparkled in the light. Her deep-green eyes were so captivating, even far away, that Iggy feared looking into them.

She hurried to Lecque and gave him a big hug. "Welcome back, Brother." Then she stepped back and stared at Iggy, who dropped his stare. "And what did you pick up on the way?" She walked up to Iggy, who was still on the horse, and looked him up and down.

Lecque gave a sarcastic chuckle. "Raraesa, meet Iggy. Iggy, you may dismount the horse now. And try not to fall off."

Raraesa gave Lecque an inquiring head tilt, perhaps curious about his sarcasm. "Otherwise, how was your journey?"

Lecque pulled Raraesa several feet away out of earshot of Iggy. "I watched a Death Knight kill a Nostaw Warrior. That is when *he* showed up. Then last night we were attacked by two Baisd Bheulachs. And to my surprise *he* killed both of them."

"What!" Raraesa gasped.

He looked back at Iggy, who was simply standing there. "He arrives, and our land goes out of balance. It is obvious he is from a land much different from ours. Neither of us knows how he got here."

Raraesa glanced at Iggy. "He is young."

"When I questioned him on the ride here, he said he was your age, fifteen. Though he does not look any older than eleven."

"That does not say too much for where he is from. Where *is* he from?"

"Some place called Suck Your Hanna Pencil Place. "

Raraesa put her hand to her mouth and laughed. "What? Suck your hand?"

"I know." Lecque laughed.

"He is so scrawny. If they are all like him, he and they pose no danger to us. What do we do with him?"

"I do not know. Bring him in and get him some food, if you would. He will have to stay with us for now. Try to become his friend and find out more about him but be careful. There is more, a lot more. We will talk later. I want to get the horse settled down, watered, and fed first. Oh, he asked me if I was a Wiate."

"What?"

"I am just as concerned. Either he is a spy, a sorcerer, or I am not sure what. See what you can find out."

They walked back to Iggy, who still stood beside the horse, looking at the ground. Raraesa sized him up and down. Without commenting on his strange fashion, she walked into the cottage. "Come with me. I will get you something to eat."

Iggy followed her silently. He stopped just inside the front door and looked around the room. The floor was packed dirt. There was a small wooden table and stools in one corner, and an open-hearth fireplace with red-hot embers that filled half of the adjacent wall. On the left side of the room were two wooden partitions that jutted out, giving privacy to whoever was behind it. Iggy assumed that was where they slept.

"Take a seat," Raraesa said, pointing to one of the stools at the table. She placed a bowl in front of him. "I hope you like stew."

"Thanks," Iggy said quietly. He picked up a wooden spoon, then took a taste of the stew, and in moments he was downing the last spoonful; he hadn't realized how hungry he was.

Raraesa took a seat opposite him at the table. "Hungry, were you? Do you want more?"

"No, thank you," he said quietly.

For a moment, there was an uncomfortable pause. Raraesa stared at him as he stared at his bowl. Then she plastered on a comforting smile and broke the silence. "Tell me about yourself. Where did you get those clothes? I have never seen clothes like them."

Iggy was quiet for a few moments. "This is not real. Is it?"

"I assure you, everything here is real."

"But how? How can I be in this place, in this... world? I've hidden from a Death Knight, been anointed by a Nostaw Warrior, and attacked by things called Baisd Bheulachs." His eyes scanned the room, then settled on her.

"A Death Knight and a Nostaw Warrior? I have never heard of anyone actually seeing either of them. Or living to tell about it. But the Baisd Bheulachs, Lecque tells me it was you who killed both of them. I am very impressed. Why not tell me who you are? How did you get here?"

"That's just it; I have no clue." Iggy wrung his hands. "I'm from Susquehanna, Pennsylvania. That meant nothing to Lecque. Does it to you?" She shook her head. "I was being chased by some guys—gang members—who wanted to beat me up, but my brother, John, was going to face them down." He thought of John and wondered for the hundredth time how he'd fared against Wayne's gang.

"I promise you, Lecque and I are just as confused as you are. So, start from the beginning."

Iggy tried to speak slowly and calmly, but his words came out in a rush as he told her about all he'd been through. "The next thing I know, this creature called a Nostaw is singing to me and giving me these curved swords. And Lecque tells me if I ever lose them or give them away, he'll kill me." Iggy stopped. He wanted her to understand. "More than anything, I can't believe I left John alone."

"Why did you?"

Iggy whispered, "Because until yesterday I wasn't much of a fighter. I'm not a fighter."

"Lecque said you certainly fought hard against the Baisd Bheulachs. You also asked Lecque if he was a Wiate. Do Wiates live in your land?"

"No. I don't know what a Wiate is. I have been having dreams about a place like this and a bad ruler who killed a Wiate by cutting off his head. It made the sword he used really powerful. So powerful even the ruler couldn't touch it."

The story startled her. "That ruler is Mallak. And what you dreamt really happened in the past."

"So why did Lecque get mad at me when I asked?"

She thought for a moment, then said, "Wiates are powerful people. Their power lies in their blood. Mallak had a special sword forged with special metal. It needed to touch the blood of a Wiate to make it invincible. So, when Mallak cut off the head of that Wiate—his name was Rielick—Rielick's blood touched the sword and turned it into a magic sword. What Mallak did not know was once Wiate blood touched the sword, only a Wiate could wield it. So, ever since then Mallak has killed any Wiate to ensure they do not use the sword against him. It sits on that palace veranda stuck in stone and reminds him every day that he failed. Now do you understand Lecque's concern and anger?"

"I guess I do."

"I don't understand how you arrived here. You said, 'Poof, the next thing I knew, I was in a different place.' What does that mean? Are you a wizard? Why can't you use your powers to poof yourself back to your Sucahanna, Pensavanea?"

"Do you think if I had any powers I'd be sitting here? I can't believe I'm even talking to you."

"Why?"

"Because you must think I'm crazy."

She stared at him, and he looked down at the table. "Do I make you nervous?"

"No… Yes."

"Why?"

Iggy felt the next thirty seconds were the longest, most awkward silence he had ever endured. He glanced up momentarily. She doubted his story. He could read the reaction on her face. Finally, he took a deep breath. "I'm in a strange world with a beautiful girl. Why shouldn't I be nervous? Anyway, where I'm from girls are mean and can hurt you more than guys can."

"What is 'guys'?"

"Guys—that's a word for boys. I'm confused. You and Lecque speak English, but some words you don't know what they mean."

"What is English?"

"English... English is the language we are speaking. What do you call your language?"

"Why, we call it Skye. We live in the Kingdom of Skye, so we call it Skye." She smiled as if she understood. "So, you call it English. Your land must be the kingdom of English."

Iggy shook his head and chuckled. "No, we just call the language English."

"I guess I will just stay confused. So, you were telling me about girls who are mean by hurting guys."

"When it comes to girls, let's just say I don't trust them very much... so I avoid them, and they avoid me. I had a girl ask me out to a movie once. I waited at the ticket counter, and she eventually showed up—but she was with all her girlfriends. She laughed and ignored me as she walked by."

"What is a movie?"

Iggy shook his head. "Never mind."

"Fine," Raraesa said, appearing annoyed. "Why did you not say anything to her when she walked by you?"

"Because I knew I wouldn't win." He spoke softly. "It was the smartest thing to do. Why bother?"

Their conversation continued. At first, he only stared at the table while he talked, but during his explanations, Raraesa would occasionally stop him and ask a question or two and he realized he was looking up at her. He saw by her expression she wasn't mocking him but encouraging him. Eventually, Iggy talked to her as if they were longtime friends. He wasn't sure how much time had passed, but suddenly a wave of fatigue washed over him, and he yawned. His mind and body were finally at ease in a way they hadn't been for over twenty-four hours. His eyes glazed over, and soon he was fast asleep.

∽

Lecque walked into the cottage. He looked at Iggy, who was in a deep sleep at the table, and asked Raraesa, "What happened here?"

Raraesa laughed. "Oh, some home cooking and conversation got the best of him. Come, help me get him into your bed. Then you can tell me all about your adventure."

"Wait one moment." Lecque was taken back. "You want to put him in my bed? Where then am I going to sleep?"

"There's the extra room in the barn. For now, you can sleep there." She looked at Lecque, who was shaking his head.

"Yes. You made him our guest. Now help me."

"One night only. I will not have a fifteen-year-old boy sleeping near my fifteen-year-old sister while I sleep in the barn."

"Why, Brother? You fear for me?"

"I should actually fear for him. If he did try something, you would snap him like a small tree branch."

Raraesa stood and lifted Iggy's head off the table while Lecque lifted his torso and kicked the chair away.

After they put him to bed, Lecque undressed him and brought the clothes to the kitchen so they could examine them. Lecque picked up the strange shoes, tapping the spongy soles. "I do not understand what kind of material this is. It is like nothing I have ever seen before. It has a hardness but also a softness to it. The rest is a cloth, I think, but a cloth totally different from what I could find at the finest shop. And look at the string woven back and forth, and it goes through holes with little metal circles protecting the cloth."

Raraesa looked closely at the jeans. "Brother, this is cloth, but the weave is so tight, it gives the pants tremendous strength. No loom or mill I know can make this. And look at these round pieces of metal in the corner of the pockets!"

"Then you agree, he is a wizard?"

"I do not know."

"You do not believe his story that he does not know how he arrived here?"

"I told you, I do not know."

"Well, you had better find out. I do not have time to watch him constantly. I still have no idea what to tell the town fathers. They will wish to know who this stranger is. In fact, I am not sure we should let him stay."

"You brought him here. He is our guest. For that reason, you are sleeping in the barn with the horses. We will talk more about this after a good night's sleep."

"I will be gone early in the morning. I have a meeting to attend to. Let me know when I return if you've found out anything more about our strange visitor. And keep your sword nearby. I do not trust him."

∽

Iggy's vision cleared. He was standing on the bottom step of his home in Susquehanna, Pennsylvania. "Oh, my God! What just happened?" He looked to his left, then his right. He was back in Susquehanna.

John and Aunt Gwen's voices came from inside. The front door was open.

"John! Aunt Gwen! The two of you will never believe the dream I just had! No, it was more like I was hallucinating. It was so real!" He ran up the steps.

"I can't believe you put Iggy in that situation!" Aunt Gwen seethed. "And now you tell me you have no idea where he is! What is wrong with you? What were you thinking?"

"I'm sorry, Mom. I thought he could handle it. That it would push him to—"

"Push him to what? To be like you? Well, in case you haven't noticed Iggy is *not* like you."

Iggy frowned and said, "Aunt Gwen, John, I'm right here. I'm okay."

"John, you get out there with your friends and search everywhere. Look every place possible." She pointed with dagger eyes to the open door. To herself, she whispered, "Iggy, I swear, you are going to be the death of me. I just hope to God you're safe."

"What's going on? Why are you ignoring me? I'm right in front of you."

Iggy's vision faded to black.

With a start, Iggy's eyes opened, but only for a moment. He muttered, "I'm right in front of you." Then he was fast asleep again.

8

The following day, just before noontime, after riding half the morning to Carfield, the county just west of Nilewood, Lecque walked into The Brethren Pub near the center of Brightenrid, the county seat, to meet with a member of the underground movement plotting against Mallak.

The pub had a worn wooden bar across the back of the room that five men stood at, holding wooden tankards of mead, looking suspiciously at Lecque when he entered. The bar had seen decades of use and abuse of drinks being served across it and bar fights against it, leaving it scuffed at the edges and pitted on top.

A set of wooden steps to the left of the bar led to a second floor where patrons used to sit at tables with wooden plates and pewter goblets. The bar once boasted a sunken firepit in the center of the main floor that, in a time before Mallak, was occupied by a pig on a spit, turned by a young boy whose sole job had been to make sure the meat roasted evenly. But now the fire pit was cold. Pigs and meat were scarce since Mallak now took pigs and cows as tax payment if the locals did not have enough coin to pay their taxes.

The room's light was dim, which suited Lecque just fine. He walked up the worn wooden steps and took a seat at the last table on the left, which overlooked the floor below.

Soon, a much older man joined him. His face was scarred and his nose was slightly crooked, evidence of battles fought that didn't disappear with time. This was Ankter, one of the councilmen of a town named Stagwell. His opinion was often sought for important matters. For that reason, he insisted on meeting Lecque in Brightenrid instead of Stagwell. Anonymity kept him safe.

Ankter did not greet Lecque or shake his hand. His demeanor was brusque. When he spoke, he came straight to the point. "So, what did you accomplish? Did you meet with the Affaraons? Did you hash out any agreement with them?"

Before Lecque could answer, the pub's serving maid approached with two tankards of ale and a wooden plate of hard bread. "Bread is all we have today. You shout for me if you need anything else. Though, there is not anything other than refilling your tankards."

"My travels were very eventful, but not in the way one would have expected," Lecque replied.

"Well, speak, boy—don't keep me waiting all day. Did you make it to Whiencaster, and who did you meet?" Ankter took a drink from his ale and ripped a piece of bread off the platter and stuffed it into his mouth.

"I did. I met Shaila, the Dinas Affaraon emissary. We met west of Whiencaster, near the moors where you said she would be. She was very obstinate and said she spoke for the Affaraon people. Their Adepts will not help us. They feel the runes magic they have in place is adequate protection for their people. Their Adepts feel there is nothing to be gained by aligning with us against Mallak. I tried but was unable to change her mind."

Ankter wiped his mouth on his sleeve. "Then that is that. If Shaila and her Adepts will not help, your idea of amassing this magnificent alliance between people who have been suspicious of each other for longer than history itself is dead. Mallak has an army of five thousand now. He is moving north, expanding his rule, crushing those who oppose him. I told you that you were wasting your time with this nonsense of an alliance. The people of Dinas Affaraon will not join our rebellion."

"Although I am disappointed, we could now have more pressing problems. I came across a Death Knight killing a Nostaw on my way back home." Lecque shuddered as his memory flashed back to a vision of the Death Knight.

"There you have it!" Ankter said, pounding the table with his fist. "It is done. Mallak has a Death Knight; *we* have pitchforks. This crusade is over. If Mallak has a set of Nostaw swords to display, we do what he wants us to do and that is that. Or die by those swords."

"Mallak doesn't have the swords. The Death Knight didn't take them."

"Oh, he will. He will send some of his minions out. They will cut off the hands that are fused to those swords, and believe me, he will display them."

"You misunderstand me. The swords were gone. There is nothing for Mallak to retrieve." It was Lecque's turn to wipe his mouth, and he recounted the tale of the Nostaw's death and meeting Iggy in his travels after seeing the Death Knight. Lecque was careful to leave out the part about the Nostaw giving Iggy the swords. And since he would not mention the swords, he couldn't talk about the Baisd Bheulachs and saving his life.

"Where are the swords?"

"I do not know."

"I do not like this. Not at all. A Death Knight killing a Nostaw. That boy showing up out of nowhere. None of this is good. It all has to be connected. The boy, Iggy, must go. He is a danger to us, to Stagwell, to Nilewood. You know Mallak will learn of him and come for him. When Mallak comes after that little imp, we will all be in danger. I tell you, he must go."

"And when you say go—?"

"I mean cut him loose."

"That is certain death for him. He has no survival skills."

"What is that to us?"

"Ankter, that is unacceptable." Lecque was surprised to hear himself say it and by what followed. "No. There is no reason to send this boy to a sure death. I will not have that happen." Lecque looked down, then right into Ankter's eyes. "Let me make this clear: You will do nothing to harm this boy because that is all he is—a harmless, scared little boy. I will not sacrifice him to Mallak or anyone else because you are not man enough to protect him."

"Watch yourself, boy."

"Or what? You will tell Mallak about our group of resistance fighters? The ones whose heads he has vowed to cut off. Your head is right up there beside mine." Lecque finished his ale in one final gulp, then stared defiantly at Ankter. "If Iggy goes down, so will you. Remember that."

Lecque rose from his chair and left.

9

Mallak sat alone at the less-than-elegant table in the center of the castle's main dining room. Despite the dreariness of the table before him, there was a lavish spread of roasted meat, chicken, and potatoes. He meticulously pushed his fork into the meat and cut off a piece with surgical precision. Then, with great ceremony, he lifted it and placed it into his mouth. He closed his eyes with every bite, savoring the food's flavor.

A guard approached from the opposite side of the room.

"Emperor Mallak, there is news—"

Mallak's left arm shot up with his palm toward the guard. He didn't look up or say a word. He continued to eat; his eyes closed in relish.

Mallak inwardly smiled knowing the guard stood at attention, rebuffed.

Everyone knew of Mallak's unexpected outbursts of rage. Beads of sweat formed on the guard's forehead and rolled down into his eyes, blurring his vision. Mallak knew the guard dared not move, not wanting to provoke his emperor. The discomfort was nothing compared to the possible retribution for interrupting the man's meal. Having one's tongue ripped out was Mallak's favorite.

After a good twenty minutes, Mallak wiped his mouth with his napkin. He raised his hand and motioned the guard over. "You may speak now."

"Emperor Mallak, one of our scouting parties has returned. The group requests an audience with you to share news of what they learned."

An uncomfortable silence ensued. Mallak stared at the guard, then at his empty plate, then at the ceiling before his eyes again settled on the guard. "Do you know why you are still alive after you dared interrupt me while eating?"

"Because you are kind and forgiving, Emperor," the guard said, trying to keep his voice steady.

"No. It is simpler than that. You are alive because my food was delicious, and I was in a great mood while eating it. What is it these scouts want to tell me?"

"I do not know, Emperor Mallak."

Mallak stood abruptly from his chair. He pulled his fingers through his hair and looked intensely at the guard. He started to open his mouth but stopped. He grinned and simply waved his hand. "Well, then, I think you need to bring them in so we can both find out what is so important."

"Yes, Emperor, I—"

"Go!"

The guard turned and hurried away as Mallak chuckled. He loved seeing the fear in their eyes as they jumped to his every command. With a sardonic smile, he remembered eavesdropping on one of his father's conversations—his father, the king. "Mallak," he heard him say, "just does not have what it takes to lead men, let alone the whole kingdom." *Well*, Mallak thought, *how would dear old Father feel about me now? Everyone cowers in front of me, fears me, and jumps to do my bidding.* He wondered again what Father would think, but then laughed. *He cannot think. He is dead. Because I killed him. And the guards—they are nothing more than puppets on a string, and I am the puppet master.* He laughed again.

Moments later, three scouts entered the throne room, accompanied by the guard. Mallak sighed with impatience and waved them forward. "What is it you felt was so important that you needed to tell me directly?"

The scout in the middle bowed and replied, "My emperor, when we were on patrol, we came across a Nostaw that had been recently killed."

"How do you know he was recently killed?"

"The blood around him was still liquid. It had not dried or turned to gel."

"Did he still have his swords?"

"No." The scout had a quiver in his voice.

"His hands had been severed?" Mallak asked.

"No."

"No, you say. Well, the swords were gone; his hands were intact. There was obviously another Nostaw present who was willed the swords. Did you track down this other Nostaw?" Mallak stared intently at the guard, who shook his head. "*Why not?*"

"You are talking about hunting down and confronting a Nostaw Warrior! There were only three of us. We would have been no match against such a warrior." Sensing Mallak's agitation, the scout gulped. "W-w-w-we felt it wiser to return to inform you."

The veins on Mallak's neck bulged and pulsed as his face turned an angry red. His robe abruptly began pulsing with colors, from deep purple to red then to black. "You come across a freshly killed Nostaw," he said, his voice high-pitched, "with no other bodies around. Someone or something killed that beast. Yet you do nothing to track down more information for me?"

The scouts squirmed and shifted but said nothing.

Mallak paced furiously. The pulsing colors on his robe quickened in time with his step. "The swords are gone! And you did not follow the trail because you were afraid?"

"Emperor, surely you cannot expect the three of us would have stood a chance against a Nostaw?" The scout instantly realized his mistake. He lowered his eyes to the floor, fearing what repercussion was coming his way.

"*Coward! I hate cowards!*" Mallak raised the staff in his right hand. His robe turned a deep violet as sparks shot out from it and into the crystal finial on top of the staff. "*Die!*"

An electrical current shot out from the center of the crystal and landed directly in the middle scout's chest. The scout's body stiffened, then fell backward onto the floor, a ring of smoke issuing from his chest. Then his body went still.

Mallak stumbled to the right. He used the staff to support himself. His face was beet red, the veins in his neck pulsing. "The two of you should be more fearful of what I will do to you now. You will wish you had died at the hands of that Nostaw!" He struggled for control of himself for a moment before he roared, "*Guards!*"

In seconds, ten guards rushed in, took stock of the situation, and surrounded the two scouts.

"Take them underground and show them what it's really like to be afraid. And drag that dead one out of here. Throw him into the moat so everyone can see what happens when you are a coward and put your safety before my wishes!"

Two guards grabbed the fallen scout. One of them looked up. "Emperor, he is still alive."

"Then slit his throat before you throw him in! Get out *now!*" Mallak wobbled on his feet as he made his way to his throne. His hands trembled. He looked at one guard. "You! Go find Gobus. Tell him I want him here immediately."

Moments after the guards hurried out, Gobus entered the room. He had silver hair that fell to his shoulders. His fingernails were long and pointed at the tips. He wore loose, off-white voluminous pants and a pullover shirt that ended mid-thigh and was cinched tight around his waist with a robe belt. He also wore an outer jacket that ended mid-waist. The jacket sleeves stopped just below his elbows, allowing his long-sleeved shirt to flow out.

He strode over to Mallak. Unlike the scouts and guards, Gobus looked utterly at ease.

"I sensed you needed me. I was nearby, so I came. And I was not needed elsewhere." He looked at the sweat on Mallak's forehead. "What happened? Why are you distressed?"

Mallak glared at him. "You are the great Wizard of Dark Magic. My *great* wizard. You tell me. Why am I distressed?"

"Ah, Mallak, first, I am not your wizard. I indulge you because I want to. And, second, unlike you, I know my limitations and the dangers of attempting to exceed them." Gobus crossed his arms.

Mallak checked the clasp on his robe. Fiddling with it, making sure it was tight. "It was a *simple* energy burst. I pulled it from my rage like you taught me. He went down, but it did not kill him. It only stunned him. I almost fainted. What if word spreads through my kingdom and beyond? The mighty Emperor Mallak taken to his knees, unable to smite a lowly scout! How can I rule a kingdom? They need to fear me." Mallak breathed heavy with anger.

Gobus took a deep breath in and slowly let it out. "Mallak."

"It's Emperor Mallak! You will call me Emperor Mallak!"

"If that makes you feel more powerful. Emperor Mallak, have you learned nothing from me? You are trying things far beyond your current level of training."

Gobus slowly walked around the room, his left hand, palm up, held out in front of him. An inch above the open palm was a rotating ball of pure fire, sparkling and crackling. He ever so methodically moved his right hand, palm toward the ball, over it. He waved his hand slowly back and forth, mere inches above the flame.

"I have explained that you are not the one with the power. That robe you wear holds the power. You are only a conduit." Gobus closed both hands into fists, and the ball of fire disappeared. "I have been teaching you how to channel that power, how to direct it and use it. I do not think, though, that you have listened to me. The problem is, as I have explained before, the robe needs energy when casting a spell. It finds the easiest source. Which, in this case, was you. You let your anger get hold of you." Gobus looked around. "That fire, there." Gobus pointed to the fireplace. "It is a great source of energy. As I just showed you. If you had only focused your mind on it, the energy of the burning logs would have flowed into the robe and done your bidding. Your anger blinds you to these essential components."

Mallak glared at Gobus. "What if there is no fire or energy source around?"

Gobus met Mallak's glare with a smile. "The robe will suck the energy from you until there is no energy left."

"Then what?"

"Then, Emperor Mallak, you will die."

"That is not an option. Is there no other way?"

"Hmm. Actually, there is. Ancient legends say there are crystals that store energy. That energy is limited though, except for one crystal. The center crystal from a massive magical stone. It is said that crystal holds extraordinary power, renewed constantly by the sun. If you possessed it, then your robe would have unlimited power. Thus, so would you."

"Where is this crystal?"

"I do not know. In fact, that is a question only you will be able to answer."

"Explain."

"Legend says that crystal was handed down from king to son across the ages. So, when the son became king, he would possess it. If your father, the king, had it, he would have passed it on to you. You are indeed the king... but maybe you were not the one he had chosen to replace him."

"My father died suddenly."

"Yes. We were told." Gobus paused and smiled at Mallak for a moment, enjoying the slow torment he was inflicting on Mallak. "There is something else."

"Talk, then!"

"This special crystal must willingly be given from person to person. Only then will the power of the crystal transfer to the new owner. If it is taken and not given, the crystal is useless."

"And what if that person died before giving it away?"

"Then it is said the power of the crystal would pass to the closest relative by bloodline."

"If I find who has this crystal, what if he will not give it to me?"

"As I said. The crystal would be useless."

"If I catch who has it, I will torture him until he willingly gives it to me."

Gobus shrugged his shoulder with indifference. "That might work." Gobus strolled around the room, his fireball relit in the palm of his right hand. "I understand you raised a Death Knight."

Mallak's facial muscles contorted with rage.

"Oh, stop." Gobus raised his hand. "Do you think I do not know everything you do or attempt to do with regard to magic?"

"I raised him with no problem."

"Your naivety will be your downfall. You do not know the problems you face."

"Then speak! Tell me my problems."

"You have made a fatal mistake. You have overreached. You think by creating a magic jewel, an *amateurish* jewel, and placing it in the hand of a dead soldier, that you've created a Death Knight loyal to you? How naive. Did you wipe out his soul? *No.* Did you wipe out his memory? *No.* He will only follow your commands as long as it is beneficial to him."

"You take me for a fool! I know all that. I will wipe out everything about him. And when he is loyal to me, he will raise the next army of Death Knights that are loyal to him, and that will happen only when he is loyal to *me!*"

Gobus shook his head. "You are a fool. You were not ready! You do not have the power to turn him yet. You want an army of the dead, but you cannot control their leader."

"What do I need so I can control him?"

"Stop worrying about power and *get that crystal*. Not that I think your vanity will allow it."

"Who has it?"

"Ahh, you are repeating yourself again. As I said, I do not know. My advice is to look inward into your own family. You may or may not find what you are looking for. But in the meantime, I suggest you practice focusing on external energy sources. Try to control your anger. You were close to death today. If you had let your anger and your rage flare any longer, I might be standing over your lifeless body. And I warn you, you can only push your Death Knight so far. Be careful. And find that crystal."

Mallak dismissed Gobus with a wave of his hand and, once alone again, stood deep in thought. The muscles of his jaw clenched tight as the rage boiled inside him. "Kylian, I am glad I did not kill you. I will make you tell me about the crystal and where it is hidden."

10

Consciousness came slowly back to Iggy, for real this time.
His thoughts drifted to Aunt Gwen and John. Then he opened his eyes, and his surroundings hit him: the walls of stacked stone, the hay-filled mattress on the dirt floor. These could not be denied. He saw old clothes, not his jeans and shirt from before, folded on a stool. He lifted the covers and was shocked to find himself in only his underwear. He blushed, wondering if Raraesa had undressed him.

Leonard would die laughing. The first time a girl takes his pants off, and he's asleep. Leonard. He was probably in homeroom, wondering where Iggy had gone. Everyone probably thought he'd run away because he was so scared. That part was true. But Iggy didn't think he was in a safer place.

Instinctively, he reached up and touched the amulet around his neck. Relieved it was there, he rolled out of bed and got dressed in the strange clothes. The shirt was cream-colored and made of wool. The tan pants were of a similar fiber blend. The clothes were comfortable and fit him well. They were well worn, obviously belonging to someone else. But the clothes were the only things on the stool.

"Where are my swords?" He swiveled his head and looked around the room. Iggy placed his hands behind his back. "I wonder?" He felt instant warmth and, pulling his hands around front, saw that each hand held a Nostaw sword. "Wow. That is so freaky."

Iggy took a moment to wave them around as if he were fighting off an invisible attacker. Then he put them behind his back, and they disappeared once more. "Even freakier."

A sweet smell from the cooking area made him move faster. He was hungry. All thought of swords disappeared from his head. Walking around the partition, Iggy saw Raraesa standing near the open hearth.

"Ah, Iggy, you are awake," Raraesa said, turning. "Have you rested?"

Iggy's heart jumped. She was as beautiful as he remembered. "Yes, I did. How long did I sleep?"

"Well, you fell asleep at the table yesterday midafternoon. Lecque and I put you to bed, and now it's midmorning of the next day. Come, sit down. You must be hungry. I hope you like porridge." Raraesa scooped some out of a pot hanging over the fire and placed a bowl of it on the table for him.

Iggy took the wooden spoon, filled it with a bit of the food, then gingerly tasted it. "This is good." He immediately devoured it.

"Would you like more?"

"Yes. Definitely."

Raraesa filled his bowl a second time. When he was done, he looked up and saw Raraesa at the wooden table, her head down, sewing. Feeling safe because her back was to him, he finally took a long look at her. She was beautiful. Her mid-shoulder-length hair was light red with a brownish tint that looked brighter when she turned her head and the light caught it at a different angle. She was well-toned, possibly because of the hard work she did. She carried herself confidently and would have been one of the popular kids at school, one of those girls who never would have acknowledged his presence.

She turned to face him, and he blushed and quickly looked away.

That moment was not lost on Raraesa. She moved to sit across the table from him. "You told me how you felt the safest when you do not draw looks to you. I exchanged your clothes for what you have on. That way you can blend in."

"What about my sneakers?"

"What are sneakers?"

"What I was wearing on my feet. What do I wear on my feet?"

"So that is what they are called. You cannot wear those here. They will be noticed. This is a small village filled with wary folks who notice everything that goes by them; we must go to the nearby town of Stagwell. There is a leather cobbler there. He may have some old boots that fit you. We can trade some eggs for them. Until then, I have some very old ones. The front parts are torn, and the toes are not covered."

Raraesa sat tall in the saddle and reached out a hand to Iggy, pulling him up onto the saddle behind her. He tensed as their bodies touched.

"What do I hold on to?" He held his arms stiffly by his side, not wanting to touch her.

"Hold your hands straight forward on either side of me." As he did, she gently took hold of them and pulled them around her waist. "There. Now you have something to hold on to." As she walked the horse down the path, she said, "Hold me tight. I won't bite you."

Iggy slowly increased the tightness around her waist, realizing this was the first time he'd held a girl; a big grin formed on his face. *John,* he thought, *if you could see me now.*

His confidence grew as they made their way through the beautiful countryside. The open trail they were on was flat and smooth. The forest on either side was lush, filled with willow, juniper, and yews, the canopies in some areas so dense that only tiny streams of light filtered through to the ground below. They passed just a few other small farms like Lecque and Raraesa's now and then. Some had sheep, others had cows or pigs in their pens, although the animals were few. Life here seemed tranquil despite Raraesa saying folks were wary.

He estimated it had taken them thirty minutes to reach the outskirts of town. Raraesa stopped the horse, and they dismounted. "We'll walk from here." She took the reins and walked in front of the horse. Iggy trailed behind. "Come on." She turned and held out her hand.

He looked at Raraesa's hand. Should he take it? Or was she telling him to hurry up? He took a deep, quiet breath, extended his hand, and took hers in his.

"Where did you get that beautiful crystal you wear around your neck?"

"It was my mother's. When she died, my aunt gave it to me. I wear it all the time. It keeps her memory alive for me."

"I am sorry she died. You must miss her."

"I was young, so I don't have many memories of her. That's why I wear the necklace."

They walked across a field where a group of five teenage boys were throwing rocks. The game was simple: they picked a rock, and whoever threw it the farthest was the winner. Spotting Raraesa and Iggy, they stopped and ran over to them. They all looked to Iggy to be about his age. One kept looking at Raraesa in obvious admiration.

"So, Raraesa," the boy said, "you decided to grace the town and us with your presence."

"Frankie," Raraesa replied evenly, "if I had known you were in this field, I would have taken another route. I see no one has any work for you today."

"Who is this plab?"

"Don't you call him that! His name is Iggy, and he is with me."

"Hey, Frankie," one of the other boys said, "let us see how far his scrawny arms can throw a rock."

"What are the rules?" Iggy asked.

"There are none."

"Do you have to throw it?"

"What are you, an idiot? How else are you going to get it across the field? You going to kick it?" Frankie broke out laughing. "Here, you can use my rock."

Iggy took the rock and looked at Raraesa's horse. He walked over to it and withdrew the bow lashed onto it.

"Do you have a piece of cloth about this big that I can use?" He held his hands out about one foot apart, looking at Raraesa.

"I do." She pulled a piece of cloth out of the saddlebag.

Iggy took the bow and attached both ends of the cloth onto the bowstring, leaving a pouch.

He smiled calmly at Raraesa. "Glad you are wearing pants and boots. Will you lie down here on your back with your feet facing the field and raise your feet with your knees slightly bent?"

Raraesa did as she was asked. Iggy took the bow and placed Raraesa's booted feet inside each side of the bow, resting the bow horizontally against the soles of her boots. He took the rock and placed it in the pouch. Standing behind her, he pulled the bow string very taut, moving the rock in the pouch up and down, judging the angle. The wooden bow creaked as it was pulled to its limit.

"Bombs away!" Iggy yelled, releasing the bow string. The rock flew through the air at least five times the distance of the boys' longest throws.

Raraesa looked through her knees and jumped up before the rock landed. "Wow! That is wonderful! Where did you learn that?"

Iggy smiled at her and whispered, "I do know some things." He turned to Frankie. "I win."

"As I said, he is with me." Raraesa turned and took her horse's reins in one hand and Iggy's hand in the other, and they walked to town.

They held hands all the way to town to Iggy's delight. Eventually, the dirt path changed to a wider dirt road filled with broken cobblestone. The buildings were a combination of stone and wood with none rising over two stories. The buildings were worn like the cobblestone, as though maintenance had been minimal over the last decade. A few people pushed their carts down the streets.

In the time before Mallak, the carts had been filled with potatoes and onions, others loaded with barley or beans. But now the produce they were bringing to barter—because coins were mostly held for Mallak's taxmen—barely covered the bottom of their carts.

Raraesa led the horse to a stone structure with an open swinging wooden door. Adjacent to the building stood a rail held up by two posts. Raraesa tied the horse to this and called inside. "Ansel! It's Raraesa. I will leave my horse here while I go into town."

A big man wearing a leather apron showed up in the doorway. Iggy intuitively knew from studying history in school that he was a blacksmith. His face was as worn and leathery from the heat of his blacksmith furnace as the apron wrapped around his torso. The skin on his arms not covered with soot had a healthy glow, uncommon with blacksmiths.

"Sure." His voice was deep and serious. "Who's your friend?"

"This is Iggy. He will be staying with Lecque and me for the time being."

Ansel looked him up and down. His gaze lingered for an extra moment on the crystal amulet around Iggy's neck. "Where are you from, young man?"

"Pennsylvania," he blurted before Raraesa could answer for him.

"Hmm." Ansel scratched the stubbles on his chin with his blackened hand. "I guess that is in a part of the land I have not been to."

"Yes," Raraesa jumped in. "That is very far from here, in the south. The town is so small I do not even think it is on the maps. Less than fifty people live there. His family experienced a terrible tragedy. Sadly, he is all alone now, so he will be staying with Lecque and me. If you could spread word so the townspeople know not to be concerned, we would appreciate it. We should go now, but we will see you soon." She waved over her shoulder as she led Iggy away. "Iggy, you must keep your past a secret."

"Why? Because they won't believe me?" Iggy kept his head down as they walked.

"Just the opposite, because they will believe you, and that is dangerous." She stopped walking and looked at him intently. "The people here are afraid, they are suspicious, and they are scared for themselves and their families."

"Why?" Iggy looked around, bewildered. What he saw were people keeping to themselves as they walked, little to no eye contact. There was no joy in their steps. "People look afraid. Of what?"

"Our 'Emperor' Mallak." She looked around to make sure they were alone. "They are afraid of who he is, what he can do, and what he has done. He rules these lands with terror. He has many spies. Unsuspecting villagers get visits from Mallak's soldiers in the dark of the night that make unspeakable threats if they do not watch out and report things back to his guards." Raraesa looked him dead in the eye. "As far as anyone knows, you are from the south, from a very small village. Lecque found you alone, wandering, and felt bad for you. Your parents have died, and you are alone. Until we get things sorted out, you will be staying with Lecque and me. Got it?" Her eyes bored into his.

"Got it."

11

"What a pleasant surprise," Kylian rasped. "I have a visitor. And of all people, it is my brother, the emperor. I do not think you have ever visited me in my humble residence. I apologize that it is a bit dusty, as this prison cell has but a dirt floor."

"Quiet!" Spit spewed from Mallak's mouth.

"Brother, what is wrong? I fear you are in distress. Your voice is higher and squeakier than I thought was possible. Did you *come* here to seek some guidance from your locked-away brother? I'd invite you in to sit and talk, but, alas, there is only one stool, and it sits at an angle. I'm afraid you would fall off it onto the floor. I'll sit and you can stand." Kylian sat expertly balanced on the angled stool and folded his arms. "Tell me, brother emperor, how can I help you?"

"Tell me about the crystal."

"The 'crystal'? So cryptic a question. Brother emperor or emperor brother, whatever you want to be called, you will have to be clearer in what you are asking."

"The *crystal!* Did the king—"

"Our father, who you killed?"

"*Did* the king tell you about a powerful crystal?" Mallak stared intently at Kylian.

"A crystal that had power. Hmmm. He did. He said there was a crystal that had enormous power and was handed down from king to king for safekeeping. And it was never to be used, only protected from misuse." Kylian smiled at Mallak. "I guess he did not give it to you before you killed him. Maybe because you were not supposed to be king. Or was it that he thought you would misuse it?"

"Enough! Did he give the crystal to *you*?"

"... No." Kylian's smile widened to a sarcastic grin.

"Liar!"

"Maybe yes—maybe no. You will never learn from my lips. What are you going to do? Lock me in a dirty dungeon for fourteen years and throw away the key? Hmm, oh yes, you have already done that."

Mallak stormed out of the dungeon.

"Come back anytime, brother emperor. I have so enjoyed our little talk."

⚜

Ulric, Mallak's highest commander, one who was loyal to him, stood still and silent in the throne room, his hands folded in front of him.

Ulrick watched Mallak's rant, matched with a sweeping back and forth pace in front of the throne reach a level of fury he had never witnessed in all his years of serving him.

With Mallak's unpredictable personality, Ulric would not give him any reason to direct that fury at him.

"When my brother married, the king gave him land to the west of here."

"Yes. I remember that area. It is now under the kingdom's control."

"There was a manor house there. Kylian lived in it."

"Yes, I remember the house and the land. We used to ride there, you, Kylian, and me. We played in the fields and hunted there when we were young."

"Quiet! Did I ask you that?" Mallak's words spewed out. "Is it still standing?"

"I am sure it is, My Emperor."

"Go there, with soldiers. Tear that house down, board by board, brick by brick. Inspect each piece. You are to bring me any jewels, fine stones, or crystals that you find there. Throw everything else into a pile and burn it. I want no evidence left of the house or that my brother lived there. Do you understand me?" Mallak spat the last words out with a venomous tone as his robe pulsated with colors and he instinctively reached for the robe's clasp, making sure it was secured around his neck.

"Yes, Emperor Mallak."

"Do this in one day. Do you understand?"

"Yes, Emperor Mallak."

"When you return, I have another chore for you."

"Yes, Emperor Mallak."

"One last thing. You are in charge of my army? Is that correct?"

"It is, My Emperor." Ulric perspired.

"Then tell me, head of my army, what is taking so long in taking over Port Havolee?"

"The pass through the Black Cairns. The resistance keeps ambushing us. The pass is narrow and deadly for our soldiers."

Mallak simply waved his hand, dismissing him.

After a thirty-minute ride west of Castle Maol, Ulric sat in his saddle, his horse standing still, occasionally snorting and neighing. He looked across the field to the left of the manor house as a slight warm breeze rolled across his face. His memory flashed back to hunting with Kylian and Mallak. They were just kids, around twelve years old. Mallak was his same age, and Kylian was two years younger. They had grown up together and had a childhood bond.

My, how things have changed, he thought. *And others had not.*

He remembered commenting to Kylian that day how he was concerned about Mallak. "It seems," Ulric had said to Kylian, "that Mallak enjoys killing things."

"Why do you say that?"

"When you and I shoot an arrow into an animal and kill it, we always bow our head and give thanks for its sacrifice, so we have food on the table. But when Mallak shoots something, he glares at it and smiles as it dies. I asked him about it."

"And what did he answer?"

The answer should have warned him, should have warned everyone. But they were just kids. "He said he enjoyed watching things die and marveled at their suffering and struggling for their last breath. And as they closed their eyes for the last time, he wanted the creature's last glimpse in this world to be of him."

Snapping back to the present day, he shook his head, then dismounted. Upon arriving, the twenty soldiers he had brought with him began to systematically empty each of the nine rooms and pile the contents onto the dirt in front of the house. Everything was broken and smashed. No hiding place was left unveiled. The soldiers knew what they were looking for. Jewelry, shiny stones, crystals were to be brought to Ulric for his examination. Then the building itself was dismantled board by board, stone by stone and laid in a separate pile. When the sun had set, torches were set up. Their work continued through the night until there was nothing left to examine, nothing left to break.

Ulric felt the pangs of sadness as he looked over the pile of rubble that was once a home. He had enjoyed dinners with Kylian and his new bride in that house. He enjoyed watching her pregnancy blossom. He had not been around for the birth.

He had been with Mallak charging through the towns and counties. Killing and killing—there was so *much* killing. Mallak had put him in charge of his army. He rationalized that he had had no choice. It was kill or be killed. Soon, much of the kingdom had yielded to Mallak's wishes.

When he returned, he was told to bring Kylian, his wife, and his child to Mallak. He had knocked on Kylian's door with extreme sadness. Kylian had told him his wife and child were gone. He would not say if the child was a boy or a girl. And he would not say where they were. Kylian went without argument with Ulric to be presented to Mallak. Kylian also forgave Ulric and said he understood the difficult situation he was in, and from that moment on Ulric had used all the influence he had with Mallak to keep Kylian alive.

~§

Ulric stood before Mallak in the throne room.

Mallak sat on the throne with unnatural calm. "Tell me," Mallak demanded, "what did you find?"

Ulric stood stiff and at attention before his childhood friend. "We did not find any crystals, gems, or even simple shiny stones. It was clear that robbers had broken into the manor and looted it many times. I am sorry; what you were looking for wasn't there."

Mallak stared at the dark smoke-smudged ceiling of the throne room that once boasted inlaid murals of the countryside. Now not even the most colorful tile showed through the dirt and smudge that had risen from the fire pots scattered throughout the room to keep it warm and lit.

Mallak gave a sardonic smile, then looked down at Ulric. "I have another task for you. Find the Past Seer. Take him to where the Nostaw's body rots. Have the Past Seer find out what happened there."

He waved his hand and dismissed Ulric, then went back to staring at the ceiling.

~§

Iggy and Raraesa walked out of the cobbler's store. On Iggy's feet were worn leather boots. They had no holes in them and they fit. Raraesa had to barter hard. The cobbler wanted coin, but Raraesa only had eggs. The cobbler agreed only after Raraesa promised to bring him six more on her next trip to town. They didn't hold hands this time. Iggy wasn't confident enough to reach out first. He was satisfied with relishing the recent memory of the touch of her hand, the casualness with which it had happened. That moment was what he thought it would be. That moment vanished quickly as reality reminded him where he was. Pangs of loss rolled over him. He withdrew into himself for a moment, looking only at the cobblestone street in front of him.

The smell of baking bread wafted through the air as they passed a house with someone inside, baking it. It reminded him of walking into the local bakery at home with Aunt Gwen. Finally, he looked up. He accepted that getting home was up to him. He should face it. Being what John called a wuss would not do. Also, there was Raraesa, who appeared to like him. It was time for him to buck up and rise to the challenge.

"Iggy, are you well?" Raraesa asked.

Iggy stopped, thought, then continued their walk. Knowledge was power, and he had a lot of questions. "Tell me about this land now that no one is within earshot."

"What do you mean?"

"Well, how big is Skye? What is to the north, south, east, and west of here?"

Raraesa shrugged casually. "North of here the land stops. There is an angry sea, with whirlpools and rocks that shatter all boats that venture onto them. Then north of that is the Island of Cambria. That is where the Nostaw live. West of here is most of the Kingdom of Skye, which ends where it touches the mountains where hot melted rock rolls out of them. The land ends to south in the vast sea. The kingdom is bordered on the east by the Black Cairn Mountains that run from north to south of the kingdom. And, lastly, east of the mountains is the Plains of Clouds."

"What is the Plains of Clouds?"

"There's a gap in the Cairns where the land drops straight down. As far down as the Black Cairns are high. Actually, so far down no one has ever attempted to scale down the sheer cliffs. You cannot see the bottom because it is completely covered by clouds that run past the end of your vision. No one knows what's down there or what it looks like."

"Wow, that's creepy."

"I agree."

"So does the guy, Mallak, rule over the entire Kingdom of Skye?"

"No. There is land to the north and south, and Port Havolee that's east of the Black Cairns, protected by a very narrow pass that is still free of him. I am concerned that will not last. He is building a large army. It is just a matter of time before the entire kingdom comes under his evil rule."

They continued walking down the street, and Iggy casually asked, "Have you ever heard of Liquid Fire?"

"No. What is that?"

"Did Lecque tell you about the Nostaw Warrior and how he gave me his swords?"

"He did."

"His *special* Nostaw swords?"

"Yes, he did. And he was very surprised."

"That's not the only weird thing. It was something the Nostaw said to me before he died. He said the only way I can get home is to fulfill a quest, which starts when I dip the swords into Liquid Fire."

"I have never heard of such a thing. I'll ask Lecque; maybe he knows."

"I don't think so. I already asked him. He was clueless too."

"Clueless? What is clueless?"

Iggy laughed. "It means he doesn't know either."

Raraesa glanced around, hoping they were not causing a scene. "Are you hungry?"

Iggy sighed. He couldn't ignore the baking bread aroma. "I guess so. But what I really want is a heaping plate of mac and cheese."

"What is this mac and cheese?"

"Macaroni and cheese. It's what my Aunt Gwen would make for me when I was having a bad day. She called it my super comfort food. She taught me to cook, and we'd make it together. While we made it, we'd talk. Which was also comforting."

"Aunt Gwen sounds very special."

"She was… I mean, is."

Raraesa stopped and looked at him askance. "Of course, I know what cheese is, but what is mac? I know a family with the last name of Mac."

"Figures, I get sent to a place that doesn't know what macaroni is. Do you have spaghetti?"

"No."

"You don't have any type of pasta here, do you?"

"Iggy, I have no idea what you are talking about. What is macaroni, spaghetti, or pasta?"

Iggy shrugged. "I guess I could show you."

"I would like that."

Iggy thought for a moment, then smiled. "Do you have eggs, flour, salt, pepper, cheese, and dried mustard?"

"We have a block of cheese wrapped and saved in the root cellar. I have herbs from our garden. Mustard seed is too difficult to get. Lecque brought back a small bag of salt on his last trip to Port Havolee; he has some way to get to it. I can give you a few pinches. Do not tell Lecque. He is saving it for curing meat."

"I promise. We could crush the herbs. And we will also need butter and milk. Oh, yes, and flour."

"Butter takes so long to churn; we usually use lard. The milk and eggs we have from our cows and chickens. And I have flour to make bread."

"Well, if you really want to… I could show you how to cook it, but only… if you really want to."

Raraesa smiled with a slight head tilt. "I would really like that."

After retrieving their horse from in front of Ansel's blacksmith shop, they walked toward the field, when Raraesa stopped. Frankie and his friends were still throwing rocks across the field.

"Are we taking a different route?"

Raraesa smiled sheepishly. "No. Climb up." She helped Iggy into the saddle and adjusted the stirrups for his feet, then climbed on behind him. She pushed him forward and took the spot, settling in behind him. "That is better."

"What are you doing?"

"You are taking the reins."

"But I don't know how to ride a horse." *And*, he thought, *I like riding with my arms around you.*

"By the time we get to the farm, I promise you you'll know how to ride." She threw her arms around his waist and held on.

Iggy looked at her arms encircling him. *I could get used to this, though.* "Well, then"—he smiled a big grin—"I could use a lesson or two on how to ride."

Raraesa kicked her heels into the horse, and they were off. Iggy responded to the death glares from Frankie with a casual nod of his head and a confident smile. The rest of the ride was filled with instructions on how to control, direct, and bond with the horse so one rides symbiotically with the animal. Iggy was an eager learner as Raraesa leaned forward with her chin on his shoulder to grab the reins and show him how to do it right. By the time they rose over the hill above the town, Iggy had the horse in a comfortable trot and gave every indication he had been riding for years. It didn't hurt that Raraesa was nudging the horse with subtle kicks of her heels.

※

Southwest and a half day's ride from the dead forest that surrounded Castle Maol was an old-growth forest so widespread it took two days of riding by horse to reach the other side, where it met rolling grass plains that extended to the horizon. Narrow barely distinguishable trails crossed and crisscrossed this oak and pine tree forest. It was a place that one could easily get lost in and stay lost if one did not want to be found.

So, it was with some surprise to the sixtyish-year-old man who sat on a log to see Ulric slowly ride up on his horse. Beside the man was the horse-drawn cart that carried his worldly belongings. He tended a fire and was cooking a rabbit on a wooden spike.

"Ulric, my old friend. It has been, why, over five years since we have seen each other. This cannot be by chance. But how did you find me?" Quitee stood up off the log he sat on.

"Hello, my friend." Ulric dismounted. "You are correct; this is not a chance meeting. And to answer how I found you"—he chuckled—"these woods may be vast, but I still know who enters and leaves them and where they hide when they choose not to leave. It is my job to know these things."

"Just so, just so. Come sit beside the fire and tell me why you are here."

"I have a task for you."

Ulric sat as Quitee pulled the rabbit off the fire, cut off a piece with a small knife, and passed it to Ulric. "I am listening."

"Mallak needs you to look into the past for him. A dead Nostaw Warrior."

"Dead, you say." Quitee pondered. "That is a lot harder than someone alive. It will cost you double." He held out his hand.

Ulric reached into the pouch tied onto his waist belt, pulled out some silver coins, counted them, and dropped them into Quitee's open palm.

Quitee looked at them and laughed. "I said double."

Ulric pulled out eight more coins and dropped them into Quitee's palm. "I was just seeing if you were vigilant." He, too, laughed.

"So why do you do this?" Quitee asked.

"Do what?"

"Work for His Mightiness the emperor."

"I do not know what you are talking about."

"Stop the charade, my friend. Or do you forget I am a Past Seer? It is easy to read your past with you simply sitting next to me. And do not worry. Your secret is safe with me. I hold many a person's deepest secrets in this head." Quitee tapped his forehead with his finger.

"And what secret is it that you think you know?"

"Your wife, your son. Whom you have brilliantly hidden from Mallak."

Ulric's face tensed up. Quitee allayed his concerns. "." My friend, relax. There is not enough money in all of Skye to have me divulge such personal secrets. I do not play those types of games. I divulge the past to those who pay me but, as a Past Seer, I still live by a code of honor. So, I assume you stay loyal to him to protect them

Ulric sighed. "There is great truth in that. Mallak is very dangerous, and he is not right in the head. I figure if I can stay one step ahead of him, they will be safe."

"I would do the same thing if I had a family. But, alas, I am a traveling harlot for hire. My kind, Past Seers, are few and far apart nowadays. If we congregate in one spot, we would be a target. Mallak saw to that. So, we scattered like birds in the wind. He only looks for us when he needs us."

"I understand. Let me ask you the same question. Why do you do what you do?"

"Do what? Look into the past? That is what I do."

"No. Why do you work for the emperor if he killed off most of your kind?"

"It is a task. A paid task. I have no long-term allegiance to the emperor or anyone other than myself. I am paid, thus I work. I hold momentary allegiance to the coins in my pouch. When the task is done, I move on. Until the task is done, I am a bought-and-paid-for Past Seer. That is also a Past Seer's code." Quitee took a bite of rabbit. "How long a ride is it to this dead Nostaw?"

"Two days and one half of the next day."

"Then we stay here tonight and leave in the morning. Eat up, my friend, then we sleep."

12

A few hours later, Iggy and Raraesa stood by the table in Raraesa's cottage, looking at the ingredients they'd gathered that he needed to make mac and cheese.

Iggy began. "The first thing we need to do is clear off an area on the table so we can make the pasta dough for the macaroni, which is the 'mac' part of mac and cheese."

They quickly set about clearing off the wooden kitchen table.

Iggy took a moment and looked around the room. It wasn't a bad place; he felt safe and in control. He glanced at Raraesa, and a slight smile curved his lips. Not bad, cooking with a beautiful girl—life could be worse. Much worse. For the moment he forgot where he was and how he had gotten here. His shoulders relaxed, he took a deep healthy breath in, and thought, *You got this.*

He looked at Raraesa with a grin.

"Now we start with the dough." He scooped a pile of flour onto the table, then he cracked six eggs and poured them into a well in the center of the flour. He looked at Raraesa. "Now you use your hands and mix." Iggy dug his hands into the mixture, stopping after a moment to look up at Raraesa. "Why don't you try?"

"Very well."

Within moments the two were mixing and kneading pasta dough. Iggy was in his happy place as he pushed and folded the dough.

"Now, we need to roll the dough out thin and flat."

He picked up the rolling pin he'd used to crush the herbs, and after rolling out the dough, he showed Raraesa how to cut it into long strips, then crosscut them, so they had small, rectangular pieces. "You finish cutting the pasta while I cut up the cheese blocks. That's for our *mise en place*."

"What is *mise en place*?"

"It's a French phrase. It means 'putting in place.' Think of it as getting all the ingredients measured and prepared before cooking them."

"I see… but what is *French*?"

Iggy thought for a moment before he replied, "That is best left for another day. It's a long answer that frankly isn't important now. While I slice the cheese, you finish cutting the pasta."

After Iggy finished with the cheese and other ingredient preparation, he said, "We need to boil some water. Can we hang a pot over the fire?"

"Yes." Raraesa took a pot from the cupboard, filled it with water, and placed it on a hook that hung over the flames.

"Perfect. I need to start on the *roux*."

"The what?"

"It's another French word—never mind. Can you melt that lard in a pot?"

Soon enough, they had a pot of water hanging over the fire to boil. Raraesa grabbed another pot, placed the lard in it, and melted it over the fire. Then she removed it from the heat.

"Now we add the salt, pepper, herbs, along with the flour. Then we slowly add the milk and stir it until the whole thing is smooth. Next, we cook the mixture until it starts to thicken." Five minutes later, Iggy smiled. "Now we drop the cheese in and mix until the cheese is completely melted."

Soon the other pot with the water came to a rolling boil. "Next, we simply scoop up the pasta and drop it into the water." When that was done, he folded his arms. "Now we wait."

Raraesa stood beside him, appearing intrigued and full of anticipation over how this concoction called mac and cheese would taste. "How will we know when it is done?"

"It should be done when the pasta floats to the top. But I still like to check it, so I pull out one piece of pasta—called a noodle—once in a while and sample it." He showed her, and when a noodle felt just right in his mouth, he fished one from the pot and gave it to her. "Here, taste this. This is how it feels when it's done."

She did and crinkled her nose. "It tastes bland; it has no flavor." There was disappointment on her face.

"Don't worry, we still have more to do. That's where the magic comes in. The pasta texture's good. Help me strain it." Iggy grabbed clean rags and carried the pot to the sink. With Raraesa's help, who held a piece of cheesecloth since she didn't have a strainer, Iggy poured the pot of boiling water and the noodles into it. "Shake it up and down to drain the water, then put the noodles back into the pot."

Raraesa followed Iggy's directions. He then poured the sauce over the pasta. "We stir a few times, cover it, and let it rest."

"Iggy, now I know you are playing a game with me; food does not get tired and does not need to rest."

Iggy cracked a smile, then laughed, which annoyed Raraesa. "Nooo, it's a cooking term for when you let food sit so that it continues to cook in its own heat."

"You were not jesting at my expense?"

"No. I don't make fun of people. I know how hurtful that is. One final stir, then we eat. Could you get two bowls and spoons, please?"

Iggy scooped out two deep bowls of mac and cheese for them. "Prepare to be carried away on a cloud of tasty pleasure."

He took his first spoonful. It tasted slightly different from the stuff back home and had a different texture, given the lard rather than butter and the flat instead of round noodles, but it was still delicious, hitting the right notes.

"Now, that's good." He looked at Raraesa.

Raraesa stopped for a moment and put her spoon down, "This is tremendous, and you are brilliant. I love mac and cheese!" With total spontaneity she reached across the table, grabbed Iggy's head with two hands, and planted a kiss on his right check.

Iggy froze for a moment then touched his fingers to the check that was kissed as he stared ahead in wonderment.

Raraesa scooped the last of her mac and cheese into her mouth. She swallowed with a satisfying smile. "I can't wait for you to cook something else for me."

"Neither can I, Raraesa."

❧

That evening, Iggy lay in a makeshift bed in the barn with an ear-to-ear grin. *What a day.* It could not have gone any better had he planned it.

Rolling over, he fell asleep, and his happiness faded. His dreams swirled with thoughts, confusing thoughts. He wasn't flying above the land, he was running… and he was afraid, very afraid. There, up ahead, he saw a cave. He ran into it and stopped. Bending down, he panted hard, trying to catch his breath. Eyes—there were many eyes staring out of the dark at him. Everywhere he turned, there were eyes. The darkness disappeared, and he was bathed in light. But he was in a cave! There, on the walls, torches lit one at a time, increasing the illumination that seemed focused on him. Spinning around, he was surrounded by eyes.

The cave opening was blocked.

In unison, a chorus of voices chanted, "Give us the swords. Give us the swords."

Iggy fell to his knees and covered his ears, but the voices penetrated his hands.

"Give us the swords!"

"Here they are, then!" Iggy yelled back as he pulled the swords from behind his back and tossed them into the darkness.

Silence. Only silence. To Iggy, it dragged on and on. It was so quiet he could hear his heartbeat.

Then, one voice came out of the darkness, "You are not Tilead. You must die."

Many swords, Nostaw swords, appeared, enhanced by the torchlight reflecting off them. All coming closer to Iggy.

The chanting started up again. "You are not Tilead. You must die."

"No!" Iggy screamed.

He bolted upright in his bed, covered with sweat, his heart pounding. The remainder of the night was fitful as he tossed and turned, but he eventually he fell back to sleep.

13

The next morning Lecque sat at the table after feeding the horses, cows, and pigs. "Where is Iggy?"

"Still sleeping," Raraesa replied as she fixed a bowl of gruel and bread and placed it on the table for Lecque, who sat and ate.

"What have you discovered about him? Is he someone we need to be concerned about?"

"Honestly, Iggy is harmless."

"He was not harmless the way he killed those Baisd Bheulachs. He is just untrained."

"He is like a scared rabbit, though. He has no idea why or how he ended up here. He talks about amazing things from where he is from. And he knows strange facts. None that are relevant to us. He is a kind, sweet young man." Raraesa sat with her own plate and ate.

"Sweet, you say." Lecque stopped eating for a moment. "Yet, he has a pair of Nostaw swords. I met with Ankter yesterday in Brightenrid. He wants Iggy gone. He feels he is a threat, a danger to the town and to our cause."

"I have told you I do not like or trust that man. He does not care about us, our cause, or even this town. He only cares about protecting himself. I feel, Brother, he is a coward and one who is a real danger to us!" Raraesa's tone was sharp and full of annoyance. "When are you going to take me to those meetings?"

"You know they will not accept your involvement."

"Because I am a girl."

"That is correct."

"I am one of the best with a sword for my age. You taught me yourself. I can be helpful if it comes to a battle."

"Just keep practicing. If it does come to a battle, I would want you beside me."

Raraesa nodded. Then, suddenly alarmed, she asked, "You will not let them hurt Iggy? Yes?"

"Do not worry. I told Ankter that under no circumstances was Iggy to be harmed. I agree he is innocent. I just wanted your opinion."

"Tell me, then, do you intend to teach him how to defend himself? How to use those swords?"

"If only I could. The Nostaw race has stayed secluded for many generations. Their fighting skills with their swords are legendary. It is said that only a Nostaw Warrior can pass down the teaching of those swords. Those swords, it is also said, have powers that are beyond our knowledge. But he does need to learn how to protect himself. I think you are the best one to train him."

"That will be interesting." She smiled. "He keeps talking about this quest and having to dip the swords in Liquid Fire to bring them alive. Have you ever heard of Liquid Fire?"

Lecque shook his head. "No, I have no idea what that means. Anyway, today I will meet with Lachlan. He wants to buy one of our milking cows. We need to sell one of them to pay the taxes."

"Where is the coin you earned from your last trip to Port Havolee?"

"We cannot use that. If we do not sell a cow, people will ask how we came to have that much coin. We cannot draw suspicion to us. I do not want them to find out I'm a runner to the port for contraband goods."

"I do not like you doing that. One day you will be caught."

"I will be careful. And tomorrow I must also go to Ginside for a meeting. I want to take Iggy with me."

"Why?"

"I want Madam Trinity to evaluate him."

"You know she's crazy."

"I am not sure she is as crazed as people think. Anyway, there is more to him than meets the eye. And I agree that he has no idea either. Madam Trinity might have some answers to some of our questions about who, or what, he is."

"Here, I want you to try this." Raraesa put a bowl in front of him.

"What is it?" Lecque looked at the bowl with suspicion.

"It is called 'mac and cheese.' Try it."

Lecque took a spoonful. After sniffing it, he tasted it. Finally, he said, "This is very good. Where did you get it?"

"Iggy made it. There is more to Iggy than your eyes can see."

"Well, at least he is good for something!" He wolfed down the mac and cheese. "Now, I have to go." Lecque got up just as Iggy entered the cottage. "Iggy, I am taking a trip to the city of Ginside tomorrow. I want you to meet someone."

"All right! A road trip. I guess on horseback you can't call shotgun?" Iggy looked from Raraesa to Lecque then back to Raraesa.

Lecque and Raraesa stared at Iggy and simultaneously shook their heads.

"What is shotgun?" Raraesa asked Lecque in a soft voice.

"No idea." Lecque replied as he walked out the front door.

"Iggy, sit. I have breakfast for you." Raraesa spooned out a mixture of what looked to Iggy like watery mashed potatoes.

After a moment, he tasted it. "This isn't bad. What is it?"

"Breakfast gruel. It's a little bit of this and a little bit of that."

"Aunt Gwen called it leftover surprise."

Raraesa laughed. "That is true. It is always a surprise what it will taste like. Today, it is not that bad."

⇗

Bright and early the next day, Iggy and Lecque set out on the three-day ride to Ginside. Iggy was pleased to see he had his own horse to ride. The morning air was cool and crisp; a subtle breeze rustled the tops of the trees. For the first few hours, Iggy and Lecque rode quietly down the path that meandered through the forest. Around midday the forest thinned and eventually stopped. Iggy gazed far ahead, and as far as he could see, dark-green hills rolled up and up, not into mountains but into foothills.

Spectacular, Iggy thought as they rode up to higher elevations. Late in the afternoon, Lecque stopped and dismounted next to an outcropping of boulders that stood twice the height of his horse and were twice as long on the open treeless hill.

"We'll camp here tonight. The wind usually comes from that direction. If we stay on this side, we should be warm. Search around for any dead brush or bushes you can find so we can have a fire to stay warm tonight."

By the time the sun was setting, they had gathered two armfuls of dried sticks and had a small fire going. Sitting close to it, they talked. Iggy had again arranged stones in a small pyramid as he had the first day he had met Lecque. Satisfied they would be comfortable through the night, they both sat around it.

"So, tell me more about the suck your hanna pencil neck place you came from."

Iggy chuckled and realized this was the longest he had spent with Lecque other than the first day they had met. He had been so caught up with Raraesa he hadn't noticed the lack of interaction with Lecque or that Lecque disappeared for entire days. Something he'd attempt to discover more about on this trip.

Lecque, on the other hand, was bowled over when Iggy told him about cars, planes, and especially television. Iggy held off on telling him about landing on the moon and cell phones—he'd save that for another time.

The second day was filled with Iggy laughing and Lecque disbelieving. "You will not make me believe that you touch a piece of metal and you are able to talk to another person on the other end of your kingdom and it is not magic."

"I told you yesterday, it is called science."

"No, it is magic. And I think this is more in the realm of black magic."

Iggy laughed. "So, you think I am a black magic wizard?"

"No, I think you are the lowly jester for a black magic wizard."

"You're saying I'm full of it, then."

"Full of what?"

"Never mind." Iggy laughed even harder.

They had passed through some high meadows on the third day, and then finally returned to a landscape with trees, though they were widely spaced apart. Sunlight blazed through to the grass, and the lack of a forest canopy allowed the grass to grow as high as the bellies of the horses. They trotted along the path beaten down from prior travelers, easing their way as their long journey continued.

A warm, dry wind blew across the open field and swirled around the Nostaw's lifeless body, unmoved from where it fell several days before. Ulric and Quitee approached with apprehension, expecting to see a body ravaged by vultures and other scavengers. Surprisingly, the body was untouched.

Quitee began the task at hand by inspecting the area around the fallen Nostaw. He had the unique ability to study an area and investigate its past by seeing what had taken place there.

At the sight of the fallen Nostaw, Quitee and Ulric's horses stood uneasily abreast, their heads swaying back and forth. They smelled death, not natural death, but death from demonic evilness, which had kept the scavengers away. Ulric and Quitee dismounted and walked to the lifeless Nostaw.

Quitee carried a ceremonial staff inlaid with rune symbols. Upon approaching the Nostaw, he held the staff aloft.

"You must stay there, my friend. Do not approach closer and do not enter my circle."

Quitee stood motionless for a short time in front of the body. Then, taking a few steps back, he slowly drew a circle around the Nostaw, his staff cutting the ground with ease. When the circle was complete, Quitee stayed within it. He struck the staff down with a fluid motion, driving it into the ground. With both hands now free, he raised his palms toward the sky and chanted a few words in a language Ulric had never heard before. Then Quitee stopped and stood, waiting, peering intently at the drawn line. The line in the ground pulsed a dark gray, growing darker as the seconds passed, as if sucking in the surrounding light, lending a shimmer and blurriness to anything near it, giving the line a life of its own.

When Ulric looked at it, he felt a chill. The horses snorted and whinnied. Ulric held tightly on to their reins to keep them from bolting in fear. He told the horses "All is well," trying to convince himself things truly were well.

⸻

Quitee bent his head down and shut his eyes. His hands remained extended in front of him, trembling in spasms. Then his head twitched from right to left and back again, at first slowly, then at a faster pace, as if scanning the pages of a book. He was turning back pages, not of a book, but of time itself. He twitched faster until two figures walked backward into the circle, then hovered over the Nostaw.

Quitee's head stopped. Then he moved his right hand in front of him from left to right, and time moved forward again. He watched a Death Knight hover over the motionless Nostaw before leaving. Moments later, two figures—one tall, the other younger and smaller and wearing strange clothes—entered the circle and stood beside the Nostaw. Quitee leaned forward. The figures were hazy from the waist up. He could not clearly see their faces or features. He had never encountered this before. Both figures had red auras shimmering around them, blurring them to Quitee who, in frustration, twisted his head back and forth, up and down, trying to peer through the fog of his vision.

He made his way around the Nostaw until he was on the same side as the two figures.

Quitee watched the smaller of the two kneel, then saw as the Nostaw spun his swords around the small one's neck. The vision cleared slightly in that moment, though not enough for Quitee to make out any clear details but enough to make out a pulse of energy coming off the smaller figure's chest.

"Yes," Quitee said in a low mutter, "you, little one, you are the powerful one. And, by your clothing, you do not appear to be of this land."

The swords suddenly spun and were in the hands of the small one. Then the Nostaw was dead. Moments later, the two blurred figures walked out of Quitee's time circle and were gone.

Quitee walked back to Ulric and informed him of what he had seen.

"We must ride directly back to Mallak. We must inform him that whoever has those swords wields great power," Ulric said.

"You must inform him, for my job here is done, and I am going in a different direction." After Quitee mounted his horse, he turned to Ulric. "A free piece of knowledge. To see the future, you must be able to see and comprehend the past. And I see in the future a prophecy that might become reality." He dug his heels into the sides of his horse and in moments was at a full gallop across the field.

⁓

As Lecque and Iggy neared the town of Ginside, they slowed the horses and let them walk. They dismounted at the edge of town, left their horses at the stable, and headed to the center of town.

Ginside was once a beautiful place, laid out around three-square grassy parks no more than a hundred feet from edge to edge. They were surrounded on all four sides with streets now filled with loose and missing cobblestones. The streets around each park were lined with two-story brick buildings in disrepair, with window shutters that hung at different angles and grime that covered the buildings' outer walls. Large oak trees interspersed in the parks gave shade to unstable wooden benches. The grass desperately needed a good cutting. Ginside, same as other towns and cities under Mallak's control, was decaying from lack of funds, due to high taxes.

They stopped at a small entrance that led them into an inn. Lecque stepped up to a counter. The innkeeper, an old woman with a weatherworn face, came from behind the front desk. "And how may I help you?"

"Good day. We need a room for two," Lecque said.

She looked them over. "How many nights?" she snapped.

"Two."

The innkeeper grabbed a key and dropped it on the counter. "Six coins. And we do not barter for rooms." She held out her hand, palm up.

Lecque opened a leather pouch dangling from his waist and paid her.

"If you want dinner, we serve it in the pub. Tonight, you are lucky; we have fresh meat. And we have two troubadours entertaining us. Be advised: the meat is sparse and the room is small. We do not have much joy around these parts anymore. So, when we have meat and entertainment… well, the seats and the food will go fast. You will find beds upstairs." She turned and walked into the pub without saying another word.

After climbing the steps and entering the room Iggy flopped onto a bed with a satisfied smile on his face. "Man, even straw feels good after lying on the ground for two nights."

"Let us get something to eat and then back to bed early. There is someone I wish you to meet in the morning."

They entered the bar through a side entrance that extended out from the inn. The room got quieter as folks looked at them guardedly from seven wooden tables surrounded by stools that had seen better days. The woman who had checked them in was behind the bar taking orders and serving drinks alongside a very rotund man who sported a bushy fiery-red beard.

The room was filling up, but, as luck had it, Lecque found a table with two stools to the left of the tiny foot-high stage that was more akin to a platform. Moments after sitting, a barmaid walked over to them.

"What can I get for the two of you?" There was no enthusiasm in her voice.

"You have any mutton?"

"No. All out. We rarely have mutton, so it goes fast."

"What do you have, then?"

"Stew. Meat and potato stew. No idea what kind of meat, though."

"Then we will both have stew, with plenty of bread. And two mugs of ale."

The barmaid turned and walked away before Iggy could object. "You ordered ale for me?" Iggy asked in hush tones.

"I did. Is that a problem?"

"Where I'm from, I'm considered too young to drink ale. Don't you have a drinking age here?"

"The age to drink is simple, if you want a drink, you can have one. So, do you want an ale or milk?"

"Ale is fine. I am on my way to becoming a Nostaw Warrior, after all." Iggy whispered so as not to be overhead as he sat up straight in his chair and squared his shoulders.

In a short time, the food and drinks arrived. Lecque wasted no time digging into the stew. He chased every mouthful of food with a swig of ale. Iggy was just as hungry and followed Lecque's lead, spooning in mouthful after mouthful. He left the ale untouched.

"If you let the ale sit too long it gets bitter and heavier. Best to drink it fresh… or if you do not want it, you can pass it over to me." Lecque held out his hand.

"No, I'll give it a try." Iggy raised the mug to his lips and took a tiny sip. He held it in his mouth for a moment before swallowing it.

"Well?" Lecque asked.

"Well, what?"

"I assume that was your first taste of ale. What did you think of it?" Lecque had a smirk on his face.

"Not what I expected. But not horrible." Iggy returned the smirk as he took a gulp this time. After a few more mouthfuls he felt his emotional protective wall lowering. "So what are we doing tomorrow?"

"I told you there is someone I want you to meet."

"Yes, you did. But you didn't say who. So, who am I meeting with tomorrow?"

"Her name is Madam Trinity. She can see things."

"Sees things? Like what things?" He leaned into Lecque and whispered even more quietly, "Can she tell me about the Nostaw and these swords?" Iggy took another mouthful of ale.

"I do not know. I hope she will be able to tell us how you arrived in Skye, why you are here, and how to send you home. If she cannot, I am hoping she might be able to find out from her governing council of Interpreter Adepts."

"And what and where is this council?"

"I do not know that. That is a tightly guarded secret."

Iggy took another mouthful of ale. He looked at the glass, disappointed to see it was almost empty. "Another tightly guarded secret. And what does this council do?"

"It rules their land."

"And where is their land?" Iggy's words were slurring, and he was talking louder.

"No one knows."

"Another guarded secret. Got it."

"And speak even softer. I do not want anyone to hear our conversation about Nostaws or you having the swords."

Thirty minutes later, after their second round of ale arrived, Iggy was slightly giddy. He raised the mug and took a deep swallow.

"Iggy, go slow. We have a long day tomorrow, and the last thing I want is to be dealing with you throwing up all night and then dragging along with a headache tomorrow."

Iggy looked around; the room had filled. Every seat at every table was taken, and more men and women stood by the walls. Up on the small rise that was the stage, the woman who had checked them in earlier took the center.

"Welcome all," she started. "If you have not eaten, I am afraid you are out of luck. The mutton and the stew are no more. But there is plenty of drink to go around." Cheers erupted around the room. "Let us give a warm welcome to the traveling minstrels Trafagla and Fernando, who will sing, play, and spin a few tales for us."

Trafagla took the stage and rhythmically clapped her hands; everyone in the room took her cue and clapped along. It had been such a long time since most had laughed and relaxed. For the moment, they felt safe and let down their guard, if only for the moment.

Iggy was impressed by the way she walked and carried herself with the true confidence of an entertainer, smiling and greeting the audience. She might've been in her mid-twenties, with a deep cinnamon complexion, dark-brown eyes, and shiny black hair that was full and flowed with her every move. She was slightly taller than he was and wore a knee-length skirt and a flowing blouse embroidered with flowers.

The male minstrel, Fernando, took a seat on the stool on the stage and strummed a tune on his guitar. Trafagla walked to the edge of the platform and sang. It was a catchy tune, and the words were rather silly. It was about a pig farmer whose pigs were smarter than he was. The pigs would only eat chicken. If the farmer wanted to fatten up the pigs, he would eventually run out of chickens. When the farmer realized the chickens grew faster than pigs and he made more money selling chickens, he let the pigs go. He thought he was so smart, but the pigs returned every evening for their dinner, a modest amount of chicken, which the farmer happily gave them because if it wasn't for those dumb pigs that only ate chickens, he would be a poor pig farmer instead of the modest comfortable chicken farmer he was.

By the end of the first song, the crowd was smiling and clapping to the tune as Fernando strummed. The two continued, song after song. Iggy had taken Lecque's advice and sipped his second mug of ale slowly, learning to enjoy the flavor. As the evening progressed, he found himself captivated by Trafagla.

"For our last bit of entertainment," Trafagla said, "I want to tell you a tale. A tale about greed, death, and manipulation. A tale about stolen valor and stolen lives. About a would-be king and his prophecy."

The crowd suddenly went quiet, the anticipation palpable. Iggy looked around. It was as if this woman on the stage had pushed a button to silence everyone. Even the barmaid had stopped serving and took a position at the bar, staring at the stage.

Iggy leaned over to Lecque and spoke softly, "What's going on? Why has the entire place gone quiet?"

"It is the story. At the end of every troubadour show, one of them tells a story. Sometimes it is a tale about our past or what could be in our future. Other times it is a dark, scary story. Or just a whimsical tale. Either way, everyone wants to hear it, so… shhh." Lecque put two fingers to his lips.

Trafagla took a deep breath and began:

"Beatherd Meadalsy was the ruler of Skye seven hundred ninety-three cycles ago. Which we in Skye call years now.

"It was a time of uncertainty and flux within this great land. What this land lacked was stability and harmony. Beatherd attempted to calm the masses by marrying a common girl, Corie Ruteghas, whom he absolutely loved.

"Peissawag Cindergleam arrived on their wedding day. Now, Peissawag was a dwarf wizard that folklore foretold through the ages would bestow wonderful gifts on people, or, if angered, he would bring poverty and plague upon those he visited. That day he was happy, for he saw that

Beatherd's marriage to Corie was founded in true love. As a wedding gift, he gave them a stone. But not just any stone. It was a stone he had personally mined from an incredibly special quarry. And this stone was the size of the king's bed itself. Its height loomed a foot taller than the king, who stood six feet tall himself."

Trafagla stopped and took a drink from the mug on a small table on the stage.

"One would rationally think this stone was too big and too heavy to move. But Peissawag was a wizard, and this stone was as light as a feather. He placed it on the marble floor of the great throne room. Then, Peissawag informed the newlyweds that the stone had many powers. But the one bestowed upon it for their wedding gift was the power of health, happiness, and good fortune for his kingdom.

"And good fortune their kingdom had, for their crops were plentiful. Their land lived in harmony, for the surrounding kingdoms all made peace and grew in their own prosperity. Happiness spread to all corners of the land."

Iggy looked around. Everyone was mesmerized by Trafagla's tale. He turned back to her and sipped his ale as she continued.

"When Beatherd's rule had come to its end, his son Lloyd took the throne. He inherited the good fortune that had been bestowed upon the kingdom. When his reign was over, he passed it onto his son, Merrick, who passed it onto his son, Apevan. A few years into Apevan's rule, Cinead, the emperor of Acmodael, arrived. Acmodael was—or I should say is—an island to the far north of here. Far off into the water... no one knows exactly where. It is also said that even if it was found, no one could reach it."

Trafagla stopped for a moment and pondered before asking the audience, "If no one had seen it, was it a myth or a rumor? Did this land really exist?" She looked around the room, making eye contact with a man in the corner, then with a woman near the front of the platform. She looked to the right then to the left. No one answered her. "Some questions will go unanswered, I guess. Let me resume.

"Cinead informed Apevan that he wanted the stone so his land could

prosper. Apevan was wise. He told Cinead that he could have the stone if he and only he could move it. Try as he could, Cinead could not.

"*Cinead roared with rage, 'If I cannot have the stone, then neither shall you!'*

"*With two hands, Cinead unsheathed his mighty sword and raised it above his head. The sword began glowing a blinding red, then he brought it down upon the stone.*

"One would think that sword was no match for solid stone. But you would be wrong, for Cinead's sword was a powerfully magic sword— magic and power no one knows about in this day and age.

"*When the sword struck the stone, the stone shattered into many crystal pieces, as many as there are trees in this land. And these magical crystals flew out of every opening of the castle and were flung to all corners of the kingdom. It is said that whoever holds the centermost crystal has at their hands immense power.*

"And what, you may ask, about the magic sword?" Trafagla looked around the room at the patrons.

"Well, the stone wasn't without its own magic. *When the sword hit and shattered the stone, the stone retaliated. The sword that was in Cinead's hand disintegrated into dust. And from that moment on the Kingdom of Skye lost its harmony and good fortune. The end.*"

Trafagla placed one hand on her waist and the other behind her back, then took a bow. The patrons in the bar erupted with clapping and hoots of praise.

Iggy turned to Lecque, who was clapping hard. "What does she mean, 'the end'? That's not the end. It leaves the story unfinished."

Lecque responded with a disapproving look. "Iggy, it was a great story. Do not ruin the moment. Clap and be happy."

Iggy begrudgingly clapped.

Trafagla walked around the room with a mug, stopping at each table. The patrons dropped coins into the mug and expressed thanks for being entertained.

When she stopped at Iggy's table, Lecque dropped in a coin. "Thank you for such great song and entertainment this evening," he said.

Trafagla looked at Iggy and smiled. "And did *you* enjoy this evening?"

Iggy blushed. Her eyes up close momentarily mesmerized him. Her smile was warm and yet mysterious. "Well, yes. The songs were very entertaining. But... ."

"But?"

"But the story is left unfinished. You just ended it with 'the end.' There must be more. What happens next?"

"Why, Iggy, this is the story." She motioned around the room with her hand. She smiled at him, then walked away.

Iggy looked at Lecque. "What does she mean, 'this is the story'? That makes no sense. That's not an answer."

"That was the end of her story. It is her story to tell as she chooses."

"But how did she know my name?" Iggy asked, alarmed.

"I'm sure she heard me call you by it. If it concerns you, why don't you go and ask her how she knew your name, while I finish our ale." Lecque dismissed his concern with a wave of his hand.

Iggy looked around but didn't see Trafagla. She was nowhere in the bar, and patrons were leaving. He circled the exterior of the room, but to his dismay she was not to be found. But he did see the owner of the inn.

"Excuse me," Iggy said.

"Yes, young man, how can I help you?" she asked, more pleasantly than when they had arrived.

"I wonder if you know where the lady performer went? I would like to ask her a question."

"Ah, young man. She is not that kind of a girl." She frowned.

"What kind of a girl? I just need to ask her about how she knew my name. Did you see where she went?"

"Oh, I am sorry. I thought you wanted to bargain with her, uh, for her favors... for the evening." She gave a quiet laugh as she looked Iggy up and down. "How foolish of me. You are clearly still a boy. But, to answer your question, she and her companion are gone. They never stay long after they perform. I am not sure why. They collect their money and leave. I am sorry, I cannot help you."

"Yeah, me too." Iggy turned and walked back to where Lecque had just finished the last drops of ale.

Lecque smiled. "Did you find her?"

"No."

"Come. Let us get to bed. We have had a long day today and will have another long day tomorrow." Lecque got up, and Iggy followed him.

After settling down in their beds, Lecque turned to face Iggy. "I'm curious. Why *were* you so upset with the end of the story?"

Iggy thought for a moment, then answered, "Stories have to have a beginning, middle, and an end. Her story only had a beginning and a middle."

"But wasn't the end when the sword got turned to dust and the stone shattered into many pieces? And did she not say 'the end'?" Lecque sounded proud of his reasoning.

"No, saying *the end* does not make it the end. I want to know what happened to Cinead. He didn't have his powerful sword anymore. Did Apevan take him prisoner or kill him? What about all the stones that flew to all parts of the kingdom. Did they have any value as little pieces? And what happened to the Kingdom of Skye after the stone was destroyed? By saying 'the end,' it left more questions than answers by telling the story in the first place."

"But that would be a separate, different story." Done with the issue, Lecque rolled over in bed to sleep.

Iggy, seeing he would not win this, agreed. "I guess you're right." He, too, rolled onto his side to sleep.

14

They rose shortly after sunrise. Iggy felt miserable. He had a pounding headache. They had a breakfast of bread and started down a road already filled with vendors setting up their stands. The items were sparse. Some vendors sold used and repaired clothes; others were starting small fires to cook whatever chicken or meat they could get a hold of for those passing by. A few had been lucky enough to have fresh fruits and vegetables they could sell for the local farmers. All in all, it was a depressing place to live and work. Today there was an unmistakable tension in the air. Iggy saw soldiers walking through the stands with keen eyes checking everyone up and down, on guard, ready to pounce.

Lecque noticed this also. They walked by one stall, and Lecque asked, "Why are all the soldiers out so early in the day? What's going on?"

The stall owner replied, "A soldier patrol was ambushed and slaughtered yesterday, every last one of them. The rumor is they were robbing a farmer who was bringing his produce to town to sell, and they were also trying to have their way with his daughter. Then arrows flew and struck the soldiers down.

They are looking for strangers. They think they have taken refuge in town. They say the arrows were special, made by master hands. Some say it was the work of Scathach." He looked at Iggy. "Do not worry—all they have to do is take one look at him and know it was not you." He smiled and turned back to setting up his stall.

The stall keeper was correct, for as they walked by the soldiers, they were essentially ignored. After three blocks of one-story shops, Lecque led Iggy to a two-story building. There was a sign hanging out front that read "Madam Trinity."

Iggy followed Lecque through the door into a parlor with two well-worn wingback chairs and an aged, worn couch. Iggy sensed movement to his left and turned. A short, pudgy woman who looked about sixty years old walked into the parlor. She had a bulbous nose under a cap of snow-white hair. Thick glasses perched on the nose, making her eyes look unusually large.

She smiled and jumped up and down. "Lecque! How good to see you." She skipped over to him and gave him a generous hug. "Oh, Lecque, Lecque, how I have missed you!" She stood back and snapped her head toward Iggy. Then did a pirouette and faced him. "And who do we have here? No, no, no, do not tell me, Lecque, do not tell me." She jumped closer to Iggy and quickly looked him up and down. "Oh, you are special, very special. Who are you?" Her head turned quickly to Lecque then back to Iggy. "I know who you are. You are... Do not tell me, do not tell me. I give up. Tell me, who is he?"

"His name is Iggy," Lecque said.

"I know that, yes, I do, for I am Madam Trinity." She looked at Iggy. "Iggy, you say. Yes, yes, I knew that. What a strange name. Iggy... hmm... what does that mean? What does Iggy mean?"

Iggy was wide-eyed with disbelief. *This woman is crazy.* "It is short for Ignatius."

"Ignatius, you say. Iggy Ignatius. What a silly name. Iggy Ignatius come over here." She grabbed him by the arm and pulled him over to one of the wooden chairs by the round wooden table. "Sit, Iggy Ignatius, sit."

"It's Iggy or Ignatius, not Iggy Ignatius."

"Yes, yes, I knew that. For I am Madam Trinity."

Iggy watched as Trinity waved her hands through the air, then out of nowhere a deck of oversized cards popped into her hands. She sat and shuffled the cards faster than Iggy would have thought possible. The cards flew through her fingers, then suddenly twelve flew out of her hands and landed faceup in two aligned rows of six. Trinity flung the remaining cards into the air, and they vanished. She stood and leaned over the two rows of cards, looking at them, then at Iggy.

"Yes, yes, oh my. Yes, yes. You are a special one." She spun to Lecque. "Yes, Lecque, he is a special one. I will take him to the council of Adepts today."

Iggy jumped up from his chair and sidestepped over to Lecque, concern on his face. "Lecque, you're not gonna leave me with… her? Are you?"

"Yes. I trust her. I have a meeting I must attend." Lecque turned to Trinity. "When do you need me back to get him?"

"Oh, yes, this will be fun. I would say by midafternoon. We have things we need to do, Iggy Ignatius and I."

"It's just Iggy," Iggy repeated stubbornly.

Trinity grabbed Iggy by the hand. "Come and sit again. We have cards to look at, to guide us."

Iggy sat back at the circular table and viewed the cards laid out in front of him. They were not typical playing cards, nor were they Tarot cards. They were covered with intersecting lines that formed nonsensical figures.

Madam Trinity turned and walked Lecque to the door. "Now you shoo, run along and leave this lovely young one with me. He will be safe with me. Yes, yes."

"There is something different about him. I was hoping you could find out and let me know," Lecque whispered to her at the door.

Madam Trinity simply smiled and prodded Lecque out the door, then quickly shut it behind him.

Moments after Lecque left, the front door opened. "Trinity!" A high-pitched female voice floated through the air. "It is Mayven. Are you here?"

"Stop, Mayven! Do not enter." Trinity turned to Iggy, circled her right hand through the air in an arc, and pulled a card out of thin air. "Iggy, take this," she whispered. "Hold it tight in both hands and stare at the picture. No matter what happens do not look up. Do not stop staring at the picture."

Iggy did as she asked.

"Yes, Mayven, you may enter my parlor now."

Mayven walked around the corner into the parlor. "Really, Trinity, since when are we so bossy? 'Do not enter my parlor. Now enter my parlor.' What are you trying to hide from me?"

Trinity had a gleeful grin. "Yes. Yes, yes, this is marvelous. Tell me, Mayven, what do you see?"

"I see my friend jumping up and down in her parlor acting like a fool. That is what I see. Why, what should I be seeing?"

"Nothing else." Trinity clapped her hands together. "Oh, this is marvelous, so marvelous. So, Mayven, what is the reason for your visit?"

"I saw a man leaving here moments ago." She turned her attention to the door. Instinctively, Madam Trinity and Iggy looked there too.

When Iggy looked up, he became visible again. Madam Trinity shot him a look and motioned for him to concentrate. He did and invisibility returned just as Mayven turned back to them.

"I came to warn you," Mayven continued, "the soldiers are looking for someone. One of their patrols was ambushed yesterday, and all the soldiers were killed. They are rounding up all the males and questioning them. I wanted to warn you to be careful."

"Killed, you say? Marvelous, just marvelous. Now you must go. Yes, yes, you need to go. Thank you for the warning. But as you can see, there is no one here, so I have no need to worry. Good-bye, now."

"I do not know why I bother with you sometimes." Mayven turned and left.

Trinity spun to face Iggy, who was still staring at the card and gripping it tightly. "Did you see that?" She jumped up and down. "Iggy Ignatius, you can put the card down now. Did you see that?"

Iggy lowered the card. "Did I see what? Other than another nutcase staring at me, ignoring me as if I wasn't here."

"Yes, yes, yes! That is just it—she did not see you. You were invisible to her. You, Iggy Ignatius, are very special indeed, for you were invisible."

"I'll play along. How was I invisible?"

"The card, the card, it is a magic rune card of invisibility. And you made it work. You are an incredibly special person, Iggy Ignatius."

"Yes, so you say. And for the last time my name is Iggy, or Ignatius, but *not* Iggy Ignatius."

"Yes, yes, so you have told me. Now we must go. The Adept Council awaits." She stopped and pondered for a moment. "But the soldiers are stopping everyone." She leaned into Iggy and stared into his eyes. "You didn't kill any soldiers, did you?"

"No."

"Yes, yes. Grab that card; we must go now." Trinity led Iggy to the door. "Now, you hold that card in two hands out in front of you and stare at it as we walk. And again, never look away from the picture on the card." She clapped her hands and jumped up and down. "This will be exciting, yes, exciting."

They walked down the middle of the cobblestone street. People walked by with their heads down, not making eye contact. They were very afraid. Farther down, the street was filled with soldiers stopping and questioning everyone, but mostly the men, lining them up against buildings, yelling and threatening them, demanding answers.

Trinity, with Iggy in tow, bounded down the street until she stopped next to one of the soldiers. "What are you doing?"

The soldier looked her up and down and quickly opined that she was crazy, so he ignored her, which did not sit well with her.

"Hey! I asked you, what are you doing?"

"If I tell you, will you go away?"

"Yes, yes. I promise."

"We are looking for the killers who ambushed our fellow soldiers a half day's ride on the road west of here. You would not know who they are or where they are, would you?"

"Oh yes, yes, I have seen them." She giggled.

"Really? I bet you did. And where did you see them?" There was deep sarcasm in his voice. "And do you know where they are now?"

"Well, I haven't traveled out of the town in days. But my little friend here just arrived. He might have seen something. You should ask him." She waved her hand to Iggy, who stood frozen as he held the rune card in front of him with a death grip, staring at the lines drawn on it.

The soldier looked where Trinity had just pointed and clearly saw no one. He stared down at her. "Move along, lady. I don't have time for your nonsense. Leave now, or I will have you arrested."

"Very well. Come on, Iggy Ignatius, let us go."

Iggy followed her to the corner, where she walked down an alleyway between two buildings and stopped. Iggy stopped beside her.

"You are a crazy lady! What were you trying to do back there?"

"Oh, Iggy Ignatius you were safe," she said merrily. "Didn't you see that he could not see you? You were invisible. Yes, yes, invisible."

"For the last time, my name is… oh, never mind. What does it matter?" He shook his head. As he did so, he caught sight of a narrow space in the dark alley—an alleyway within an alleyway. "I hope we're not going in there?"

"You can see that path?"

"Yeah, why?"

"That path is a secret portal path. It is camouflaged by the runes drawn into the walls on either side. Only those highly trained in rune magic can see through it. Yes, yes, Iggy Ignatius, you are a very strange person."

"Yeah, so I've been told."

"Let us go. And you can lower the card. Once we enter this portal, no one will be able to follow us." Trinity entered the tight path between the buildings. After a moment's hesitation, Iggy stuck the card in a pouch attached to the rope belt holding his pants up and followed her.

They made their way along a corridor between the buildings, turning left, then, after a while, turning to the right. Finally, they came to a door. Trinity placed her right palm against it, and the wood glowed with multiple colors then disappeared. In front was a garden filled with flowers in full bloom. Flowers Iggy had never seen.

There was a row of prickly cacti with roselike flowers three times the size of any roses he had ever seen sitting on the top of each cacti. And row upon row of open-blossom flowers protruded out of the ground with no apparent stems.

"You like our lovely flower garden?"

Iggy looked around at the deep-jade-green-colored garden of grass bordered by connected flowering bushes and shrubs. A lone ornamental statue of a butterfly stood to the left, neatly interwoven with the garden and nature itself. The flowers were a wonderful gathering place with all the bees buzzing around—

Iggy heard a fluttering of wings. He saw what looked like a human no taller than the height of his knee, flying around inches off the ground. It had golden hair and alabaster skin that glowed as it pruned the flowers with small sheers.

"What is that? Hmm, I mean, who is that?""

"That, Iggy Ignatius, is a Glaistig. One of our garden fairies. They take care of our beautiful flowers. I believe her name is Viridi."

The Glaistig was now trimming flower bushes and shrubs nearly as tall as it was. Looking around, Iggy saw marble stepping-stones here and there that guided visitors around the garden. Vines and roots playfully crept through the gardens, eager to expand their foothold.

"They are different from flowers I'm used to. They are very beautiful."

"Yes, yes. Let me show you a few of our rare plants." Trinity walked over to a bed. "This is the Borago Officinalis. Its green leaves are used in cooking, and its blue starlight flowers are used by our healers. And this one over here"—Trinity jumped to a plant to her right—"this one is an Epilobium Caerulea." It rose to the height of Iggy's waist and had golden yellow flowers. "The inside of the bigger stems is used to create a sweet jam, and our healers also use the seed pods that appear later in the year." Next, Trinity simply stopped and straightened. "We are done talking about plants today. Follow me." She turned and walked to the garden's exit.

Iggy shook his head and trotted to catch up with her as they exited the garden and entered a path that meandered through tightly cropped bushes that stood two feet above Iggy's head. It reminded him of a corn maze in Pennsylvania that he and John visited one year around Halloween.

After seven left and right turns, they finally exited the labyrinth and faced a castle. A very strange-looking castle. Archway after archway filled the lower level. Looking through the archways Iggy could see the entire ground level was inlaid with flat stones that were all three strides across, creating a patio about the width of a football field that spanned the length of the entire castle that sat above it.

The castle was made of oddly shaped weathered fieldstone. On the left were stone steps that led straight up the outside to the upper level, easily fifty feet in their air. The steps were only two feet wide with no railing. They stopped at a platform with a door set back. To the right, carved out of the ascending stone wall, was a serpent's head that rose from the ground to the highest point of the castle and ended with the mouth displaying massive fangs.

Iggy turned around in a circle. Behind him, there was no town, just open fields. "Where did Ginside go?"

Trinity waved her hand nonchalantly. "Oh, it is over there somewhere." She looked confused and waved in the other direction. "Or, it might be over that way. I am not really sure. I get so confused and turned around sometimes."

"Where are we?"

"Why, Iggy Ignatius, we are in Dinas Affaraon." Trinity smiled at him.

"And where is Dinas Affaraon?"

"What a silly question. It is right here, where we are. Come on." She began to climb the steps.

"Wait!"

Trinity stopped. "What? What is wrong?"

"I am not going up those steps! There's no railing, and it's straight up!"

"Well, of course you are. How silly. How else do you expect to get into the castle?"

Iggy pointed through the closest archway. "Through there."

"Do you see any steps in there?"

Iggy walked to the archway and looked in. "No."

"Right, so we take the stairs right here. Come, come." She stared at Iggy until he walked back to her. "All right, then, up we go."

Trinity stood straight and walked up the steps with no regard to the height or the lack of railing. Iggy started behind her. When he was at least twenty feet up, he looked down and instantly bent forward to hug the steps. He continued upward on all fours like a dog or cat would, all the time muttering over and over, "I hate high places."

Finally, he made it to the stone platform and lay on his stomach. After a few moments, he rolled onto his back. Opening his eyes, his view was filled with Trinity staring down at him.

"That was a very strange way to climb steps. Why did you not simply walk up them?"

"What about falling?"

"When you walk on the ground, do you tip over?"

"No."

"Exactly. You put one foot in front of the other and walk. Walking up steps is the same thing as walking on the ground. One foot in front of the other. Now, come on, you strange, special little boy, we have to see the council."

Trinity turned and walked through the door at the back of the platform. Iggy followed her. Once across the door's threshold, they were standing on the edge of a wide-open arboretum with birds flying around and butterflies flapping their wings, moving from flower to flower. The air was sweet and fresh. Above was the open clear blue sky dotted with clouds floating by. Looking behind him, he saw a freestanding door frame, with the door he had just come through closed. No walls or ceiling there either.

"What is this place? Who lives here?"

"Why, Iggy Ignatius, I already told you we are in Dinas Affaraon. And who lives here? Why, of course the Affaraons live here. The leaders of their council are the Interpreter Adepts." She smiled at him. "Let us go. The council is waiting for us."

"You've said that. I am hoping they are as knowledgeable as I've been told. But how do they know we are coming?"

"Oh, you silly boy, they just know." Trinity continued down the path. "And you have heard about them?"

"Yes." This time Iggy smiled and said nothing more.

They came to an opening around a bend with benches arranged in a circle. Four middle-aged men were casually sitting there. They all wore multicolored robes, and one had a few butterflies landing on his open hand, feeding on something in his palm. Another one, who was asleep, had a bird sitting on his head. The other two men were chatting.

Trinity and Iggy approached.

"Good morning, Interpreter Adept Ezether," Trinity said to the one with the butterflies eating out of his palm.

"Good morning, Trinity."

"Good morning, Interpreter Adept Arekius," Trinity said to the one with the bird on his head.

Still appearing to be asleep, he replied, "Good morning, Trinity." He opened his eyes and raised his head. The bird stayed put.

The two deep in conversation stopped talking and faced Trinity.

"Good morning, Interpreter Adept Gudius," Trinity continued.

"Good morning, Trinity."

Iggy watched this, transfixed at this weird greeting and feeling as out of place as if he he'd landed in Alice's tea party.

Last, she addressed the one remaining man. "Good morning, Interpreter Adept Ildor."

"Good morning, Trinity."

With the formalities over, Trinity walked into the center of the circle of benches. She turned and motioned for Iggy to join her.

Ezether said, "So, this is the remarkable young man you informed us about."

"It is. Oh, yes, it is. Yes, it is. This is Iggy Ignatius," Trinity said with a giggle.

"Too young," Ildor said. He crossed his arms in front of him, signifying he had decided.

"Yes, I agree. Too young," Gudius also said. He also crossed his arms.

"I do not see much potential in him," Arekius said.

The three looked to Ezether for his proclamation. "Come closer." Ezether motioned with his hand to where Iggy should stand.

After a moment's hesitation, Iggy complied. Ezether stared at him, looking him up and down. Then his eyes fell on Iggy's amulet. "Where did you get that crystal you are wearing?"

"It was my mother's."

Ezether continued to stare at it before looking Iggy in the face. "I see a lot of potential in you, young Iggy. The problem is, you do not realize your potential. I also see in you that you have a quest to complete." He turned to the others. "I agree with the three of you. He is too young." He looked at Trinity. "That is our answer. When he is older and wiser, he may return."

In unison, the four said, "We are done; you may leave now."

"Oh, very good, very good." Trinity seemed giddy with joy as she clapped her hands and jumped up and down. "Let's go, Iggy Ignatius, we are done here."

"No! How do they know about my quest? I want to know what

they know!" Iggy turned to the Adepts. "Tell me about my quest. I need information. How do I complete it? I demand you tell me!"

"He demands," Adept Gudius said as the other Adepts broke into laughter.

"Oh, Iggy Ignatius, they won't tell you. You heard what they said. You are too young. Let us go." Trinity turned and walked out of the circle.

Iggy followed her, confused and angry. Once they rounded the corner, Iggy stopped short, saying, "Wait a minute!"

Trinity stopped and turned to Iggy.

"What was that? What just happened back there, and who were they? And why won't they tell me what they know? What I need to know. And how did he know about my quest? And how can they think I'm too young for a quest when I've already got it? What kind of sense does that make?"

"Why, they are the Interpreter Adept Council. They are wise and know a lot about… well, a lot. And they didn't tell you what you wanted to know because they simply did not want to. And what just happened? They evaluated you."

"What do you mean, they 'evaluated' me? They were a bunch of clowns sitting in a garden with butterflies and birds."

"What is a clown?"

"A clown… it's… it's a jester, I guess you'd call it here."

Madam Trinity looked hard at Iggy. "Oh, no. They are not jesters. They are very wise and powerful men. They were simply resting in the garden, taking council. Then they set about their work." She wagged a finger at Iggy. "Do not underestimate them, ever."

"Tell me what they meant, that I was too young, then."

"The law in our land is one is not allowed to be formally taught runes magic until he or she is sixteen years old. You are only just fifteen, if I am not mistaken."

"How do you know my age?"

"I, too, know things." She gave him a sarcastic smile.

"You said they evaluated me. How? They didn't even talk to me."

"They did not have to." Her voice was singsong happy again. "They looked at you. That is all they needed."

"Really? And what did they conclude by looking at me?"

"Why, they concluded what I did... with a slight variation. They decided that you indeed have great potential. But you are still too young, and you need some maturity. Nonetheless, they agreed you have great potential." Trinity clapped her hands.

"Potential for what?"

"Potential to be trained as a Runes Interpreter Adept, of course. One day you will be an Adept of the power of the runes."

"And why do you think I will be able to become a... a Runes Adept? You just met me—and what is a Runes Adept? And, really, what are runes?"

"Oh, you silly boy. Runes have magic in their letters and words. And why you? That card I had you hold up. The one that made you invisible. Only a person trained in the power of runes could have controlled that card. But you, you, Iggy Ignatius, have no training. What you did was spectacular. You did not even know what you were doing. It was natural. Yes, you are special, incredibly special! But now we must go."

Trinity walked down the path to the freestanding door frame and opened it. They both walked through it, and Iggy was again on the platform, with the treacherous stairs without rails.

Trinity started down the stairs as if she had no worries about falling. Iggy, full of rage, stormed down the steps behind her, too angry to care about falling to his death. Trinity gave him a smile when he reached the bottom.

He saw her smirk and looked at the stairs. "One foot in front of the other," he said defiantly, looking at the stairs.

"And back into town we go." She turned and retraced their route until they exited the alleyway. They were back on the side street in the town of Ginside. Trinity stopped before they entered the main street.

Her eyes peered deeply into Iggy's, which unnerved him.

"What just happened, where we were, this portal we used to get to the location in Dinas Affaraon. That is a *secret* you may not tell anyone. Not even Lecque. It must be kept a secret for their safety and yours." Then she suddenly laughed and returned to her giddiness. "Anyway, they would not believe you. Come along, Iggy Ignatius."

15

Mallak donned his dark pulsating robe, tugged it closed, and stared out the window. His back was to Ulric, who stood silently with his hands clasped behind his back.

He had just given Mallak the details of Quitee's visions at the death site of the Nostaw. It had been received better than Ulric had anticipated. He had expected a fit of rage, but Mallak was lost in thought.

Turning, Mallak finally spoke. "Interesting. Quitee wanted a closer look. The energy repulsed him. It stopped him. The past was seeing into the future. Quitees future. Anticipating him. Protecting those two figures." Mallak thought for a moment. "Was that energy projected from inside the person? Or was it an outside energy field, like a protective cocoon?"

"I am sorry to say I do not have that answer, My Emperor. But Quitee said that the little one has powers that make him a dangerous adversary, of that I am certain." Ulric waited for an angry tirade to start. To his surprise, Mallak simply waved his hand dismissively. Ulric understood that despite his long friendship with Mallak he was being dismissed, so he turned and walked out.

The Death Knight came out of the dark shadows in a far corner of the room, after Mallak's signal to approach. The odor of rotting flesh quickly spread in an ever-widening radius around Mallak. This putrid smell would offend any reasonable person, but it pleased Mallak; the scent reminded him of the power he wielded. Mallak smiled at his creation, his creature of death.

Mallak narrowed his eyes as he gazed upon the Death Knight and took one more slow, deep breath in, savoring the noxious odor. "You are my greatest creation yet. You cannot be killed. You are already dead. I can send you back to your hole in the ground forever. Until you are dust. I pulled you out of that nothingness. So why do I feel so-so... so *disappointed* in you? Word comes to me there is a Nostaw in my kingdom." The veins in his neck bulged. "I sent you to kill it. Instead, you left it alive! And you did not bring me his swords!"

A voice rose from deep inside the creature. It resonated as if being projected from a tunnel far away. "You do not scare me, Mallak. For I am Death, and nothing you do can harm me. You think you have given me something wonderful? You have not. You have raised me from my grave, where I was at rest, at peace. I am bound to you, to do your bidding. But when someone dies by my hand, how they die is up to me. I decide whether it is quick or slow and painful. And, lastly, I do not gather souvenirs for you or anyone."

"I have the power to smite you into the ground!"

"That is not a threat. That is my wish. And you would be wise never to threaten me."

There was a long pause, and the only sound was Mallak's breath as he huffed with frustration. "Find that boy and his companion. Kill them both. Those are my orders. Or you will walk this land endlessly... in misery. Now go."

"Do not be so sure of yourself. There is another way for me to return to my grave. And if I can make it happen, you will be the one who fears me." The Death Knight turned, receded back into the shadows, and was gone.

16

Lecque entered the small back room at The Goat's Head Inn near the outskirts of Ginside. Ankter sat at the head of a table that also held two companions, Magnus and Euan.

Lecque took his seat and poured himself a mug of ale. "I hope you are all well and fine," Lecque said, greeting them with a nod.

"We are doing just fine," Magnus replied. "Now that we are all here, shall we start? Lecque, you had a meeting with a representative of the Dinas Affaraons. Ankter informed us prior to you arriving that they will not join our fight against Mallak?"

"That is correct. They feel their runes are strong enough to protect them. They feel this is our fight and do not want to expose themselves to any danger." Lecque lifted his mug for a drink.

Euan said, "Those gutless swine. Don't they know that when Mallak gains more power, he will blow through their runes with a wave of his hand? Yes, they are safe now, but they are so shortsighted."

"I've heard that Mallak has rolled over the province of Boulderglen. It was a massacre. Anyone who gave even the slightest indication of opposing him was slaughtered," Magnus said. "You must sway the Affaraons to our side. We need their help."

"It took me a long time to even make contact. I will have to come up with some leverage to use with them. As of now, all communications have been cut off," Lecque said.

Ankter jumped into the conversation with disdain in his voice. "I want to bring up this boy who has come out of nowhere."

Lecque looked at Ankter with dagger eyes. "That boy is of no concern to this meeting. He is under my care."

"He is dangerous," Ankter grumbled.

"Yes, as dangerous as a little boy can be. Are you afraid he will stomp on your foot when you are not looking?" Lecque sneered.

"Since he has arrived, bad things have happened. Mallak is on the move, forcefully reclaiming lands his father once ruled over. He is sending soldiers around to enforce his draconian laws. There are Death Knights being brought back from the dead and armies forming. They say Mallak is obsessed with more control and power. I told you at our last meeting that this rebellion is over. We have no chance," Ankter said.

"And you blame this on Iggy? He is a little boy. He cannot even defend himself." Lecque laughed.

"I am warning you, Lecque—" Ankter began.

"No, I am warning you. Leave Iggy alone. You are more concerned about a small, frightened boy than the one we should be concerned about. Iggy is under my protection. Any attacks on the boy will be considered an attack on me."

The meeting adjourned, and Ankter stormed out.

As Lecque started to walk out, Magnus stopped him. "We must keep on working to grow our ranks. Mallak is becoming too dangerous."

"We will defeat him. I will give my last drop of blood to that cause."

Magnus placed a hand on Lecque's shoulder. "I promise you, we will avenge your father."

Lecque exited The Goat's Head Inn, turned down the street, and was unceremoniously pulled into a small alleyway between two buildings. Before he could react, a knife was pressed against his throat. In front of him stood Ankter leaning into the knife. His warm, stale breath flowed over Lecque's face and made the hairs on the back of his neck stand on end.

Ankter brought his face within an inch of Lecque's as their eyes met.

"You listen to me. I have a wife, two daughters, five grandchildren, and three farms. I will sacrifice you and that little kid to keep them safe. You will not put me, or them, in danger. Get rid of that kid." Ankter removed the knife and left.

✍

Once Iggy and Trinity were back at Trinity's, Iggy sat wordlessly at the table for a long time. Trinity had gone into her kitchen and returned with some tea, which she poured into a teacup for him.

"What now?" Iggy asked.

"Why, silly, we drink our tea."

Iggy folded his arms and stared at her. "Show me another one of those magic cards."

"Oh, Iggy Ignatius, you silly, they are not magic cards. They are runes cards. You are the one who makes the magic."

"Fine, whatever. If I am so special, test me with another one."

Madam Trinity returned Iggy's stare. Her demeanor changed to one of seriousness. "All right, I will." She waved her right hand in the air, and the cards instantly appeared. She thumbed through the cards, pulled one out, and handed it to Iggy. Her voice remained serious. Gone was her singsong cadence. "This card is the card of truth. Take it. You cannot use it on me. Runes do not work on me. But, be forewarned—you may not always want to know the truth. Sometimes things are kept from us to keep us safe, in here"—she pointed to her head—"in here"—she swirled her hand over her body—"and, lastly, in here." She placed her hand over her heart.

Iggy took the card.

Her singsong voice instantly returned, "Now Iggy Ignatius, we drink our tea, and we wait."

"Wait for what?"

"Drink, drink," Trinity said, drinking her tea without saying another word.

Iggy followed her lead and drank in silence.

When they were done, they placed their teacups in their saucers. Trinity smiled as the front door opened and Lecque walked in.

"There, our wait is over. Lecque has returned." She winked at Iggy. "I told you all we had to do was wait."

"How did you know?" Iggy then muttered to himself softly so not to be heard, "Oh, never mind; you'd only give me a foolish answer."

Trinity spun her head to Iggy. She had heard, to Iggy's surprise and embarrassment. "No answer is foolish. Only how it is interpreted will make it sensible or, as you say, foolish."

Jumping up out of her chair, she skipped to Lecque and gave him a hug. "Oh, Lecque, it's so good to see you again. Yes, yes, your little Iggy Ignatius is a very special person. You must, and I insist, must bring him back to me for a long, exceedingly long stay. Promise me you will."

"Well, we could stay another day, if you wish. Do you want me to leave him with you and I could come get him tomorrow morning?"

Iggy jumped up. "No, I'm good. We can go." Iggy bounded over to Lecque's side. "I am not staying here. I am leaving with you." His eyes pleaded with Lecque, who chuckled.

Iggy and Lecque walked back to the inn. "That Madam Trinity is dingbat crazy."

"Don't underestimate her. She has powers that cannot be explained."

For a moment he thought about telling Lecque about his adventure with Trinity. But then her warning stopped him. For now, he would keep it to himself.

"It is early enough in the day," Lecque said. "Why don't we start our trip back home. If we leave now and ride all afternoon, we can make it to Limestad. We can stay there for the night. That will at least put us a half day closer to home."

"And a half day away from that crazy lady."

❧

The day was growing long, and the sun was getting low when they entered the outskirts of Limestad, which looked stark to Iggy, with its murky wooden rooftops, chiseled stone walls, and dismal overgrown surrounding woods. Overall, Limestad was just a dreary place.

"This place doesn't look too inviting," Iggy said to Lecque as they stopped at the stables and dismounted.

"It is a crossroads town. People pass through for a meal and to sleep. Not too many people live here. Let us head inside." Lecque and Iggy tied up their horses and walked to the tavern.

A sign hung near the front door: "The Ghost Raven Tavern." The outside was covered with mud-plastered walls and stacked stone that made up most of the building's outer structure. It was nearly impossible for Iggy to see through the dirt-covered windows.

Entering through the old wooden door, Iggy and Lecque were welcomed by suspicious stares instead of people laughing, talking loudly, and openly having a good time. Consistent with its name and considering the outside of the tavern, it was as stark as Iggy expected. The busy barmaid greeted them with nod. "Find a seat, if you can. I will come find you."

They found a table with two unoccupied stools. Soon the barmaid came over to them.

"What can I get you two?" she asked with not a hint of a smile.

Lecque looked at Iggy. "Ale?"

Iggy nodded.

"Two mugs of ale and whatever you're serving for dinner. We are two hungry men."

Iggy smiled inside. It felt good to have Lecque call him a man. He took a moment to swivel his head and look around the room. Squared wooden beams supported the ceiling. The walls were covered with trinkets and mugs of different styles, hanging from hooks. The tavern was filled with travelers who, judging by the boots and cloaks, seemed its primary clientele.

Suddenly, four soldiers burst through the front door. "Everyone stay where you are!" one of the soldiers barked. "We are looking for a young boy and a male roughly between the ages of twenty and thirty.

Tell us what you know. If we find you are hiding information, you will die a slow, painful death."

Iggy looked wide eyed at Lecque who gestured with his hand to remain calm.

An elderly man got up and defiantly walked up to the soldier. "Listen, you—you can't barge in and threaten us. We've done nothing wrong. There are many young boys in town, as well as men between twenty and thirty years old."

The front door opened for a second time. This time the putrid smell of death permeated the bar, followed by the Death Knight.

Iggy froze in his seat and stopped breathing for a moment. It was the same Death Knight he had seen standing over the Nostaw Warrior. Lecque grabbed him by the arm and squeezed. "Stay quiet and still. Do not draw attention to us."

The Death Knight walked up to the soldier and the elderly man. In a guttural voice, it demanded, "Who is this?"

"He is a defiant one."

The Death Knight reached out and grabbed the elderly man by the shoulder. Before the man could scream, he had turned to dust that scattered on the floor at the Death Knight's feet. "You!" The Death Knight pointed to the next patron. "Have you seen a young boy with a man between twenty and thirty years of age who are not from this town?" His lifeless face moved close to the patron as he extended his rotting hand to grab the patron's shoulder.

"Yes! Yes! They just arrived! There! Over there!"

Everyone turned toward Iggy's table. It was empty.

"Do you take us for fools?" the lead soldier demanded. "There is no one there."

Iggy and Lecque sat frozen at the table behind the invisibility rune card. Iggy stared at it as hard as he could, trying to ignore his shallow, rapid breathing. Lecque sat wide-eyed, his heart pounding, his right hand on his sword.

"They were there moments ago!" the patron said. "They must have slipped out."

Lecque sat there looking at Iggy, his expression showing he was clearly baffled as to why no one could see them.

A dwarf was sitting next to the bar. He looked at the Death Knight, then back at Iggy holding a rune card and sitting frozen like a statue. The dwarf did nothing.

The Death Knight stared intently at Iggy and Lecque's table without moving. The room was quiet, and the tension mounted with every heartbeat. The Death Knight stared at the table. Then, without saying a word, he turned and walked out.

The head soldier shouted, "If you see them, send word to us or you will end up like that one." He pointed to the pile of dust on the floor. He and the other soldiers stormed out of the bar.

The dwarf quickly made his way to Iggy's table, where Iggy was still holding up the rune card. "Boy, put down that card, get your things, and leave. When they see you suddenly visible again, they will be as afraid of you as they are of that walking dead thing."

"You can see us?" Iggy asked.

"Of course I can. Now go!"

In the commotion of the bar, patrons circling around the pile of dust on the floor to get a closer look and others simply pouring out of the bar in sheer terror, Iggy lowered the card. In that instant, those looking around the room for any other signs of danger saw Iggy and Lecque suddenly show up at what moments before had been an empty table. Gasps shot out of the mouths of those patrons who had just witnessed this.

Iggy and Lecque jumped up from their table. "That dead thing was looking for us! Why was he looking for us?"

"We gotta go. *Now!* Follow me!" Lecque demanded.

They pushed their way through the crowd and to the door as fast as they could. Iggy bumped hard into the dwarf and sent him flying to the floor. The dwarf grinned as he picked himself up.

When they were outside, Lecque grabbed Iggy and pulled him around the side of the building. "We need to make our way back to the stable. What was that thing you held out in front of you that stopped them from seeing us?"

"It was an invisibility rune card. Trinity gave it to me."

"A what? Never mind. Do it again so we can get to our horses."

Iggy reached into his pocket. He pulled his hand out in a panic and checked his other pockets. With an anxious stammer, he said, "It's gone! I must have dropped it in the bar. We have to go back and get it!"

"No! Too dangerous. Stay behind me and say nothing. We will stay in the shadows and head to the stables."

Lecque turned to Iggy, who was trembling. He grabbed him tight by both shoulders. "Listen to me. You need to focus. That is the only way we are making it out of this town alive."

"But what do they want with us?"

"That is a question I also want the answer to. But you need to get hold of yourself. I need to rely on you. Can I rely on you?" Lecque looked at Iggy.

Iggy took a deep breath in, exhaled, and focused. "Yes, you can. What do we need to do?"

"Follow me." Lecque peeked around each corner, and after making sure there were no soldiers, they moved to the cover of the next building.

Following that strategy, they were soon at the back of the stables where their horses were. Lecque listened for a while, and after hearing no voices, he slowly opened the rear door and then entered.

"They will see you if you leave with your horses, and if you stay, they will also find you," the stable owner called from the darkness of one of the horse stalls. "The soldiers are searching every building. It is just a matter of time before they show up."

"Please hide us," Iggy pleaded. "We've done nothing wrong. I don't know why they are looking for us." Iggy looked around. "Up there!" He pointed to the hay loft. "We can hide up there."

Lecque shook his head. "That is the first place they will look."

"Follow me," the stable owner said.

They followed him into a stall. He took a rake and pulled back a mound of hay that the horse occupying the stall was eating. The man bent down, pulled on a latch, and opened a trapdoor. "Both of you, quickly. Down there. There is a ladder. I will cover the door with the hay, and the horse will stand on it. I will come and get you when half the night is over. Then you can sneak out of town."

Iggy legged it down the ladder without hesitation. "Lecque! Now! Let's go!"

In moments, they were sitting on the dirt floor in a pitch-black room. Neither of them knew what was down there with them or how big the room was. None of that mattered. For the moment, they were safe.

It was a different story above them. Moments after the stall was put back to normal, a group of soldiers stormed in.

"We are looking for a young boy and an adult male who's traveling with him." One soldier drew his sword from its sheath and pointed the end at the stable owner. "Tell us the truth or face my wrath. Have you seen them?"

"I have not. And word has spread about what your Death Knight did to one of the townspeople who defied you. I have no desire to face that fate or the end of your sword. Feel free to search the stable. I have nothing to hide." The stable owner walked over to a stool and calmly sat.

The soldiers wasted no time. They searched every corner of the stable and came up empty. A soldier looked up at the hay loft. "Take a pitchfork into that loft and jam it down until you hit wood. Go over every section of it. Make sure they are not hiding in the hay."

They were done in a short time. Having not found anyone, the lead soldier gave one final warning, "If you see them and give them any help, it will be the end of my sword into you... or a pile of dust on the floor." He turned and left with his soldiers.

Iggy sat in the dark, his knees pulled up to his chest, his arms wrapped around his knees and his head buried in his arms, deep in thought. He shuddered at the idea of being turned to dust by a Death Knight, and he had no idea why that might happen.

Then Sandy's face popped up in his mind's eye, and he had to laugh at himself. Here he was with a monster, a *real* monster of death chasing after him, and he's thinking about an old fear. How absurd he was back in Susquehanna for being afraid to talk to Sandy. *Wow, how pathetic I've been.* How he wished those were still his only problems in life. He vowed he would never be pushed around by bullies again.

Iggy lost track of time as they sat in the dark on the cold, damp dirt floor. "Any idea how long we've been down here?" Iggy whispered to Lecque.

"None. I was wondering the same thing." Lecque reached out and grabbed Iggy by the arm. "You did good up there. Tell me more about that invisibility card."

"Trinity gave it to me. She tested it out on me in front of a group of soldiers who must have also been looking for us when we were in Ginside. She had me hold it in front of myself and just stare at it. The soldiers couldn't see me, so I guess it worked. She gave it to me and said it would keep me safe."

"And you thought she was crazy? That crazy woman saved us."

"I guess she did. That card was so special. I can't believe I dropped it. I am sorry. I was so focused on getting out of there."

"You did just fine. You thought quick enough to pull the card out. You saved us. Honestly, I was terrified. You are more like me than you think."

"I'm nothing like you."

"You have no idea, Iggy, no idea." Lecque took in a deep breath. When he let it out, he added, "When I was around your age, I lived with Raraesa and my mother and father. My father was one of the guards who protected King Ancelmus, Mallak's father. The king was kind, gentle, and generous. The people loved him. My father was honored to protect him. King Ancelmus had two sons. Mallak and Kylian.

Mallak knew his father favored Kylian and wanted Kylian to be the successor to the throne.

"Mallak was not going to allow that to happen. Mallak's desire to be king was much stronger than his love of family. One day, the king, queen, and Mallak's wife, along with the king's spiritual advisor, were on a carriage ride through the countryside. The troops with them that day were all loyal to Mallak. All except my father. The carriage stopped on the edge of the woods. When my father dismounted and demanded to know why they had stopped, Mallak came out of the woods, snuck up behind him, and ran his sword into his back. He was not man enough to do it face-to-face, coward that he is. After having the king, queen and his wife dragged out of the carriage, he slew the king and queen as his wife screamed for mercy."

Lecque stopped for a moment.

"Enraged, the king's spiritual advisor shouted, 'For your savagery, in his eighteenth year your son and his three brothers will rise up and smite you dead! You have been warned. You cannot stop this prophecy.' They say Mallak laughed and ran his sword through his pregnant wife. 'Now,' he said, 'I have no wife or son.' Moments later he killed the spiritual advisor too.

"When they returned, the official story was they'd been attacked by a band of roving thieves, and in the battle that took place, my father, the king and queen, Mallak's wife, and the spiritual advisor had lost their lives. Mallak imprisoned his brother, Kylian, on ridiculous charges that he was behind the attack. Of course, we all knew otherwise. One day my mother was in town when Mallak and his entourage rode by. Instead of bowing, she started shouting out and calling him a killer.

"That evening soldiers showed up at our farm. My mother hid me and Raraesa before they stormed in. She put up a fight, but, in the end, they killed her."

"I'm sorry. I didn't know."

"There's no way you could have." Lecque placed a hand on Iggy's shoulder. "Raraesa was only six. I was about your age. We gathered up all the valuables and money my parents had hidden in the house and ran away. We were on our own. The money did not last very long. We lived in the woods two counties over for close to a year, hunting for food, then we worked on farms or at blacksmiths, stables, inns, even making arrows for hunters, working anywhere to raise money. Finally, we landed in Nilewood.

"Raraesa worked for an old lady on her small farm who needed help. Her husband had died and she had no children. When she did die, she left the farm to Raraesa; it's where we live now. I took work with the underground. I have a way of slipping into Port Havolee past Mallak's soldiers. You could say I was a smuggler bringing contraband from the port to the villages controlled by Mallak. The good thing is, I don't think Mallak knows who we are or even that we even exist. But he might, one day."

After what seemed to be an eternity, the hatch above them opened. No light spilled in. "You are safe to come up," a voice from above said.

Iggy emerged from the hole first, then Lecque surfaced. "It has been a while since the soldiers and that dead thing were seen on the streets. It is the middle of the night. I think if you leave now, you can slip out of town."

"Do you know which way they went?" Lecque asked.

"They took the west road out of town." The stable master gave them a small package. "Here, I wrapped up some bread and cheese for you. I am sure you are hungry."

Iggy took the package. "There are not enough words to thank you for what you have done for us. I hope one day, somehow, I can repay you. But, for now, I can only say thank you."

The stable master replied, "Just remember as you grow that the greatest gift to give someone is to help them in their time of need."

After saddling their horses, they walked them out the back stall door. The stable owner stood in the door, and as he watched them leave, he said only loud enough for himself to hear, "And we Wiates have to look after each other... at all costs."

ᛰ

Iggy and Lecque continued to make their way through the shadows of the buildings, leading their horses, until they reached the road. They mounted and quietly left, headed east. They had said not a word between them, having agreed on total silence.

Lecque finally pulled up on the reins and stopped. "Let us get into the forest here and spend the night. No fire at all."

Both dismounted and walked their horses deep into the woods until they found a clearing. After tying the horses to trees and matting down an area of grass, they both lay down.

"Lecque, talk to me. Why are they chasing us?"

"That's what I want to know."

"And who was that little guy who was able to see us?"

"I do not know, but forget him for the moment. What did Trinity say about that card? Can anyone use it?"

"I don't think so. She said I was destined to become an interpreter-wizard-master-adept guy or something like that because I was able to use it. Like that's gonna happen."

Lecque didn't respond to Iggy's remark. After looking up at the dark sky for a moment, he said, "We need to stay quiet, so let us try to get some sleep." He rolled over and shut his eyes.

Iggy went over and over in his mind where he had placed the card. The last thing he remembered was having it in his hand when he banged into that short guy who fell onto the ground. Finally, due to sheer exhaustion, his eyelids drooped and closed, and he drifted off into a restless sleep.

ᛰ

The morning sun filtered through the trees and warmed Iggy's face. He opened his eyes with a start and looked around. The forest was not how he expected it to look. In the dark of the night, he had imagined it was filled with thorny bushes and twisted trunks of trees that exuded danger from their bark. Instead, the light of day showed pine, silver birch, and alder trees that provided just enough openings for light to pass through for vibrant ferns to spread in the flat ground below. Off to the right was a three-story-high towering oak.

A gentle breeze flowed through the trees, rustling the leaves. There was a smattering hodgepodge of yews and osier willow bushes that filled in some open spaces.

In the distance, Iggy heard a medley of nature's noises, most of which were small creatures scurrying around the forest. For a few moments, he was relaxed. No one was chasing him. He was in no hurry; he simply looked around and listened to the nature that surrounded him.

Iggy stood, and his movement woke Lecque.

Lecque stretched. "Well, Iggy, let us go home."

"I couldn't agree with you more. Do you think that dead thing is out there looking for us?"

"I am sure it is. But it did not find us in the night, so let us hope it is still going in the opposite direction." Lecque untied his horse, as did Iggy. They walked through the woods. After an hour they emerged onto a trail that Lecque recognized. "This will take us back to Nilewood. But keep a sharp eye out for soldiers."

In Ginside, the dwarf made his way through town and stopped at his destination, Madame Trinity's. He pounded on the door with no regard for the early hour. After many rounds of pounding, the door opened.

"Medyr!" Madam Trinity said. "Why are you here so early?"

"I took this off a young boy yesterday." He held up the runes card he had pickpocketed off the stranger when he'd purposely banged into him at the bar. "I recognized it as one of yours. How did he get it?"

"Come in." Trinity opened the door wide and let him in. He followed her into her sitting room and sat. "Why, Medyr, I gave it to him. And why did you take it from him?"

"Soldiers and a Death Knight came looking for them. The boy held it up. Who taught him that? He is clearly untrained."

"Oh, Medyr, you should not have taken that card away from him. This is an extremely dangerous situation." There was no singsong happiness in Trinity's voice.

"I stopped a dangerous situation by taking that card away from an untrained one."

"No, the dangerous situation is that rune cards and their spells do not work on those brought back from the dead." Trinity stared at him.

"You mean that Death Knight could see them all the time?"

"Yes…" Trinity's voice trailed off.

17

The normal three-day ride back from Ginside to Nilewood took Iggy and Lecque four days. The extra day was required out of an abundance of caution. Whenever they heard or thought they heard other travelers they'd stop and hide behind the closest stand of trees, bushes, or rocks.

On the fifth day, Lecque and Raraesa sat at their all-purpose table in front of the fire hearth, finishing their breakfast. They'd let Iggy sleep so they could talk without him present.

"I have to tell you," Lecque said, "one minute Iggy is cowering in the corner and then the next he is producing invisibility spells to keep us safe. And you still say he is harmless?"

"I tell you, Brother, either he is the best actor and wizard ever or he is harmless and clueless." Raraesa shrugged.

"Madam Trinity agrees with you. But she was more definitive. She said Iggy was extremely naive about his powers. Though she did not say what those powers were. She did say he was very special and important." Lecque stopped with his mouth open as if he had something else to say.

"And? What are you not saying?"

"Ankter made it perfectly clear at the meeting that Iggy must go. He has no idea of what has been going on. He is a suspicious person and blames all the latest ills of this county on Iggy."

"And? What did you say?"

"I agree with you. Iggy is naive and harmless, at this time. And he is incredibly special. I told Ankter and the others that Iggy is under my protection and is not to be harmed."

"Iggy is in danger. Ankter, and I am sure the other members, are also against him. A Death Knight is chasing him. What do we do?"

"I think we start by training him. You must turn him into a strong swordsman and a natural fighter. If that is possible. Although, I am not sure he has the strength to lift a sword." Lecque chuckled. "But, for now, I have chores to take care of. The needs of running this farm does not stop because we have a guest." He got up and left.

✧

Iggy finally woke up. He had had a fitful sleep and was exhausted. Last night the three had talked at length about the Death Knight and Madam Trinity. Though Iggy kept what transpired at the Dinas Affaraon Council to himself. For now, he would heed Madam Trinity's warning to not tell anyone.

After breakfast, Iggy and Raraesa walked out to the side yard, where there was a chicken coop. "We must collect the eggs and bring them into town to sell them. That helps us keep this little place running. But mostly it pays the monthly taxes."

"Can I come in and watch how you get the eggs?"

"No, because you will be the one getting the eggs." She grinned.

"Uh, I don't think so."

"I do. Go. In the coop." She pointed.

Iggy entered the coop with great hesitation. He looked around. "Where are the eggs?"

"Under the hens. Stick your hand under them and gently pull them out."

Raraesa waited. At first she heard the gentle clucking of the hens, which quickly grew louder. Then there was a squeal that sounded like a little girl.

"Eeeee! Move! Eeeeee! Ohhhhh! Eeeeee!" Iggy squealed.

Suddenly the squeals from Iggy and the clucking stopped. Iggy walked out of the hen coop, covered with hay but with a triumphant smile on his face and a basket full of eggs. He placed them on the ground. "It's not funny. Those things are vicious. They were trying to gang up on me and pluck my eyes out."

"Oh my goodness." Raraesa laughed so hard she was held her belly. "You are beyond funny. They are just small hens. Perhaps they were fearful that you were going to take out your swords and slay them!"

"That's exactly what I did."

Her laughter faded. "I've been wondering. Where are they?"

Iggy reached behind his back. When his hands came forward, each held a Nostaw sword. "Here they are."

"But I don't understand. I saw you from behind. You are not wearing a sheath. They weren't there."

"I know. I don't understand it either. Watch." He placed the swords behind him and then showed her his empty hands. "See, they're gone now."

Raraesa said nothing; she just stared at him in amazement.

"I don't know why the Nostaw gave me these swords. I wish I did. I don't know what I'm supposed to do with them."

"I do not have any answers for you," she said as they walked into the cottage and placed the eggs on the table.

"I'm sure he does." Iggy's gaze went to Lecque, who'd just walked in the door.

"And what is that you are sure of?" Lecque asked as he came to the table and sat.

Iggy produced his swords and abruptly and firmly placed them on the table and sat. He reached into his waist pouch and momentarily glanced at his truth runes card. Holding it tightly in one hand below the table, he looked up. "I need you to tell me about these swords. And about the Nostaws. If I'm to figure this out, I need information."

Raraesa joined them, folding her arms in front of her. Iggy stared at Lecque, his eyes demanding answers.

Lecque broke Iggy's stare and looked at Raraesa, who simply shrugged. "Tell him."

"What we know is only through rumors, legends, myths. Anyone who has ever run into a Nostaw has never lived to talk about it. They are ruthless killers."

"But you knew about the swords, the Blinak Ritual."

"I told you—rumors, myths."

"Tell me about their land."

"Cambria. To the far north, on a separate piece of land across the sea."

"Maybe I should go there and talk to them. Try to figure this thing out. After all, I am a Nostaw Warrior now."

"You are not a Nostaw Warrior, and I doubt you would survive the journey. The sea between Skye and Cambria is covered with rock shoals. If you were lucky enough to guide your boat through them, you'd be sucked down below the surface by one of the many whirlpools. It is impossible to reach Cambria by water."

"Then how did that Nostaw get here? These swords—what is so special about them? They appear to be normal swords. Heck, they don't even look very sharp."

"I have no idea how he arrived in Skye. For a Nostaw to become a warrior he must go on a quest. He must prove himself a man, and by fulfilling that quest the swords become magical. They become indestructible... they change. Then and only then will the Nostaw become a warrior."

"And his quest was given to me."

"It appears so."

Iggy released his grip on his truth card, then slid it back into the pouch. In that moment the spell was broken. The three sat there, saying nothing. Finally, Raraesa broke the silence.

"Well, let us take these eggs to town and sell them."

It was late morning when Iggy and Raraesa approached the town. Raraesa's questions for Iggy were less about the swords, which neither of them could explain, and more about his strange life in Susquehanna, Pennsylvania. Iggy and Raraesa laughed and talked, unless near a home or passing a person, until they reached town.

"You really want me to believe that you pick up a piece of metal and talk into it, and someone in another town can hear you and talk back?"

"Yes, but that person has to have a cell phone too."

"And you want me to believe that you can sit at home and look at something like a mirror to watch a play that was done on the stage yesterday or the week before?"

"Yep, it's called television—or TV for short."

"You must think I am a simpleton. I suppose you snap your fingers and can jump from one town to another?"

"No, that's only in stories. Of course we can't do that."

"Well, at least there is some sanity in your Sucha… Suqa… Suck Your Handa, Pennsylvania. I am glad you still need horses to get around."

Now Iggy laughed. "Susquehanna. No, we don't use horses. We have cars."

"Cars?" Raraesa stopped and turned to him.

"A car is a… a cart with four wheels, but without a horse. You sit in it and drive it to wherever you want to go."

"What makes it go?"

"An engine. I'm not about to explain it other than to say it's not magic. Trust me, it just works."

After selling the eggs to a market stall, Iggy explained pizza to Raraesa. He went through the different toppings he and his brother would get and explained what a pizza restaurant was, along with the feeling he would get from the aroma.

As they approached the blacksmith where Raraesa's horse was tied, Iggy felt the hairs on the back of his neck rise. He knew this feeling. Leonard had teased him multiple times, saying he was psychic for his ability to sense danger. He saw movement out of the corner of his eye. In moments, he and Raraesa were surrounded by Frankie and his friends. Frankie blocked their way.

"What do you want, Frankie?" Raraesa demanded.

"We've been following you two around. Why is *he* with you?"

"What if he is? What's it to you?"

Frankie turned to Iggy. "You think you are a big man walking around holding her hand. I think she is the one holding your hand. Leading you around like a little baby. Protecting you. Let us see how she protects you now."

Before Raraesa could react, two boys were behind her. They grabbed her arms and twisted them behind her.

"Leave her alone!" Iggy yelled as he moved forward to protect her. Before he could do anything, Frankie punched him in the gut, sending him to his knees.

"We saw you were also selling eggs. We took one of them and decided to give it back to you." Frankie withdrew an egg from a satchel he was carrying.

"You mean you stole them," Raraesa sputtered.

"Yeah, you could call it that. Oh, look, it cracked. I guess it is no good to eat anymore." Frankie turned to Raraesa and smashed it on her head.

The other boys erupted in laughter.

Iggy gasped for air and looked on in horror.

Frankie rooted through Raraesa's satchel. "My, my, what do we have here?" He looked at Raraesa and the boys holding her, then with a smug grin turned to Iggy. "See, little boy, no one has to hold you. Raraesa, on the other hand, is a fighter. You are simply helpless. Look at you, clutching your belly, on your knees." Frankie opened Raraesa's satchel and pulled out a handful of flour to add to the egg in Raraesa's hair.

Iggy, furious and without thinking, yelled, "Leave her alone!" He lunged at Frankie, his fists balled up. But before he could strike, Frankie again punched him in the gut, sending him to the dirt again, where he balled up in a fetal position and moaned.

"Hey! What's going on here?" Ansel the blacksmith stormed out of his shop, a hammer in his right hand.

"Run!" Frankie yelled.

The boys released Raraesa and ran across the nearby open field as fast as they could.

Raraesa knelt next to Iggy. "Iggy! Are you all right?"

Iggy gasped for air without replying.

Ansel reached down and lifted Iggy up with ease. "Come inside, you two—let us get you cleaned up. Looks like you will both be just fine."

Raraesa looked at Iggy, who refused to make eye contact. He stood frozen and stared at the ground as he clutched his abdomen. "Iggy, it will be all right," she said.

"No, it won't. John was right. It's time I learn how to fight," he mumbled. Then, without looking at her, he followed Ansel into the shop, dejected.

The ride back to their cottage was tense and quiet. After what seemed like an eternity for Raraesa, they finally arrived. Iggy climbed down from the saddle wordlessly.

"Iggy, please talk to me."

"No! I am totally humiliated and embarrassed. What was I thinking, that I could protect you? I couldn't even protect myself!"

"You did try. You attempted to help me. Frankie did not fight fair."

"I need to go for a walk. I need to be alone." Iggy left the cottage without looking at her.

৵

As the day wore on, Iggy still had not returned. Lecque arrived home after selling a rooster to a neighboring farmer. Raraesa told him what happened and how badly Iggy had reacted.

Lecque sat at the table and poked an iron in the fire. "How else would you expect him to have reacted? Did you think he would pull his Nostaw swords out and threaten them? Hell, if he had I'd be more concerned."

Raraesa sat across from him. "I am at a loss as to what to say to him."

150

"You want me to talk with him?"

"Yes. When he returns."

Lecque took one last bit of bread and washed it down with a swig of ale. "How long has he been gone?"

"Ever since we got back around midmorning."

"Well, I better go out and find him."

"I hope he did not walk to the lake on the far side of the woods."

"You did tell him never to go there?"

"No, I did not." She shook her head and mumbled, "Shite." Then she said, "You must go make sure he did not wander there."

As she turned her back to him, Lecque distinctly sensed she was more upset that Iggy was gone than she would have been a day ago—his sister cared for this boy more than he'd realized.

⁓

Iggy walked through the woods along a narrow dirt path. How long he had walked and in what direction, he didn't know; he only knew he was lost. The sun was sinking lower in the sky, casting long shadows on the ground from the surrounding trees. His mood had long ago changed from self-recrimination to worry. Thinking he heard voices, he stopped and listened. He turned his head, trying to pinpoint the source. He followed the voices, to sneak up on them; he was good at hiding. If there was danger out there, he wanted to know.

When he got close to the voices, he slipped behind a tree and peered down an incline to the shores of a lake with a cascading waterfall at the far end. Two soldiers sat by a fire, arguing. "We should just kill her," he heard one of them say.

A young woman, perhaps in her late teens, sat a few feet away, her hands tied around the base of a tree. Iggy stayed behind the tree, puzzled. This girl was surely not a danger to the two soldiers. They wore armor, had swords by their sides. She wore only a pullover shirt and mid-calf loose-fitting pants.

She was the one in danger. She needed help.

Instinctively, he backed away, to get far from the danger. But then he stopped. He thought of Raraesa, egg splattered on her head. Then he thought of John. *I am tired of losing.* He stared at the helpless woman. He couldn't—wouldn't—leave her.

With all the courage he could muster, Iggy did what he did best. He moved quietly and unseen, using his brain instead of his brawn.

He crept silently through the bushes and underbrush, placing each foot gently in front of the other. Soon, he was behind the tree the girl was tied to.

In a quiet hush, he spoke. "I'm here to free you. Don't move at all. Pretend I'm not here. I don't want them to look this way."

Iggy heard a soft voice whisper, "Thank you."

She obeyed as Iggy unknotted the rope and released her.

"Here's what we're going to do," he whispered. "I want you to sneak around the tree when the soldiers are distracted. Pick your moment and move away quickly. No looking back. We'll lose them in the forest. With all that armor they're wearing, they won't be able to chase after us very quickly."

She turned to him. "They have horses," she murmured. "Follow me."

Despite the immense danger he was in, he sensed he could trust her. He thought she was around his age but more stunning than he'd thought a girl could be. Her beauty was unnatural, as if it were created by movie or TV magic. Her eyes were hypnotic and sparkled with color—or was it *colors?*—he couldn't decide. Her voice was sultry and soothing. Her blond hair cascaded off her shoulders, flowing to and fro with every movement of her body. For an instant he forgot they were in danger.

The soldiers were laughing raucously at a joke.

"Let's go," she said. Without hesitation, she ran behind them with Iggy on her heels. Iggy marveled at her courage.

They followed a narrow path that skirted the edge of woods to the left, with the lake to the right. As they ran down the path, the forest gave way to a cliff that was inches from his shoulder. Less than fifty feet in front of them, the path disappeared behind the waterfall.

"Hey," one of the soldiers called out. "You don't want to do that. Do not go there!"

"It will be all right," the girl assured Iggy. "Hurry."

"You are in danger!" a soldier shouted. "Stop!"

"Look, they're not even trying to follow us," Iggy remarked, looking over his shoulder. This struck him as strange, but to his delight she held out her hand. He reached out, placing his hand in hers.

Iggy followed the girl. They ran behind the waterfall and into a dead end. The path stopped at a solid stone wall.

Confused, he turned to the girl whose hand he was grasping. She was no longer the beautiful girl whose looks had captivated him. Instead, what held his hand was a hideous monster.

He pulled his hand out of its grip. It had the head of a Gila monster, with cobbled green skin, a black tongue, and razor-sharp teeth. It stood right where the girl had just been. Iggy faltered as the horrible creature blinked and saw something familiar in its eyes. His stomach dropped. She was the monster.

This she-monster grabbed Iggy and threw him behind her. He slammed his head into the rock wall, struggled for a moment to stay conscious as his mind clouded, then everything went blank.

The monster stepped out from behind the waterfall and roared at the soldiers, who retreated into the woods.

❦

Lecque knelt behind the cover of a bush on a knoll overlooking the lake. The events had unfolded before he could intervene. As he watched the waterfall, he knew Iggy would not be emerging from behind it. He waited an extra few minutes, shook his head, and silently backed away, making his way to his horse. After mounting up, he headed home. He wanted to scream in anger, but didn't; he didn't know if the soldiers would hear him. He balled up his fist and smashed it into his thigh a few times. Iggy was his responsibility, and he had let Iggy and Raraesa down.

When he returned to the cottage, he told Raraesa what happened. The villagers called those creatures Liminades. Raraesa knew the legends. The hideous water creatures were beautiful, irresistible women on land. Liminades lived in water and lured their prey with their magical beauty. Once under their spell, they were never seen again.

"Why did you not help him?" Raraesa screamed at Lecque.

"There was nothing I could have done! Yes, I could have fought off the two soldiers. But you know the stories about the power of the Liminades. No one has ever defeated one of them, and no one has ever survived once they have them under their power. There is nothing more we can do for him."

That night they retired on angry terms.

Raraesa could not sleep. Tears ran down her checks. *I never got to taste pizza.* The thought of being alone, cooking in the kitchen without Iggy, left her heartbroken. She had enjoyed her talks with him, all the fascinating things he had told her about his world. She tossed and turned, all the while replaying the special time she had had with him.

18

The darkness engulfed Iggy. "You are not Tilead. You must die!" Over and over the chanting rose, louder and louder.

Iggy stood firm and spun around. In his head pounded, *I am Tilead and you are now Tilead.* Iggy opened his mouth. "I am Tilead."

"Give us those swords."

"Kill him!" came multiple voices. "Yes, kill him! He is not Tilead. He is not a Nostaw. He sullies our race. He must die."

Iggy's vision faded to blackness, and as quickly as the darkness surrounded him, it lifted. Sound filtered into his ears—at first far away, then growing louder until it leveled off at a normal volume. The memory of a sharp-toothed monster stopped him from opening his eyes. He lay there, listening. What he heard confused him. Instead of the raspy breath of a monster hovering over him, ready to devour him, he heard birds chirping and leaves rustling as a breeze blew through trees.

Iggy lay immobile, listening for any sound of movement. Hearing none, he opened his eyes. At first, only a tiny slit. Then ever so slowly, completely. He was alone, on a comfortable bed. The room was built out of beautiful carved limestone with two arching glassless windows on opposite sides of the room to allow for a cross breeze. He was fully dressed.

He remembered Raraesa and Lecque. *This can't be happening all over again.*

The sheets were creamy white and silky smooth, unbelievably smooth. The door to the room was shut, so he lay there and turned his head, taking a more detailed look at the room. The walls were made of stacked limestone with shelves cut into the stone. The ceiling was vaulted, also made from stone. He guessed it to be around twenty feet high.

He felt no pain, so he concluded he wasn't injured... yet.

He climbed out of bed, feeling somewhat safe. Cautiously, he looked through one of the arched openings. In front of him was an expansive field filled with apple trees, pear trees, and other hanging fruit he'd never seen before. The grounds were meticulously groomed with greenery in every direction.

This calmed him. Stepping back, he walked to the opposite wall and the other arched window. He hesitated for a moment, then peeked out and saw a stone walkway that circled an inner open-air garden.

"I see you are awake," came a female voice from the garden.

Iggy jumped back. He flattened himself against the wall, to be hidden from view.

"Please come and join me. You are safe now."

Iggy recognized the voice—the girl he had untied from the tree. The girl who had turned into a monster.

"Maybe it's better if I stay here. You're that monster."

"Yes, indeed, I was." She chuckled. "Are you afraid I'm going to eat you?"

"Maybe."

"If I wanted to eat you, don't you think I would have done that already?"

"Hmm, I suppose so."

"Then open the door and join me here—because if you do not, I might be *forced* to eat you."

"Why should I believe you? For all I know this is one of the games you play before you kill me."

"Well, I guess you'll just have to take that chance."

Iggy weighed his options. Do nothing and stay here where he was trapped. Or go outside and hope he could outrun or outsmart her if he had to. He cracked open the door and peered out. The garden was peaceful. He heard birds chirping and singing to each other. He stepped out onto the walkway and looked up and down. Scattered throughout the walkway were waist-high flowerpots that held evergreen bushes.

"Over here."

Iggy walked with hesitant steps into the garden. He checked around to make sure he had an escape route. As he planned, he saw that the garden behind the pots was spectacular, filled with a cornucopia of exotic flowers. He saw orange, pink, red, and bicolored amaryllis, roses in an array of different colors, from small tea roses to five-foot-tall flowering rosebushes.

He recognized the flowers from the gardening catalogs Aunt Gwen liked to pore over. They used to spend hours talking about what to plant each spring. Many of these were rare, breathtaking varieties. There were ruby-red miniature calla lilies surrounded by deep-purple lilacs. Iggy knew his flowers, but he couldn't figure out how these plants were all in bloom simultaneously. Back in Susquehanna, they flowered at different times of the year. Nonetheless, he took in the view from one side of the garden to the other, allowing the profusion of flowers to soothe his nerves.

He stopped still when he spotted her in a nook in the left corner. She looked back at him and smiled disarmingly. She wore a belted multicolored knee-length skirt and a short-sleeved bright-green shirt.

"Come sit beside me." She patted the spot on the bench next to her. "Let me introduce myself. My name is Nyreada. And what is your name? And why did you help me?" Her voice was soft and soothing.

Iggy didn't move forward. "No, thank you. I think I'll stay over here. My name is Iggy. Why did I help you? Because it was the right thing to do."

"Please come and join me."

"Uh, I don't think so; you can turn, uh, really bad in about two seconds."

"Do not worry." She smiled at him. "That monster look was just an illusion. I did not really turn into that. I simply made your mind see a monster and made you think I was one."

"Why? And what happened to the lake? Where's the waterfall? Where are we?"

"You are in Fryscar."

"Fryscar? Where is Fryscar?" Frustration and annoyance were clear in his voice. He could not fathom being in yet *another* new place with no idea how he got here.

"Well, Fryscar is… here. We are in the land protected by the Plains of Clouds."

"We can't be. There are no clouds above us, only sky and the sun." He pointed at the sky.

"Yes. The clouds are also an illusion."

"And the endless sheer cliff—is that an illusion too? How is that possible?"

"Oh, those cliffs are very real. Very tall and sheer. As for the clouds. Look up. Tell me what you see."

Iggy looked up again. "I see blue sky, scattered clouds, birds flying, and the sun over there. This is all under a dome of clouds?"

"Yes… and no."

"What do you mean, yes and no? We are either under a dome of clouds or not."

"When you saw me as a monster, that was an illusion. It is the same thing." She stood and walked over to a row of orchids, then bent down to smell one.

Iggy followed her to the orchids, but he kept a safe distance so he could get a good look at her. The hypnotic eyes he remembered seemed normal, now. They were green. Her voice was soft, but the sultriness had disappeared. The blond hair was unchanged and still flowed off her shoulders and down to middle of her back. She was his height, but he had no idea how old she was.

So, he asked. "How old are you?"

"Why do you ask?"

"I was just curious if you were a hundred-year-old pretending with another illusion to be young."

"I am sixteen."

Iggy relaxed more. "I'm sorry, you were telling me about a dome of clouds."

"I was." She smiled at him, and her dimples came into full bloom, which Iggy did not miss. "When people from your land stand on the cliff and see a valley of clouds way below them, all they see are menacing clouds. They do not see our land."

"How do you make such an illusion?"

"I am sorry; I cannot tell you that. I am not allowed."

Nyreada strolled around the garden with Iggy following. She stopped here and there to breathe in deeply of the fragrance of the diverse flowers that filled the garden. She turned to Iggy.

"The cloud dome is like a protective canopy over our land. It gives us complete shelter from other people, keeping us safe from invasion. You only see a massive expansion of clouds. Only those who know the secret of how to open the doors to this kingdom can enter. To us here in Fryscar, that cloud shield is invisible. The sun shines through it. The birds fly as high as their wings will take them without touching the shield. Breezes flow and rain falls. But, from up there, all you see is a lake and a waterfall near the edge of the cliff and clouds."

"But, then, how could I get in?"

"Because you were with me."

"So why the monster illusion?"

"To scare the curious away. There are a few portals into our land, and each has sightings of monsters. Beautiful women who trap people, never to be seen again. The stories scare off trespassers, making sure that no one stumbles into one of the portals." Nyreada looked at Iggy and smiled.

"Until now," he said.

"Yes. Everyone in the area around that lake fears it." She stopped and looked him full in the eyes. "Why did you save me?"

"I had no idea about terrible monsters or any of that. I'm usually not one to purposely put myself in any danger. I guess I helped you because you needed help. I've been in that position before. Recently, as a matter-of-fact, and someone helped me. You were alone. I couldn't walk away and leave you to those soldiers."

"Well, I thank you. You saved my life. No doubt they would have done some nasty things to me. Then killed me so there would be no tales told of their misdeeds. I owe you a great debt." She walked up to him.

He tensed, and then his eyes widened as she simply leaned over and lightly touched his hand. He felt a gentle warmth from her touch, and he blushed.

Before he could sort this out in his mind, an elderly woman walked up. "*A pleasant seh to mirn, tah yunta ke kpep ya.*"

Iggy had never heard this language. His ears perked up.

"*A pleasant seh to kpep,ya,*" Nyreada replied.

"I'm sorry, I don't understand," Iggy said.

The elderly woman reeled in shock. She stepped back and glared at Nyreada.

"*What is this? You jursiks yuj surface-dweller to our land? You ih ba yots ma danger!*"

"*He is my wajah. He saved yow peh no has my hakneru.*" Nyreada responded.

The women paused for a moment, then turned to Iggy and said, "*Hello, are kpep,ya Hungy?*"

Nyreada's scowl turned to a smile. She turned to Iggy. "This is Samaita. She greets you hello and asks if you are hungry."

Iggy smiled at Samaita. "Ah. Yes. I hadn't thought about it, but I am hungry."

"*Please jursiks ba ngge to dobak,*" Nyreada said to Samaita.

"What language were you speaking? I've never heard anything like it before." Iggy was naturally intrigued. He was interested in most languages and thought them simple to learn. He recognized this one was a mixture of English with a different base root.

"Here we speak Tinte. You do not need to worry. I will translate for you," Nyreada said as she sat at a small table on the far side of the garden.

Iggy followed and joined her.

A short time later, Samaita returned with a plate full of various cut fruit. She placed it on the table.

"*Thank kpep,ya,*" Nyreada said.

"*You are minti,*" Samaita replied and walked away.

"I'm guessing that was 'thank you' and 'you are welcome'?"

"Indeed," Nyreada said, impressed. "Please enjoy the different fruits grown in our homeland." Nyreada gestured to the plate and fork.

Without missing a beat, Iggy picked up a piece of fruit that looked like nothing he had ever seen before and nibbled it. Then, after realizing he liked it, he took a big bite. "What kind of fruit is this?"

"Kolabalin. Otherwise known as Nectar of the Land."

Iggy tried all the fruits on the plate and thought each was delicious in its own unique way. Nyreada sat there while he ate and stared off into the garden.

"How did this place come to be below the clouds?" Iggy put his fork down and waited for an answer.

"There are some things I am forbidden from telling anyone outside of the Plains. You will just have to accept the fact that it is."

Soon, Samaita returned. She addressed Nyreada. "*Ke are summoned so mirn,tah Oedsuer chambers. Ka is ehpecting your presence.*" Not waiting for a reply, Samaita turned and walked away.

"What did she say?" Iggy asked.

"Oedsuer, our town leader, wants to see me immediately. Most likely it is about you being here."

"Is that a problem?"

"Not if I have any say about it." She carried herself with poise and confidence. "Do not worry," she added, "you are safe here. It is just… well, you are the first from Skye ever allowed here. That is why we have such an elaborate and frightening mythology. No one dares come near the water for fear the scary monster will kill them and eat them. Our best protection is fear. And as soon as that fear is diminished, our danger of invasion from the people of Skye increases."

"What do I do?"

"You just stay in the garden and enjoy your fruit. I will be back shortly." She strolled through one of the stone arches and disappeared down a hallway.

⟡

Nyreada climbed a flight of stone steps and stopped in front of a thick wooden door. She stood there for a moment collecting her thoughts, then knocked as she pushed the door open and walked in. She was in a room with walls of stone and arched glassless open-framed windows. The ceiling was twenty feet high with stone bookcases that towered from the floor to the ceiling. Books filled them, tightly jammed on the shelves.

Casually leaning against one of the stone bookcases was an overweight man in the latter years of his life. He had a dark neatly cropped beard with salt-and-pepper hair. He wore a tan shirt tucked into an intricately woven belt with inlaid blue beads. The belt wrapped around a knee-length kilt-like skirt that had evenly spaced stipes of alternating red, green, blue, and yellow. He was holding and leafing through an encyclopedia-sized book.

"Oedsuer, you wished to speak to me?" Nyreada asked.

He stood without acknowledging her for a moment, reading one page, ignoring her. Nyreada was not surprised. She knew she simply had to wait patiently. When he wanted to speak to her, he would.

Finally, Oedsuer shut the book. He walked silently to a stone desk and sat on a wooden chair. The only item on his desk was a clock inlaid into an intricately carved single piece of stone that shone with multiple colors. Draped over the top, carved from the same piece of stone, was a strange flying animal with its tail wrapped around one side and then forming the base.

"You have a Tipei clock," Nyreada said.

Oedsuer put his hands behind his head, closed his eyes and took in a deep breath, and slowly let it out with a sigh. He opened his eyes and focused on Nyreada.

"We are not here to talk about my new clock. Where do we begin?" Oedsuer paused for a moment. "Tell me about this boy you brought back with you. And *why* you brought him here."

Nyreada steadied herself. "First, I need to tell you some background. When I was on my way to the portal, two soldiers came out of the bushes and tried to stop me. I was able to project my monster. I fully believed it would scare them away, as it always has. But one of them had a rope. He threw it around me and pulled me down, startling me. I lost my concentration, and my monster apparition disappeared. They tied me to a tree."

"And your package?"

"It was secure around my waist."

"Go on."

"The soldiers sat away from me by their fire. They were arguing what to do with me. One of them said they should just kill me with arrows so they did not have to get too close to me. Then somebody whispered to me from behind the tree. It was this boy, Iggy; he cut my ropes and set me free. He wanted me to slip away into the woods with him, but I got him to follow me. We made it to the portal, but Iggy fell and hit his head. He wasn't awake when I checked him."

"Why did you not leave him?"

"I was afraid the soldiers would kill him. He saved my life; I had to return the good deed. It is our way."

"And here we are," Oedsuer said. "You have the bag of stones?"

"Yes."

"I fear your decision to bring this young man here is going to cause more problems than if you had let the guards take him."

"Why?" There was defiance in her voice.

"This boy—" Oedsuer cleared his throat. "This boy is the first ever brought through the portal into our world. In all history, no one has done this. That is how we have stayed safe. You have broken one of our most important laws. What do we do now? There is no precedent for this. The word is already out. I have heard many communication birds have been sent to the Ministers. It is only a matter of time before they get involved. I can only guess what that involvement will be." Though Oedsuer spoke calmly, there was a mix of irritation and concern for Nyreada in his voice.

A flutter of wings came from one of the open window arches. A hawk with a wingspan that just cleared the five-foot-tall windowless arch soared in and landed on a wooden pedestal. The bird was muscular; it exuded power and strength. Its shoulders and back were a mixture of orange, red, and brown feathers. Its head was lighter in color with streaks of gray mixed in. The tail was a grayish white, as was the bird's belly. It had enormous talons. A blue cylinder was strapped to its right leg.

"Well, so, we do not have to wait any longer." Oedsuer rose from his chair and walked over to the majestic bird of prey. He opened the bird's leg pouch and retrieved a rolled-up parchment. Moments after closing the pouch, the hawk bowed, spread its wings, and with a mighty flap flew out of the room. After returning to his seat, Oedsuer unrolled the message and read it. Nyreada sat quietly. "The ruling council is summoning you and the boy—"

"His name is Iggy," Nyreada said with annoyance.

"Hmm. The Ministers of the ruling council are summoning you and *Iggy* to come before them in two days. I suggest you leave first thing in the morning; you should easily make it to Cranncairn in one day."

"What do you think the council will do?"

"I don't know. By bringing him to our land you have initiated a chain of events the outcome of which I cannot predict. The law concerning this breach was written so long ago I am not sure if any associated consequences are still valid today."

"And what does the law say?" For the first time, Nyreada's voice cracked.

"It is not pleasant. And we have other laws that now ban that sort of punishment. That is the problem. We have never had to deal with this. It has always been straightforward." Oedsuer shook his head heavily. "One last question. How many crystals were you able to bring back?"

"Only seven this time. These special rocks are getting harder to find."

Oedsuer frowned. "I fear one day we will be without crystals to keep our cloud illusion going. When it disappears, I worry about what will happen. When you arrive at Cranncairn, bring this bag of depleted crystals to the ministry building. I will distribute the new ones. We are done here. You should go and look after him, so more laws are not broken."

Nyreada left the room somberly. She had promised Iggy he'd be safe. Now she feared it was a promise she might not keep.

19

Iggy finished his fruit and studied the songbirds that flew in and out of
the garden. Two small birds landed on the end of the table and eyed
his fruit. He purposely left a few pieces on the plate and smiled. He
pushed the plate to the opposite end of the table. The two birds tweeted
with joy as they hopped onto the plate and pecked at the remains.

"It is both a beautiful and relaxing place, isn't it?" Nyreada asked.

Iggy turned, startled. Seeing it was Nyreada, he settled back. "Yes,
it is. I could stay here forever. Or at least a few days. Do you have
breakfast here every morning?"

"What is breakfast?"

Iggy chuckled. "Morning fruit. After you wake up, the food you
have in the morning is called breakfast where I come from. It literally
comes from breaking the fast from the previous night."

"Breakfast—what a silly name. We just call it food."

"How did your meeting go?"

"It went…"

Samaita approached them. "*Would kpep,ya mirn,sets hukn bato to eat?*"

"*No wi i si are finished Thank kpep,ya,*" Nyreada said.

"*Thank kpep,ya,*" Iggy said.

Both Nyreada and Samaita looked at Iggy in shock. He had used the correct words in Tinte and felt he had pronounced them perfectly.

"I was not aware you were able to speak Tinte," Nyreada said.

"I have a gift for languages. I learn them quickly."

Nyreada smiled at Samaita and nodded that she could leave.

Iggy gave out a heavy sigh.

"Are you all right?" Nyreada asked.

"I guess so. This is nice. But I need to get back. I'm sure Raraesa and Lecque, who I've been living with, must be worried. And… I don't know… I somehow think they'll take me closer to my actual home. You know, *home.*"

"Who are Raraesa and Lecque?"

"That's who I live with in Skye."

I can't even imagine what Aunt Gwen and John are thinking back home. The memory of them felt like such a distant concept, it was unfathomable. "How do I get back through that portal thing?" Iggy pointed to the sky.

Nyreada hesitated. "Before that happens, the council in Cranncairn wants to meet you. I'm sure they are curious about you and have many questions they want to ask you."

This made Iggy very uncomfortable. He crossed his arms. "When do they want to talk to me? Are they coming here?"

"We leave tomorrow morning for Cranncairn. It will take us most of tomorrow to get there."

"But what if I don't want to talk to them and I just want to go back now?"

"That could put me in the position of wishing I was back tied to that tree."

"What if the council won't let me go?"

"Why wouldn't they? You are not a danger to my people. Come, let us not worry now. We have this entire day to ourselves and another to travel. Let me show you around town. And you can work on learning Tinte." She tilted her head and gave him a soft smile.

Iggy blushed with her staring at him, so he looked down, feeling the burn in his cheeks. "I guess. We can go to town."

"You mean, *Im seyl re ndo yu so wimpuku* "

Iggy thought for a moment, then repeated, "*Im seyl re ndo yu so wimpuku.*"

"Wonderful. From this moment on we only speak Tinte this afternoon."

Iggy smiled. It was a good diversion. It would give him something to focus on to stop him from being so anxious about meeting this council.

They walked over a small rise after leaving the massive stone building that surrounded the angelic garden. Iggy saw a wonderfully laid out town in the distance; he guessed it was about two miles away. It would be a good walk. He would have time to practice his Tinte with Nyreada.

There was a soothing warm breeze, and birds sang in the background as they walked. Iggy practiced speaking in Tinte by asking Nyreada questions about her world, as did Nyreada of Iggy's situation. Sometimes, Iggy would be stumped for a word or the correct pronunciation and Nyreada would revert to Skye to explain. But, in a short time, he was speaking almost fluent Tinte, to Nyreada's astonishment. Iggy smiled. He didn't understand how his brain assimilated new languages so fast. But he did enjoy it.

"Is this land always this, this… peaceful and tranquil?"

"Yes. We have no enemies here. We only fear invasion from the Kingdom of Skye. But we have the shield of clouds, and as a last resort, we have our Exarch of Defense."

Iggy struggled with the Tinte word for Exarch. After Nyreada helped him with it, he got it correctly. "What is your Exarch of Defense?"

"Not what but who. He is our most powerful person. If an invasion were to happen, it would be he who defends our world."

Iggy thought he must lead a powerful army.

"What do you call your land?"

"Matreach," she said with a smile.

⁖

Fryscar was a lovely town. The cobblestone streets were bordered with rows of timber-framed cottages. In front of each cottage were neatly groomed gardens displaying a variety of brilliant-colored flowering plants. They walked to a stone bridge that spanned a small river that flowed through the town. The commercial part of the town began on the other side of the bridge. There were open cafés with people sitting outside, eating pastries, and sipping drinks. A stark contrast to the despairing towns in Skye.

Iggy noticed a shift in the atmosphere on the street. He saw people moving to one side and stopping and bowing their heads in reverence as a decrepit old man made his way down the street toward Iggy and Nyreada. He was thin, almost skeletal. It looked to Iggy that every step he took was labored and painful. His body twisted to the right, and his head dipped down, hanging as if it might fall off at any time but always turned to the left so he could see.

"Who is that?" Iggy asked.

"That is our Exarch of Defense. His name is Allistair."

"I imagine he leads a powerful army."

"Oh, no. It's only him. He defends us," Nyreada said reverently.

Iggy was shocked. "He is expected to defend you against hundreds of invaders?"

"Yes."

"What about ten thousand invaders?"

"Most definitely. He will defend this world all by himself."

"I find it hard to believe he could protect anyone, even himself."

At that moment, Allistair snapped his head up, and his eyes locked on Iggy, who shivered. Allistair's approach to where they stood was slow. He finally stopped in front of them. His eyes locked onto Iggy's face, and for a moment, he simply stared at him.

Iggy tried to suppress a shudder but didn't quite succeed.

"Interesting. This is the young boy I have been called to protect our world from?"

"Yes, he is. May I introduce Iggy to you. And, Iggy, this is Allistair, our Exarch of Defense."

"It's a pleasure to meet you, sir," Iggy said firmly in Tinte.

"Ah, an invader with manners. And one who speaks our language. Very interesting." Allistair took a deep breath and straightened. "I have been asked to prepare a plan in the event of a full-scale invasion."

"I promise there is no invasion. It's just me. And I am not an invader."

"Well, that is a relief. So, young Iggy, you don't think I alone could protect this land from ten thousand invaders? Or even a hundred invaders?"

"I'm sorry, sir, I meant no disrespect."

"Ha!" Allistair laughed. "None taken. For, clearly, I can see you are of no danger to our people. But, nonetheless, I have been charged with preparations. Nyreada, why don't you bring our young man to the training field later today? That way I can show him what a sickly old man can do. Ha!" There was suddenly a spryness to his step as he left.

Iggy waited until Allistair was two hundred feet away before saying, "Not that I believe in magic, but does he use magic against his enemies?"

"No. It's just him. No magic."

"Then there's just no way he could defeat even one person or even a small boy in a battle."

"Still listening," came Allistair's distinct voice from far down the road and well beyond the range of normal hearing.

Iggy's eyes widened and Nyreada laughed.

20

"Oedsuer, is it true, what I have heard?" Trafagla burst into Oedsuer's office, throwing the door open.

"Don't you ever knock?"

Trafagla stood before him in what he thought was a Gypsy ensemble. In each earlobe were two silver hoop rings that matched the size of her ears, partially covered by her shining black hair that erupted from under a deep-blue scarf. All of this was highlighted by ruby-red lipstick and a grin that went from ear to ear.

"Tell me, was I right?" The excitement in her voice was evident.

"Right about what?"

"You know I see the future—"

"Or so *you* say." Sarcasm dripped from Oedsuer's words.

"Is there or is there not a young boy from the other world in our midst?"

"Why would you think that?"

"The entire village is talking about it. So the secret is out." The excitement in Trafagla's voice was undeniable.

"Then why are you asking me?"

"It is true, then." Trafagla clapped her hands. "I must get to the council and talk to them."

"I would advise against that. The last time you stood before the council it did not go very well for you. If my memory serves me correctly, you were dragged out of the chamber yelling and screaming."

Before he could finish his thought, Trafagla was out the door without shutting it behind her.

✍

Iggy was becoming comfortable speaking Tinte. His comfort level rose as they continued through Fryscar. All in all, this wasn't a bad place to be, though he did miss Raraesa, and even Lecque's sternness. And home. *Wow, I'm living a weird life.*

"Well," Nyreada said. "Let us get our mounts and head out to the training arena. I am sure you are curious to see Allistair at his best."

"Is it a long ride? I've become good at riding horses."

"Oh, we are not riding horses."

"Then how are we getting there?"

"We are taking Rockhoppers."

"Rockhoppers?"

"Come. I will show you." She turned and walked toward a building that resembled a horse stable. Iggy followed.

The inside of the stable was as clean as the streets outside. There was no smell of the stable or hay or dirt floor he was so familiar with from Lecque and Raraesa's barn.

A man who may have been in his early twenties approached. "How may I help you?"

"We need two Rockhoppers for the day," she said.

"I will bring them out back."

When Iggy walked around to the back, his eyes widened. Waiting for them were two animals that towered over him. Each stood around nine feet high and had the torso of an ostrich, with lacy feathers in a black-and-white zebra pattern throughout the torso. Their legs were thick and muscular like a horse with three wide toes extending from hooves tipped with heavy talons. In the center of the torso, just at the base of the neck, was an eight inch-long horn with a round bulb cap and a saddlebag draped in front of it. The neck was long but twice the width of an ostrich. Attached to the end of the neck was an owl head with six eyes, three on each side of the face set in a triangle pattern.

Iggy stepped back. "Yikes. There is no way I'm getting on one of those things."

"Iggy. They are gentle. This is how we travel here. Horses are too slow." She walked up to one. "Come. I promise you will be safe." She gave a chuckle and an encouraging smile.

Iggy slowly approached and stood close to Nyreada, keeping her between him and the Rockhopper. Looking up, Iggy saw two of the closer Rockhopper's six eyes looking at him, which sent a shiver up and down his spine.

"Go ahead. Touch him." Nyreada reached up and stroked the Rock-hopper's feathers.

Iggy copied her, keeping a wary eye on the Rockhopper's head. To his surprise, the Rockhopper murmured a sound like a cat's purr.

"The feathers are soft and fluffy," Iggy said.

"Yes, they are. They are gentle beasts. Are you ready to get on yours?"

Before he could answer, the Rockhopper he was touching knelt, then sat on the ground. "But there's no saddle. How do I hang on?"

"After you get on, just hold on to the horn there. You will see." She smiled.

Iggy approached his Rockhopper with great trepidation, grabbed its horn with both hands, and pulled himself up onto its back. As he settled onto its back, the feathers rose and surrounded him, creating a natural saddle. The feathers around his legs puffed out and created a trough that his legs slid into, and a firm platform formed under his feet. The feathers, though soft, felt firm. They instantly molded around his body.

"You see?" Nyreada laughed.

Iggy's Rockhopper stood up, and Iggy tightened his grip on the horn; he was a good five feet off the ground. "How do I control it?" he called to Nyreada, who was mounting her Rockhopper.

"You just hold on to the horn and lean slightly in the direction you want to go." Leaning forward, Nyreada pet the side of her Rockhopper's neck and said, "Rockhoppers are very smart. Please take us to the Tipei Training Arena."

Both Rockhoppers nodded.

Iggy hung on, wide-eyed, as both Rockhoppers trotted across the open field. At first it was a slow trot, then they picked up their pace. Before Iggy realized, they were traveling at an unbelievable speed across the field. The two Rockhoppers, now side by side, raced across the field. Iggy held on to the horn with a death grip. He shot a momentary glance at Nyreada. She was relaxed on her ride. He glanced at her Rockhopper's legs, which were moving so fast they were a blur. Suddenly, there was a *whoomph* sound from the sides of both Rockhoppers, and wings shot out and extended. They were stiff wings that didn't flap.

In an instant, the Rockhoppers lifted gently off the ground, and Iggy was soaring twenty feet in the air. The moment they were gliding, the Rockhoppers tucked their legs under their bellies, where they disappeared. Nervous at soaring into the air, Iggy clenched his legs into the animal's torso and gripped the horn even tighter. How high would they go?

To Iggy's relief, they stayed around twenty feet off the ground. It was quiet, with only the sound of the wind passing them by. They glided for what seemed to Iggy about four miles before they dropped in altitude. When they were only a few feet above the ground, the Rockhoppers extended their legs and ran again. With another *whoomph*, the wings retracted and were gone. The Rockhoppers ran faster and faster and faster until, *whoomph*—the wings reappeared, and they were soaring again.

After the ninth or tenth time of this cycle of running and soaring, Iggy finally relaxed and enjoyed the ride. He looked around. The countryside was beautiful. The land was flat and rolling with fine green moss instead of grass covering the fields and hills. There were areas of rocks jutting out from the moss with small clear blue ponds of water sprinkled between them. The countryside was gentle and rolling with occasional rock outcroppings that shot ten to fifty feet in the air, age-worn and rounded.

Iggy's Rockhopper glided between two of the rock rises and soared around it and then around another, in an S pattern. Iggy had the wind in his face, his hair flowing behind him, and he wore an ear-to-ear grin.

He called out to Nyreada, "This is fantastic!"

"Yes, it is! It never gets old."

On one running phase, the Rockhoppers took them up a rise. They extended their wings at the very top, and the ground fell away under them. They were now easily two hundred feet in the air. Iggy held on tighter. They continued their glide, slowly sinking lower and lower. This time, when they finally reached ground level and the Rockhoppers extended their legs, instead of running faster and faster they slowed and trotted, then stopped. Before them was an open field that expanded tens of miles in front of them.

Iggy's Rockhopper knelt, then sat on the ground. Nyreada climbed off hers, so he did the same.

"What did you think?" she asked.

"That was awesome. Better than any amusement rides I've ever been on."

"Amusement ride? What is that?"

Iggy hesitated. "Never mind, it's too long an explanation."

"Come on. There is Allistair." She pointed.

Allistair was standing on a rise not far from where they stood. He had his back to them. Without turning around, he said, "I have been waiting for you." He craned his head to look at them. "Did you enjoy your ride, Iggy?"

"Yes," Iggy replied as Allistair's eyes fixed onto him.

"Good. Come over here. I want to show you what I've had set

up." Allistair motioned with his hand for Iggy to approach. "This is my field of battle." Allistair stretched his arm ahead. Spread out on the field that would have easily encompassed five football fields side by side were over a thousand full-sized straw soldiers mounted on poles driven into the ground.

Allistair stood up moderately straight, took a deep breath in, and let out an ear curdling call, "*LAS!*"

A lone bird flew toward them from way off. Iggy looked at Allistair with curiosity. Allistair returned his gaze. "Now you will see my strength." Alistair turned to the lone bird flying toward them, and Iggy followed his gaze.

In moments, the bird was on them, hovering in front, gently flapping its wings. It had the shape of an eagle with an eight-foot wingspan and massive sharp talons on its toes. Its legs and torso were covered with hard scales, and the wings' leading edge had natural armor scales on them. The bird finally landed and stood at attention, its eyes fixed on Allistair. It had a four-foot-long, five-inch-wide cylindrical tail that lay on the ground, which ended with a ball adorned with spikes. Its head also had short sharp spikes all over it with a protruding beak filled with a double row of razor-sharp teeth. Its eyes were eight times larger than human eyes and dark. Its breath had the stench of burned sulfur.

The creature's eyes locked onto Allistair, who pointed to the straw soldiers. "*Mistis kol owo,*" he said.

The creature craned its neck and shot a penetrating glance at Iggy, then it extended its wings and flew off into the horizon.

"What was that? That bird creature?"

"In Tinte we call it an *Irn Tipei*. Or, for short, a Tipei."

"That wasn't Tinte you were using."

"Correct. I was speaking to the Tipei in an ancient language called Gugb. That is the original language from the land they were from."

"What land was that?" Iggy's inquisitiveness was not lost on Allistair.

"That answer will be for another day." Allistair cocked his head to the side and stared Iggy down with a smile.

"So what did you tell it?"

"The first word was *Las*,' which was 'come.' The last thing I commanded it to do was 'attack and destroy.'" Allistair smiled. "Look over there." He pointed to the horizon.

Iggy saw what at first he took to be a black smudge on the horizon, but it quickly expanded and widened. His ears picked up a deep, low thumping that reminded him of the sound a helicopter makes off in the distance. Now it was solid black and moved like a cloud rolling across the sky. As it got closer, it continued to grow, and the rhythmic thumping got louder. It resonated in his chest. Iggy realized it was thousands upon thousands more of these flying creatures. Their wings were synchronized in their up-and-down motion. The cluster was so dense he could not see through it, and it blocked out the light from the other side. The thumping sound now pounded in his ears to an uncomfortable level.

Allistair raised his hands and called out, "*Dut gu tokpum kol mistis!*"

As soon as he called out in Gugb, the black cloud split in two and descended to opposite sides of the training field. An instant later they engulfed the straw soldiers. Iggy watched in shock as the Tipei ripped straw heads off with their razor teeth, dug their talons into the torsos, and sliced them open. Others smashed their spiked ball tail into the mannequins. Then, to his surprise, some opened their mouths and a tongue of fire shot out five feet in front of them, lighting the straw soldiers on fire. It had happened fast, and with would-be body parts— either ripped, smashed, or set ablaze—strewn over the battlefield, it was devastating. Iggy could see that no attacking army would stand a chance against the onslaught the Tipei brought to the battlefield.

Allistair turned to Iggy with his head crooked and smiled. "So, Iggy, do you have any doubts about my ability to defend this great land from invaders?"

Iggy simply shook his head. He was mesmerized, watching the Tipeis' utter savagery. "They breathe fire. Are they tiny dragons?"

Allistair laughed. "No. Fire-breathing dragons are myths. They are Tipeis. They drink Liquid Fire. That gives them the ability to breath fire."

Iggy snapped his head to Allistair. "Liquid fire! Where is it?"

Allistair stared at Iggy. "What a strange question for you to ask… and do not ask it again."

"But—"

"I will tell the Tipei they are done and can go home now." He stood up as straight as his twisted body would let him and called out in a mighty voice that boomed across the valley. "*Nal mistis kol kekp fimbap, kpek!*"

The Tipei instantly stopped their attack and pulled up, hovering fifty feet off the valley floor. The sound from their flapping wings gave a cyclical whooshing sound through the air. Yet they stayed hovering—they did not leave.

The Tipei that had arrived earlier and stood in front of Allistair flew out of the pack and again landed in front of him. After folding its wings, it looked at Allistair with unwavering stillness.

Allistair spoke to it in Gugb. Iggy gathered that he was releasing it and telling it to go free.

But the bird paid him no mind. It shuffled its feet to the right and looked at Iggy.

In that moment, time froze for Iggy. He heard only the whooshing of thousands of Tipei wings as they flapped up and down, and his heart raced.

The Tipei turned its body to face the hovering horde of birds and let out an ear-piercing scream. The horde responded in a flash and were upon Allistair, Nyreada, and Iggy. Thousands of Tipei circled around and around the three, letting off terrifying screeches as they circled them. Nyreada fell to the ground, but Iggy froze in place.

Allistair again issued his command in Gugb. The Tipei ignored their lifelong master and continued to circle them. There were so many, and they reached such a height that nearly all light was blocked out except for the occasional ray breaking through. The wind from the birds started a vortex within the tight circle, and the wind swirled around him and pulled on his clothes as he shut his eyes tight.

His amulet suddenly got hot, almost to the point of being unbearable. He yelled, not in Tinte but in English, "*Stoppppp!*"

In an instant the wind vortex stopped, replaced by the rhythmic whooshing of flapping wings. Shaking, Iggy opened his eyes. He was face-to-face with thousands of Tipei. All were staring at him with their mouths half open, showing their razor teeth. Iggy yelled, again in English, and threw his hands forward, "Go! Leave me alone!"

Every Tipei turned and shot across the valley in a dark swarm, their shadows crossing the land below.

Iggy clutched the burning amulet on his chest and fell to the ground, unconscious.

21

Iggy's thoughts rose from a deep fog. His first conscious sensation was intense ringing in his ears. It sounded like a thousand birds screeching. Next, he felt something squeezing and grabbing at his arm, shaking him. The Tipei were pulling on him; they were going to rip him apart. He opened his eyes and lashed out, kicking and yelling.

"Leave me alone! Go away!" Iggy screamed.

"Iggy! Iggy! Stop! It is only me, Nyreada. You are safe." She jumped back to avoid being struck.

Iggy stopped and focused on Nyreada. "Are they gone?"

Nyreada knelt beside him. "Yes, Iggy they are gone. You are safe. Let me help you up."

She took his hand in hers, and after a moment's hesitation Iggy stood.

Allistair walked over. "My, my, my, that was quite a display a few moments ago."

"They were going to kill us!" Iggy said.

"On the contrary," Allistair said. "They were just saying hello and making sure you were a friend."

"Do they always say hello like that?" Iggy asked.

Allistair paused, hesitating. He seemed to be deliberating whether or not to say something. Finally, he rubbed his chin and said, "Actually, no. What the Tipei did, that scene, it was rather unusual."

"I'm not sure if that's a good thing or a bad thing," Iggy muttered to himself.

"Let us get you something to drink. It will help you feel better."

Allistair and Nyreada went to get Allistair's satchel that lay on the ground. Iggy watched them deep in conversation, Allistair quite animated.

When they returned, they made a point of acting normal, as though nothing strange had happened. Iggy sat on a rock next to the Rockhoppers and sipped a drink that tasted like a sweet pear. He tried to shake off his feeling that something very odd had transpired—more than just a hello from the Tipei. Meanwhile, his head pounded, and his heart still raced.

Iggy looked up at Allistair and asked, "Why won't you tell me about Liquid Fire?"

Allistair sneered. "Young man, you are not from this world. And there are certain things, certain knowledge, that must stay in this world. So, tell me why you are so curious about Liquid Fire?"

Now it was Iggy's turn to be evasive. "I'm just curious. I heard about it in Skye."

"In Skye, you say. Hmm. All the more reason for me not to tell you. I think we are done here." Allistair turned and walked away.

"Shall we head back to Fryscar?" Nyreada asked Iggy.

Reluctantly, he agreed.

❧

Allistair waved to them as their Rockhoppers pulled away. Once they were out of sight, his facial expression turned dark and hard. "Gentle and meek? I do not think so. You are a very dangerous person, young Iggy. One I feel I will have to deal with personally. And believe me—I will stop you."

❦

Despite Nyreada's reassurances, the ride back to Fryscar was not relaxing for Iggy. Every few minutes he scanned for a massive black cloud of Tipei rolling toward them.

Iggy was quiet walking through Fryscar, deep in thought. Despite Nyreada's reassurance this was a safe and peaceful land, he didn't feel safe and was getting the impression there was a lot of danger just under the surface.

Finally, he broke the silence. "Tell me about Allistair."

Nyreada thought for a moment. "He was born with a deformity. They say he was a frail child. But they also say he was intuitive and very smart. As the years went on, the town fathers saw he had a gift with animals, so he was tested in animal communication. Because he scored so high, he was trained as a Tipei Master."

Iggy felt a pang of empathy. "What does a Tipei Master do?"

"The Tipei will only bond with one master at a time. A master goes through elaborate training and takes on the role for life. When the master is too old to continue, he passes the role to a younger trainee, who then becomes the new master."

"Is someone being trained to take over for Allistair now?"

"I'm sure there is."

"Who picks that person?"

"The current master. It is his and only his decision."

"How do they train?"

"Well, as you saw, the Tipei are fierce and ferocious fighters. Only the Tipei Master can control them. Once bonded with him, they will follow his every command. They reinforce this in training. They will never disobey him."

"Why?"

"That is just the way it is. A Tipei's only role is to protect this land. In this way, even a small, frail person can wield ominous power."

Two things nagged in the back of Iggy's mind. First, it seemed for those few seconds when the Tipei were swarming in a circle around them that Allistair in that moment did not have control over them—and that, briefly, he did. But that couldn't be.

He had to ask. "Then why did they obey me?"

"I do not know. They probably were not. Most likely Allistair was controlling them and playing with your emotions." She shrugged and walked on. She then asked casually, "I saw a glow under your shirt. What was that?"

Iggy hesitated, then as casually replied, "I have a necklace that when the light shines on it sometimes appears to glow."

"May I see it?"

Iggy lifted it from under his shirt and, without taking it off, showed it to her.

Nyreada's eyes widened. "That is beautiful." Her voice quickly became calm and casual again. "Where did you get it?"

"It was a gift from my mother." He placed it back under his shirt.

One other thing nagged at him as they walked. How could he find out about Liquid Fire without drawing too much attention to himself? He didn't want to tell anyone about or show them his Nostaw swords. But now he knew it was in this land that his Nostaw Warrior quest would be fulfilled. He would have to be cautious with how he obtained information. He wondered if his truth rune card would work here.

Iggy was up early the next morning. He was calmer after digesting the explanation Nyreada gave about the control Allistair had over the Tipei. There was no reason to believe that, after many generations of one master having control over them, his presence would disrupt the master and creature bond unless his necklace played a role. He was not fully buying Nyreada's explanation.

He pulled out his necklace and stared at it. "There is a lot more to you that I have to find out about, that's for sure." He tucked it back under his shirt.

The first hour of the ride to Cranncairn was an anxious one for him. He was on guard, scanning the skies again. The Rockhoppers did their running and gliding, no different from the previous day. The farther they got from town, the more Iggy worried about the Tipei attacking, as the majesty of the countryside was lost on him. The first hour ran into the second, and nothing happened. Iggy relaxed and stopped scanning the skies. The countryside was again spectacular.

The terrain suddenly changed when they soared around one of the rock bluffs. Iggy's Rockhopper tucked in its wings and started its run again. Iggy was mesmerized by the breathtaking view. There was an ever-expanding green valley floor that he judged to be at least ten miles wide. On either side of the valley, cliffs soared straight up to the sky. Pouring out of the rock at multiple sites were torrents of crystal-blue water that cascaded onto the valley below. The pools at the bottom of the waterfalls joined to form a quickly flowing river. The plateaus at the top of the falls held pinnacles of sharp, jagged deep-red and orange rocks.

Iggy smiled as they glided and ran across the valley floor. "This really is beyond spectacular!" he shouted to Nyreada.

"There is even more! Follow me."

She leaned left, and Iggy did the same, and soon they were soaring through the mist from the waterfalls. Iggy breathed in deeply. He was relaxed and happy. He looked over at Nyreada. This was the first time he had taken a moment to really look at her. She differed from Raraesa. Not as athletic. She had a different appeal. One he could not quite pinpoint. As with Raraesa, she was easy to talk to.

At the far end of the valley, they slowed, landed gently, and pulled to a stop. "Why don't we eat here?" Nyreada called over to Iggy as his Rockhopper landed, trotted up to hers, and also stopped.

The two sat on fine grass. Nyreada opened a pack she had taken off her Rockhopper, and after laying out a blanket, she set out food and drink.

"This is not very much, but I wanted to thank you for saving my life. I put together some delicacies from our land. I hope you like them." She smiled, and Iggy melted inside.

Iggy eyed the food. "Wow. I'm honored. What kind of food is this? I haven't seen any of these yet."

Nyreada smiled. "Well, here we have salted grilled meat from a Baj Akl snake. And these are marinated Iti thighs. Lastly, for dessert, we have pudding of Tipei Bahi."

Pointing at the pudding, Iggy asked, "That's Tipei? Those birds that surrounded us?"

"No, there is a bush that will cut you like the Tipei's talons if you touch the edges of the leaves. And the sap will burn you like the Tipei's breath. But if you manage to get the fruit off the bush, it is as sweet as any fruit and as refreshing as any mountain stream. The difficulty in obtaining it makes it ever more special." The conversation took an abrupt pause. After a moment she looked at Iggy. "I am still very thankful. You put yourself in danger to save me."

"It was the right thing to do." Iggy blushed slightly.

"Well, the right thing to do right now is eat."

Nodding, Iggy picked up the Baj Akl snake and wrinkled his nose as he sniffed it. Then he nibbled off the end and chewed it. Liking the taste, he took a full bite.

They ate, relaxed, and enjoyed conversation. Their preoccupation caused them to miss a speck moving fast across the far side of the valley. The speck was a Rockhopper; Allistair was its rider.

Nyreada stood and stretched. Iggy took that opportunity to reach into his waist pouch and hold the truth rune card. After glancing at it, he hid it in his hand.

"Do you know anything about a race called Nostaws?"

"Nothing other than you should hope to never run across one. Why do you ask?"

"I just heard stories. Allistair mentioned something about Liquid Fire. Can you tell me anything about that?"

"No. I did hear him mention it at the Tipei Training Arena. But I cannot tell you anything more about it. You ask funny questions."

"I'm just curious." He had no idea if the runes spell affected her, so he released his grip. "This has been a fantastic time. I could stay in this valley all day."

"Unfortunately, I think we must get on with our journey." She set about folding up the blanket and packed it away in her Rockhopper's saddlebag. Soon they were flying out of the valley.

As the afternoon approached the early evening, they neared the outskirts of Cranncairn, where, without guidance, the Rockhoppers stopped in front of a building. They knelt, and Iggy and Nyreada climbed off.

"Welcome to Cranncairn," Nyreada said.

Iggy looked around. Like Fryscar, the streets were cobblestone and as clean as the day they were made. Lining either side of the street were two-story brick-and-wood private dwellings in orderly rows.

A stark contrast to Ginside, Iggy thought.

"It has been a long ride. Lunch was a long time ago. I am hungry and tired. Let us get something to eat at the center, then we can go to the Inn at Riverside tonight. I hope you enjoy the accommodations. Then, tomorrow morning, we have to present ourselves before the Ministers' Council." Nyreada looked at the concern on Iggy's face. "Do not worry; they are fair men. You are in no danger. I am sure they are just curious about you and want to meet you."

They strolled through Cranncairn and soon came to a center area, which was a square surrounded by food stores. Townspeople were at most of the windows, picking up food. They then sat at the outside tables and ate.

Not knowing what to order, Iggy had Nyreada do the honors, and she got them both Woolpack Pie with Beed Dripping Chips. Iggy devoured it with an eagerness that made Nyreada exclaim, "Wow, you were hungry."

"Yes, and this was excellent." He took a swig of water and then gave her a big grin.

As their day caught up with them, they went to the inn and turned in for the night. Iggy's room was on the second floor. The Inn at Riverside was appropriately named, with a slow-moving thirty-foot-wide river that ran next to the building. The honey-colored stone exterior had ivy and moss climbing up one side with a multitude of stained-glass windows giving it an elegant presentation.

Iggy's room had a four-poster bed in one corner and a high arched ceiling. Lying in bed, his mind wandered to Raraesa and Lecque. Their small village and town were so different from this one. His thoughts jumped to Susquehanna, to Aunt Gwen, John, and Leonard, which seemed a lifetime ago. The comparisons couldn't have been starker. Given the three places, this was the first time in his young life he felt truly comfortable. That struck him as very odd.

Overshadowing that comfort were the pangs of homesickness he felt, missing Aunt Gwen, John, and Leonard. He knew they must be worried about him. And he was guilt-ridden because he couldn't help but wonder what life would be like if he lived here. In Pennsylvania he was a timid mouse, but here… he liked what he was changing into. He liked the new adventure and all it brought him. He began mentally replaying the fantastic views he'd seen on the flight to Cranncairn, then he drifted off to sleep.

He met Nyreada in the main entryway to the inn the next morning; a breakfast of fruit and breads was set up in the inn's gardens. After they ate, they made their way to the ministry building that sat in the center of Cranncairn.

"What should I expect from this meeting?"

"Well, there are six Ministers of Matreach. They are our ruling council. There is Minister Riveriron; he is the Head Minister. Then there are Ministers Sonham, Leeforth, Tritdaw, Witsaw, and Hyluita. As to what you should expect, honestly, I'm not sure. Your guess is as good as mine," Nyreada said gently, though Iggy thought he caught a hint of nervousness that he'd not heard in her voice before.

They walked down a side street to the ministry building. When they turned the corner, Iggy stopped; his mouth hung open in amazement.

"Wow! I've never seen… never even imagined anything like that. How is that possible?"

In front of Iggy was a plaza with dazzling colored inlaid stone bricks and a fountain with water of different colors pouring out of side spouts shaped like Tipei heads. At the far end of the plaza was a tree that rose two hundred feet into the air. Inlaid in the tree's trunk were sections of a castle wall. The tree seemed to have engulfed it. As Iggy looked up the enormous tree trunk, he saw segments of the stone castle jutting out of the trunk as if they were sprouting branches. The branches were twenty feet in diameter, and the tree's trunk, and castle rooms sat on the branches, perched like birds' nests.

"That is our ministry building. The seat of power that rules over all of Matreach," Nyreada told him.

"But that… The building itself. How is that possible?"

"Ah, you mean the Castle in the Tree. It just is. It is amazing. Even now, every time I see it, I am still surprised by it." She took a moment to admire it herself, then said, "Let us go. It is not wise to keep the council waiting."

The outside of the castle that was visible was built from six-by-six-foot cut-stone blocks. At the base of the tree trunk archways had been cut into the tree. Walking through the open archway, Iggy saw the base of the enormous tree trunk was hollow. The floor had highly polished blue stone inlaid into it. Iggy looked up, and his eyes widened with amazement. Along the outside ring of the cored-out trunk a circular staircase had been carved out of wood from the trunk. The living tree made up the outer circular walls that went up and up as far as Iggy could see.

The air was cool and somewhat sweet. His eyes dropped to a carved mural of Matreach that ran the entire circumference of the first level. The sky in the mural had a sun on one side and the stars on the opposite with hundreds of inlaid crystals. In the exact center of the chamber stood a shiny metal podium about shoulder height, its top flat and barren.

"This is fantastic."

"I thought you would like it. First-time visitors are always amazed."

Iggy turned his attention to the carved mural. "That mural is so intricate."

"Yes, it is what our land looks like if you climb to the highest point of this tree and look in all directions."

"It must have taken years to carve. Who made it?"

"Honestly, we do not know. It has always been here."

Iggy walked to one section and pointed to a depicted battle scene. There were hundreds of Tipeis attacking an individual. Many Tipeis lay dead on the valley floor while others were attacking from the air, their talons extended and fire spewing from their beaks.

"What does this show?" Iggy asked Nyreada.

"That was when the Tipeis were used to save Matreach from Minister Jetrix. He had taken over this land—"

"May I help you?" a woman called over to them from behind a desk, interrupting Nyreada's Matreach history lesson.

They walked up to a modern-looking reception desk. "We are here to see the Matreach Ruling Council Ministers," Nyreada said to the middle-aged woman sitting behind the desk.

"Your names?" she asked.

"I am Nyreada, and this is Iggy. The Matreach Ruling Council Ministers are expecting us."

"Indeed, they are." The woman stood. "Please follow me."

The receptionist took them to the base of the circular staircase and started up it. After three full turns around the outer circumference of the staircase, she stopped at a hallway. She turned and walked down it, her shoes click-clacking on the marble tile inlaid onto the dirt floor. Nyreada and Iggy followed. The hallway was carved into one of the enormous tree branches. Natural light shone through openings in the wood. Iggy peered through one opening and saw they were a hundred feet off the ground. As they reached the end of the hallway, the wood morphed, and they were in the stone castle.

The woman stopped in front of a bench. "The two of you will wait here. You will be called in when needed." She turned on her heel and strode away.

"The two of you will wait here," Nyreada mocked her.

"And you will be called in when needed," Iggy added.

The two laughed.

"What is so funny?" A stern voice came from the now open door to the council chamber. In front of the door stood a stern-looking older man wearing a dark robe and a black hat with a caricature of a small Tipei protruding out of the top.

Nyreada jumped to her feet, obviously embarrassed, and stammered, "Minister Riveriron! My apologies. We meant no disrespect."

Iggy for a moment stared at the Tipei on Minister Riveriron's hat and had to stifle a laugh as he thought of a bobble head doll that sat on his shelf in his room in Susquehanna.

"Surely you did; otherwise, your words would not have been followed by laughter," he said with a frown. "Nonetheless, she did not hear you. Thus, formal apology will not be required." Minister Riveriron looked at Iggy. "I assume this is the boy? The reason we are meeting?"

"Yes. This is Iggy."

Iggy instantly felt uncomfortable. He did not like the way Minister Riveriron said "*The reason we are meeting*. Iggy leaned over to Nyreada and whispered, unfortunately loud enough for Minster Riveriron to hear, "I thought this was going to be a pleasant meet and greet. He sounds too serious for that. How about you go talk with them, and I will walk around the city and do some sightseeing," Iggy said, unfortunately loud enough for Minister Riveriron to hear.

"You will be going nowhere until you are called into the Ministers' Chamber for questioning. Nyreada, we will speak with you first." Minister Riveriron pointed to the now closed door to the chamber. Then he paused. "I was not aware he spoke Tinte."

"Yes, he has been learning it since he arrived yesterday."

"I find that hard to believe. Tinte is not an easy language to learn. That will make our meeting even more interesting."

Nyreada turned to Iggy. "Just wait here." She followed Minister Riveriron into the Ministers' Chamber.

Iggy sat on the bench, his pulse faster than a few moments ago. His inner voice told him to run, but where to? He didn't know. All he knew was he was not in a good place. He no longer felt safe.

22

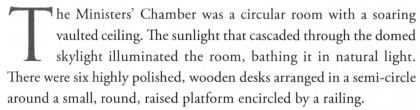

The Ministers' Chamber was a circular room with a soaring vaulted ceiling. The sunlight that cascaded through the domed skylight illuminated the room, bathing it in natural light. There were six highly polished, wooden desks arranged in a semi-circle around a small, round, raised platform encircled by a railing.

Minister Riveriron led Nyreada into the room and motioned for her to step onto the podium platform. He took his seat behind his personal desk. Five others sat solemnly at the remaining five desks, no smiles on their faces. Two hid behind beards, and one other had a handlebar mustache. They were also dressed in black robes and wore hats adorned with Tipei caricatures.

Minister Riveriron immediately called the meeting to order. "You understand that by stepping onto that platform you are bound by the truth and, despite how damaging your answers may be to yourself and others, you must abide by the code of truth?"

"I understand," Nyreada said.

"You were tasked with traveling into the other world and retrieving a package that would guarantee our anonymity and thus our safety for the next ten full season cycles," Minister Riveriron stated.

"That is correct," Nyreada answered calmly.

Minister Sonham spoke up. "Yet you not only returned with the package, you also returned with a boy from the Kingdom of Skye." There was anger in his voice.

"That is also correct," Nyreada said.

Minister Riveriron held up his hand toward Minister Sonham. "We will have plenty of time to express our… concerns with that situation. First, I would like Nyreada to walk us through how this situation arose." He clasped his hands, interlacing his fingers, and rested them on the table as he fixed his gaze on Nyreada.

Nyreada looked down at her feet and took a deep breath as she thought about the details. "It started off around the middle of the day. I made my way into the town of Stagwell. I met my contact as instructed near a local bakery and we walked around casually so as not to draw any attention to ourselves. We overnighted at the local inns. The next day we left town, sharing one horse. When we got out of town, I was given the package and dropped off near the lake. We made sure no one was following us and that there was no one around—"

"Apparently not well enough," Minister Sonham cut in.

Minister Riveriron again held up his hand, stopping any further pontificating by Minister Sonham. "Please continue."

"I made my way toward the lake to access the portal. Before I left the safety of the woods, I checked up and down the waterfront and adjacent woods. I saw no one, so I walked along the shore to the portal behind the waterfall. Two soldiers ran out of the woods. They yelled at me to stop. I have no idea where they came from but I felt safe because I projected my monster. I thought that would scare them off. Instead, one of them grabbed a rope and threw it around me. After they captured me, they tied me to a tree."

Nyreada stopped and looked directly at Minister Riveriron.

This will be a long session. She took another deep breath and proceeded with the story.

❦

Out in the waiting area, Iggy sat on the bench, his foot tapping the floor. He heard footsteps coming down the hall and the rattling of jewelry. A woman in her early twenties walked toward him with her necklaces and bracelets jangling. Her peasant-style dress and scarf flowed behind her. Iggy was taken aback by her bright-red hair that tossed back and forth with each step.

"Hello," she said as she drew abreast of him and stopped. "I have to ask, why are you sitting outside the Ministers' Chamber? Are you in trouble and waiting to meet your fate?" she asked with a slight joking tone.

"No. They just want to meet me. I guess they think I'm special," Iggy said with a chuckle. He looked at her. She had a familiar face. It finally dawned on him who she was. "I remember you. You sang and told stories in Ginside. And you knew my name. How did you know my name?"

"Oh, there are a lot of things I know. It's my business to know." She looked at Iggy, then at the-closed Ministers' Chamber door. "You know, you are the first."

"The first what?"

"The first from the other land ever to visit us. Other than, of course, me. My name is Trafagla. And it is wonderful you are continuing with your journey. Your quest."

"How… how do you know about me and my quest?"

"It is my gift. I just know things. And do not attempt to use your rune card on me. Or on anyone in Matreach. It does not work here. We are protected from it." She paused and smiled at him. "I had a dream a long time ago that we would meet right in this spot. And here we are."

"I need to know about my quest. What can you tell me? Do you know about Liquid Fire?" Iggy jumped off the bench.

Trafagla placed her hand onto Iggy's chest directly over his heart. "To find Liquid Fire, you must first bond with your heart and your soul. And with—" She stopped. Her eyes glazed over, and she looked as though she was seeing something in the distance.

"And with what?"

She replied in a singsong voice, "With a Tipei."

"How do I do that? Can you tell me? Please?"

Trafagla snapped back to the moment. "At this time... no. I do not think I can." She gave him an enigmatic smile before walking away.

"What do you mean, no? No you can't or no you won't?"

Trafagla ignored his questions, rounded the corner, and was gone.

"Maybe this place isn't as wonderful as I thought it was," he muttered to himself and slumped back onto the bench.

Nyreada continued with her story, trying to remain calm. "I was tied up for a very long time. The soldiers were arguing whether to bring me back as a prisoner or have their way with me, then kill me. I think they had settled on the latter. Then there was a voice behind me. It was the young man who calls himself Iggy. He quietly untied the ropes that bound me to the tree. I convinced him we should take the path behind the waterfall; he wanted to hide in the woods."

"Why didn't you simply frighten him by transforming? Not even a fool would have followed you then," Minister Witsaw said.

"I did change, and I completely terrified him. He fell and hit his head, which knocked him unconscious."

"Then how and why is he here, in our peaceful, protected land?" Minister Riveriron asked.

Nyreada looked around at the six Ministers, all their eyes on her. Judging her. Criticizing her. Anger rose. "He saved my life!" she spat out. "He saved our world by helping me! By allowing me to return to our world with my package! We all owe a debt of gratitude to him. He was helpless on the ground. The soldiers would have killed him, so I dragged him through the portal so he would be safe. I will not accept any criticism that I should have left him there to die! Hurting others is not out way." Her eyes darted around to the Ministers, piercing the eyes of each for a moment.

Minister Leeforth jumped to his feet and slammed his hands on the desk. "That is enough, and you will not use that tone in this Ministers' Chamber. You have put us all in grave danger. You are simply too naive and young to understand the consequences of your actions."

∽

Out in the hallway, Iggy wondered what Nyreada was being asked. For a second time, he heard footsteps on the marble floor. He looked to his left and saw Allistair walking toward him.

"Well, young Iggy, I see you have an appointment with the Ministers' council. I'm sure they will be delighted to see you." He tilted his head even more. "I can only imagine the variety and depth of the questions they have for you. They are a curious gaggle of old men." He laughed.

The door to the chamber flew open, and Nyreada stormed out. "They are a bunch of close-minded old men set in their ways." She fumed and paced in front of Iggy and Allistair.

Minister Riveriron exited the chamber and stood quietly, an unhappy look on his face. He saw Allistair with Iggy. "Allistair," he greeted him in a less-than-happy tone.

"Riveriron," Allistair returned the greeting, leaving off the title of Minister.

"Iggy," Minister Riveriron began, "the council members would like to speak with you now. Follow me."

Iggy got up from his seat when Allistair motioned for him to stay seated. "I urgently need to speak to them," he said.

"The Ministers' council has business to tend to. After we are finished with our current issue, if there is time, we will hear what you have to say," Minister Riveriron said to Allistair.

Allistair looked Minister Riveriron up and down. "I think not. I have no time for your pompousness today." Allistair turned and walked to the door of the chamber. Opening it, he turned to Minister River-iron. "You may come and hear what I have to say... if you wish." He allowed the door to close behind him.

Alistair approached the edge of the center podium but, instead of climbing onto the platform, he threw an arm over the railing and used it to help him stand up straight. Seeing Minister Riveriron had joined them, he motioned for the man to take his seat.

"What are you doing here?" Minister Tritdaw asked.

"I'm here to tell you that boy sitting out there is a natural Tipei savant." Allistair let his words hang in the air. He looked around at the six Ministers.

Minister Sonham's mouth was ajar. "That... that is impossible. There has not been a natural Tipei savant since Coronaria. That was over five hundred four-season cycles ago. Tipei Masters are hand-selected by the existing master. A natural Tipei savant! This cannot be!"

Minister Hyluita, who had sat quietly throughout the meeting, finally spoke up. "If what you say is true—"

"It is," interjected Allistair.

Minister Hyluita pressed on, "If what you say is true, then this is a very dangerous situation."

Minister Riveriron asked, "How did he learn Gugb to communicate with the Tipei?"

"He did not. He spoke to the Tipei in his native language," Allistair said. "The entire Tipei flock circled him, which they do in the bonding ceremony, when control is passed from one master to the new master. I commanded them to stop. And they *did not*. That boy out there was petrified. He yelled in his own language for them to stop, and they did, instantly, hovering in place. Then he screamed at them in total fear to leave him alone and go. His hands shot out, pointing for them to go, and in that instant the entire Tipei flock charged away from us in the direction he was pointing."

Minister Riveriron asked, "Was he aware of what he did?"

"No. He was quite shocked by it," Allistair said. "Afterward, I did not tell him the true significance of what had happened. I made it seem as though the Tipei were simply interested in his kind, since they had never seen someone from Skye before."

"Council ministers," Minister Riveriron said, "we have a major problem here. And, if we choose the wrong path, our people, our land, our way of life will be in peril."

"Yes, yes," came the reply from the other five Ministers.

Minister Riveriron continued, "Clearly we cannot allow him to ever leave Matreach. Skye can never know what our world is truly like. They must continue to know us as terrible creatures. Most importantly, we can never allow this boy to know of his true powers. Once in control of the Tipei, he could be our supreme ruler. We would be powerless to stop him."

Minister Tritdaw chimed in. His tone was not only ardent but filled with venom. "The solution is a simple one. We put him in our deepest dungeon, where he will never see the light of day again. We put him so far down in the ground that the Tipei will never hear his call to them. We also burn his voice box so there will never be any chance of him calling out to them. That is the solution."

"Agreed," Minister Sonham and Hyluita shouted.

Minister Riveriron stood. "Allistair, are you one hundred percent certain of your claims?"

After a moment's hesitation, Allistair replied, "No… not one hundred percent."

"Then I will not agree to impose such a tyrannical sentence on this boy unless you and we are all one hundred percent certain," Minister Riveriron said.

"The risk is too great to make the wrong choice!" Minister Sonham objected.

"You are correct, Minister Sonham. So, I ask you, Allistair, how can you tell us definitively that he is or is not a natural Tipei savant?"

"I will bring him to the arena and give him the final Tipei bonding test. If he is not a natural Tipei savant, the Tipei will rip him to pieces, and our dilemma is over. If the Tipei bond with him, we will have our answer," Alistair said.

Minister Riveriron asked, "If the Tipei bond with him, won't that be dangerous? He will have control over the Tipei and be unstoppable. He will have the power we fear him obtaining."

"That is where you will have to trust me. He will not have any idea of the power he will be wielding," Allistair said.

⤝

Nyreada had finally calmed down and was sitting beside Iggy when the chamber door opened. Allistair and Minister Riveriron walked out, all smiles.

"Ah, Iggy," Allistair said. "I apologize for the delay in seeing the council. I was short on time and had some pressing business to review with them." He started to walk away, then stopped. "I am going over to the apprentice training ground where the next Tipei Master is training so that one day, he can replace me—as if anyone could." He chuckled, amused at his own comment. "Nonetheless, I would like it if you would join me at the training arena. Then you can see that the Tipei are calm, trained, and present no danger to us. I know what happened with them yesterday might have been a little disconcerting."

"Yes, that's a great idea," Minister Riveriron said. "After we get to know this young man, I will have Nyreada bring him over." He smiled at them both. "Now, Iggy, the Ministers would like to meet you."

Iggy stood defiantly and looked at Minister Riveriron. "Let's do this."

Once inside the chamber, Minister Riveriron walked Iggy to the platform. "Iggy, this is what we call the platform of truth. Climbing onto it indicates you agree that every answer, no matter how difficult, is the complete truth." He gestured for Iggy to climb the two steps. "We are not here to interrogate you, so please do not worry. It is just this is the center of the room and it makes it easier for the others to see you, and for you to see them. Let me formally introduce myself: I am Minister Riveriron, the Head of this council that rules our peaceful land. I will not bore you by introducing the other Ministers. It is not necessary, for I do not foresee a need for us to meet after today."

Iggy stood on the center platform. He wanted to look calm, but his trembling gave away his nervousness. He looked at the others with a meek smile.

"We collectively want to thank you for saving Nyreada from those soldiers. We appreciate your bravery."

"You are welcome."

"You are from the place called Skye. What do you think of Matreach?" Minister Riveriron asked.

"It is an incredibly unique land."

"Yes, it is. And we are hoping you will help us keep it that way."

Iggy looked confused. "How can I do that?"

"Simply by keeping our secret and not telling anyone about it to those in Skye." Minister Riveriron's tone was gentle and reassuring.

"You can count on me. That is a promise."

"Then I think we have an understanding, and we are done here."

✍

Nyreada waited anxiously for Iggy outside the room. She prepared herself for a long wait. She herself had been in the room for some time, and surely they had even more questions for Iggy. But after just a few minutes, the door opened, and Iggy and Minister Riveriron walked out.

"Well, Iggy," Minister Riveriron said. "It was a pleasure meeting you. And, again, we thank you for rescuing Nyreada from those soldiers."

"That's it? We're done?" Nyreada asked.

"Why, yes. Did you think we were going to thrash him or lock him up for saving you? The Ministers of the council only wanted to meet him. Also, in case you were not aware, this evening there is a play on the main plaza. Why don't the two of you enjoy it together? We would like you both to return to see us tomorrow. That way we can work out the details of getting Iggy back to the other world." Minister Riveriron gave them a full-toothed smile.

Nyreada was grateful to be leaving, yet something about that smile made her uneasy.

Iggy was delighted to get to see the Tipei again. Somehow, he hoped to discover more information about the Liquid Fire. Hopefully, the Tipei would tell him.

23

Iggy and Nyreada entered the Tipei Training Arena. It was an arena the size of a baseball field, with a four-story-high, open-air ceiling covered with a thick metal mesh. It would let light and rain in, but nothing else. The ground was hard-packed dirt.

Allistair stood in the center of it, waving his arms around like an orchestra conductor.

"What is he doing?" Iggy asked as they stayed behind the protective metal fence that separated them from the arena.

Nyreada pointed up. "Look up. He's directing that Tipei."

Iggy looked up and saw a solo Tipei swooping, diving, and hovering. All its motions followed Allistair's hand directions. Allistair brought his hands together and lowered them to the ground. The Tipei responded by landing in front of him at the exact spot his hands were pointing to. The Tipei folded its wings and stood motionless.

"You see, Iggy," Allistair said without turning around, "the Tipei is completely under command of its master." He smiled as he tilted his head around to look at Iggy. "Please, open the door and enter. Nyreada, you will stay there."

"I think I'll just watch from here," Iggy said.

"They are docile and only attack when provoked or ordered to."

Allistair spun his body around but continued with his sideways look. "You are not going to provoke it, are you?"

"No. I've seen what they do when provoked… and it wasn't pleasant to watch."

"They were not being provoked yesterday. They were following my every command," Allistair said as he momentarily stared Iggy down.

Iggy entered the arena and with eyes fixed on the Tipei walked up to and stood behind Allistair.

"This is how it works: I will instruct the Tipei to listen and take orders from you, just temporarily. I am the master, of course. The Tipei will understand I am giving you orders—that you are my assistant. Then you can instruct it by telling it what to do. Advanced trainees can just point and move their hands. You see, after a while, the Tipei's mind connects with the master's, and simple gestures can control them." Allistair turned to the Tipei and spoke in Gugb to it. "*When tom gives lok pa sun command gur mir.*"

Iggy listened carefully to Allistair speaking Gugb to the Tipei. He instantly understood "*When Tom gives lok pa sun command*" as "When he gives you a command." But the "*gur mir*" threw him. "Excuse me."

"Yes?"

"What does *gur mir* translate to?"

"It means obey him."

With a little more exposure to Gugb, Iggy would have understood that "*gur mir*" translated to "kill him."

Allistair continued, "This Tipei now knows that you are its master and must completely follow your commands."

Allistair pointed to a five-foot-tall wooden pole. They were now ten feet from each other, and Iggy could smell its sulfur breath. "Let us try something simple. Instruct the Tipei to fly and land on the top of that pole on the other side of the arena."

"In what language?" Iggy asked.

"You can use Tinte or your own world language. Tipeis are able to understand the language of whoever is instructing them. Let us see how it goes."

"I'll use my own language. I wouldn't want to accidently tell him to rip my head off," Iggy said with a grin. There was something wrong here, and his mind was doing his own scheming.

Allistair took ten steps to one side. Iggy looked at him, concerned. "I am moving over here," Allistair explained, "because I do not want to confuse the Tipei. I want there to be no doubt that you are the controlling master at this time."

Iggy gave Allistair a moment to move away, then spoke to the Tipei in Spanish, *"Me entiendes?"*

The Tipei nodded.

Allistair asked, "And what language is that?"

"Spanish." Iggy smiled. "You don't understand Spanish?"

"No, no, I do not."

Iggy smiled. Iggy nodded and raised his hands and pointed to the wooden pole and said, in Spanish, "Fly to that pole and land on it."

Instantly, the Tipei spread its wings and shot toward Iggy. The moment it was off the ground it quickly banked and with two flaps of its wings was on the other side of the arena and perched on the pole.

Allistair, on the side, seemed agitated by not being able to understand what Iggy said. He appeared to be struggling to stay composed. "Very good. Now let us try something else. Order it to fly in a circle and land on that other pole over there."

Iggy called out, in Spanish, "Fly around the arena and then land on top of that pole."

To Iggy's delight, the Tipei did exactly as he had commanded.

Allistair walked back to Iggy and said, "Well, you are very talented. That usually takes three lessons with my new pupils. Let us take it up a notch. Command it to attack that dummy soldier on the far side of the arena. Tell him to first rip it with its talons, then swoop up and blast it with his fire breath."

Iggy was delighted. "Sure."

Iggy raised his hands like a conductor readying to start a symphony. "I command you to fly around the arena." Iggy circled his arms, and the Tipei followed Iggy's hand direction as if it was on the end of a string. "Now with your talons, rip!" Iggy pointed at the dummy soldier.

The Tipei folded its wings and dove at the dummy. Moments before crashing into the dummy's head, its wings deployed, and the Tipei hovered. Its outstretched talons ripped and tore at the dummy's head, obliterating it in seconds.

Iggy threw his hands into the air. "Now fly up."

The Tipei responded instantly and flew to the height that matched where Iggy was pointing.

"Now dive down and with your fire breath burn." Iggy pointed at the dummy.

The Tipei responded without hesitation. In moments, it was over. The dummy was ablaze. Iggy pointed to the arena's highest resting pole. The Tipei flew there, landed, and folded its wings.

"That was tremendous!" Iggy said to Allistair in Tinte.

"Come, we are done," was Allistair's only comment as he walked Iggy to the door between the arena and the viewing area where Nyreada was waiting.

"Nyreada, did you see that? I'm a natural." Iggy turned to Allistair. "I would like to come back, if that's all right."

Allistair did not reply to Iggy. He turned to Nyreada. "You have a very talented young man here. That is an interesting language you speak. I have never heard it before."

"We speak many languages where I am from." Iggy left it at that.

Alistair said to Nyreada, "We are done here as I, unfortunately, have some very important business to attend to. The two of you should see the festivities and the play this evening. And remember the Ministers' Council wants to see you both just before noon tomorrow."

Before Iggy turned to go, he became very serious and baited his trap with Allistair. "The other day you explained to me that the Tipei's fire comes from them drinking Liquid Fire."

"Why do you ask?"

"Just curious."

Allistair thought for a moment. He knew that the Tipei were bound by their code to kill anyone asking about Liquid Fire. Maybe this was another chance to solve his problem. He motioned the Tipei over. It instantly flew to the wooden perch just feet from where they were standing. "Ask the Tipei. Only they have your answer."

Iggy stepped closer to the bird. He spoke in Spanish again. "Could you please tell me about Liquid Fire and where it is?"

Instantly, the Tipei's beak opened. Iggy felt the warm breath and froze, thinking he was about to be incinerated. Instead, the Tipei stared into his eyes, closed his beak, and continued to stare at Iggy, evaluating him. Then, after the longest minute, it shook its head, flapped its wings, and flew off.

Allistair turned and walked out of the arena. Iggy and Nyreada missed the rage on his face as they left.

Iggy shook his head in dismay. "That didn't go as planned."

That evening, Iggy and Nyreada walked through the center of town. The pre-play festival was in full regalia. There were jugglers, fire-spinners, and jesters doing tricks for the young children and, to Iggy's delight, plenty of different cuisines to taste and enjoy. As the sun was setting, the two settled into their bench seats in front of the stage erected at the far end of the plaza. Mirrors in front of torches reflected the light onto the stage.

With a round of applause, a woman walked onto the stage. Iggy immediately recognized Trafagla.

"Welcome all, my name is Trafagla, and I am here to entertain you this evening. I will spin tales, tell you lies, tell you the truth. But, in the end, you will not care, for you will be entertained."

After many wonderful stories that Iggy and Nyreada enjoyed,

Trafagla said, "Let me finish the evening with a tale of a young boy from a far, far-off world who is transported to the world above the cloud dome."

Iggy sat up straight, hoping his uncomfortableness didn't show and bring suspicion to himself. She was telling his story. He looked around anxiously to see if anyone was looking at him. Then he thought: How would anyone know? He relaxed.

Trafagla continued, "That young man was a wizard; he could speak all languages. He was special. One of the greatest warrior races of the other land had bestowed upon him the rank of an elite warrior. The only problem was he did not know it. He could not believe it... because in his mind he was unworthy."

Iggy was amused. It was clear the story was about him. He hadn't told Nyreada or anyone in this land about the Nostaw swords or being anointed a Nostaw warrior. Iggy turned to Nyreada. "This is interesting."

"It is an old story many have told. Do you want to leave?"

"No, I'm kind of curious how it ends," Iggy replied, and he turned his attention back to Trafagla.

Trafagla paused and took a deep breath in. As she let it out, she finished her story. "And now our hero is at a crossroads. Will he take the route of goodness, or take the route of evil? Only time will tell. The end."

Everyone clapped and hooted. Iggy buried his head in his hands and muttered to himself, "She did it again. 'The end'?" Then he turned to Nyreada. "That's not how a story ends. All it did was leave you hanging. Not knowing what will happen."

Nyreada laughed. "She is the storyteller, and that is how she wants it to end."

Trafagla waded into the crowd and received her accolades as she greeted the patrons. Eventually she got to Iggy. "Well, Iggy, did you enjoy my tale?"

"Yes, up until the end of it. Do you always leave a story unfinished?"

"All stories are unfinished. Only the future finishes them. On that note, did you get the information you wanted from the Tipei?"

"No. It wouldn't tell me anything. You should know that if you see as much as you claim you do."

"Did you bond with it? With your heart and soul?" She smiled at him.

"And how would I do that?"

"Did you sing it a song?"

"A song? What song would you suggest?" There was sarcasm in his voice.

"Oh, Iggy. Maybe you are *not* ready." Trafagla turned and walked away.

"Let us head back to the inn. I am getting tired," Nyreada said as she got up.

They walked back to the Inn at Riverside in quiet.

Upon entering the Inn, Iggy said to Nyreada, "I'll see you in the morning." He climbed the stairs to his room, pondering what his next move would be.

The Ministers' council convened an emergency meeting, called by Allistair, around the time Iggy and Nyreada were climbing into bed. The council's agenda couldn't have been more different. Allistair stood before them, again declining to stand on the platform.

"There is no doubt," Alistair started, "that this young boy is a natural Tipei savant. I instructed the training Tipei to kill him if he attempted to command it. Instead, it followed his every command when he directed it in his own language. One I have never heard before, I must add. There was no hesitation, no confusion from the Tipei. This boy was in complete control. He must be stopped. He is a direct danger to us—to me—uh, to us! I, and only I, have the right to pick the next Tipei Master. I will not be usurped by... by this little boy who knows nothing about anything. I demand we deal with him strongly so that our way of life is not disrupted!"

"Then our path is clear," Minister Riveriron said.

"Yes. We must banish him to the deepest dungeon in the realm," Minister Tritdaw said.

"And we must pour a caustic agent down his throat to destroy his speaking box, so he can never even attempt to call out for Tipei help," Minister Hyluita said.

"Are we in agreement?" Minister Riveriron asked.

"Yes," the entire council said in unison.

"Are there any objections?" Minister Riveriron asked.

"I object." A female voice came from the side of the room.

Surprised by the uninvited voice, the ministers snapped their heads around to see Trafagla in the shadows of the room, leaning against the wall. She had her arms folded and was shaking her head in disgust.

"Young lady—" Minister Riveriron started.

"Don't 'young lady' me. You all know who I am, so stop with the indignation."

"All right, Trafagla, let us get right to the point. The last time you were before this council, you had to be dragged out by our guards. How did you get in here?" Minister Riveriron demanded.

"I walked in behind you before the door closed. You were all so intent on hearing what Allistair had to say you couldn't see what was happening right in front of you."

"Minister Riveriron, must we tolerate these insults?" Minister Sonham demanded.

Minister Riveriron held up his hand, stopping Minister Sonham. "I think if we are as wise as we present ourselves, we should listen to what she has to say. Then we can have her removed again, but this time to a dark cell, lest she expose the plan we have all agreed upon. You have snuck into the chamber because you feel you have something of importance to tell us. I give you the floor. Tell us, please."

Trafagla smiled and shook her head. She walked out of the shadows and then climbed the platform of truth. "I am not worried about a dark cell. All of you know my gift. I see the future."

"So you say," Minister Hyluita spat out.

She continued, "I can also see the effect different decisions have on the future. I see different timelines and their outcomes. The consequences of actions made in present day on the future." She took a breath and looked at each one of them before she continued. "You are all afraid of Iggy. So, I will tell you of our different futures, depending on what you do. The different choices you have and what you will reap if you make the wrong choice."

"Stop trying to scare us. Just tell us what you have come here to tell us so we can move on with our meeting," Minister Hyluita said disdainfully.

"Fine," Trafagla said. "There will come a day soon when we will not be able to protect our anonymity. We will not be able to find and harvest any of the crystals that create our cloud dome. That day is closer than you think. When the dome comes down, what then? Do we attack with our Tipei and wipe out the people in the other world who may threaten us?"

"I have no problem with that," Minister Tritdaw said.

"Then we would be... you all would be no different than that monster, Mallak, who is ruling the land to our west. Understand, he is getting more powerful, and there will be a day when his powers will have grown so great that with a wave of his hand he will smite our Tipei," Trafagla said.

"How does Iggy fit into this?" Minister Riveriron asked.

"Here are the different timelines I see: The first is you follow through with your plan and imprison him and burn out his voice box. I see in that timeline the destruction of our world. In the second timeline, we send him back to the surface world, and again I see the destruction of our world. The third is we send him back to the surface world, and our world thrives in conjunction with the surface world in peace and happiness. The difference between the second and third scenario is that he either tells our secret or doesn't." She stopped and looked around the room.

Minister Hyluita snorted. "If we let him return to his world with the knowledge of this world, he will tell. Then, we will perish. Not only will he bring the knowledge of our world to them, he will be able to control the Tipei, and yes, we will be destroyed. May I remind you: Tipei's are not from this land. They were brought here many generations ago by Scathach's ancestors from faraway Alkebulan."

"And it was a good thing they were. If it were not for Scathach's tribal ancestor, Nzinga, the fiercest Dahomey Warrior, and her Tipeis, the corrupt Minister Jetrix would have destroyed this land."

"We are still lucky that Scathach follows the blood oath to watch over this land. She has honor," Minister Hyluita pronounced.

"And, in return, the crystals that produce the Plains of Clouds also hides the entrance to where she lives with the Valley of the Fog," Minister Riveriron said.

Minister Sonham jumped into the conversation. "Ministers, we are getting off track. It is not Scathach who worries me. It is that boy."

"You are assuming this boy is evil," Trafagla said.

"We appear to have limited choices for a path forward if we are to protect our land," Minister Riveriron said.

"No," Trafagla said. "The only timeline that has us surviving is one that returns him to the other world."

"But we cannot let him return with the knowledge of our existence," Minister Sonham said.

"I agree," Minister Riveriron said. He turned to Trafagla. "So, you are the one who thinks you are so wise. What do you recommend?"

"The Potion of Memory Elimination," she said.

Minister Sonham exploded in shock. "This is outrageous! That is dark magic! It is forbidden! How do you know of this?"

"I've told you before. I know things. I see things. That was one of the things I saw." She had a firm look on her face. "So, I suggest the Potion of Memory Elimination."

Minister Riveriron held up his hand, stopping the conversation. "We will discuss that and what other forbidden knowledge you have later. For now, let us focus on the task at hand. The suggestion of the Potion of Memory Elimination?"

"That is impossible. That sort of magic—dark magic—has been banned for longer than I've been alive!" Minister Hyluita said. "I cannot believe you would even entertain it!"

"You do know why it was banned?" Minister Sonham demanded.

"Just in case you have forgotten, Minister Jetrix used dark magic two hundred years ago in an attempt take over this land. To essentially rule Matreach and be an emperor. He wiped his victims' memories and instilled his own perverted wishes. Those victims did whatever he slipped into their minds to do. They killed and tortured whoever he commanded them to do that to. Our people barely survived. All dark magic has been banned, including that potion. Since that time no one has been taught, learned, or used this dark magic," Minister Tritdaw said.

There was a long silence in the room. Finally, Minister River- iron spoke up. "I will need Bunyip Strand, Selkie Bone Meal, and Cinder Azollo."

"What is this?" demanded Minister Hyluita.

"Yes, explain yourself, Minister Riveriron!" Minister Sonham shouted out.

"Those are the ingredients I will need to make the Potion of Memory Elimination," Minister Riveriron replied.

"My anger knows no bounds, Minister Riveriron!" Minister Trit- daw exclaimed. "You— You have defiled this chamber! You have broken one of our cardinal laws! How dare you secretly study and learn this deadly potion! How many more have you learned behind our backs? And what is your motive? Are you a threat to this council, to our way of life?"

Minister Riveriron scrunched his eyes shut for a moment, deep in thought. Upon opening them, he looked around the room at the angry glares from his colleagues, his friends. He smiled and nodded to no one in general then he spoke in a quiet tone. "I guessed that in someone's time as the Minister of the council this knowledge would come out. So, I think it is time to tell all of you. As the Head Minister of the council, it has always been my responsibility to make sure this land is safe and secure."

"No! That is the job of this council!" seethed Minister Tritdaw. He glared at Minister Riveriron contemptuously.

Taking a deep breath, Minister Riveriron continued, "The Head Minister of the council has always known about the potion. The book of knowledge has been secretly passed from one Head Minister to the other. This has been to ensure that we are safe—since Minister Jetrix during his time as Head Minister misused this knowledge, each person chosen to be Head Minister of the Council since then has been carefully selected by the preceding Head Minister, ensuring his successor possesses characteristics that Minister Jetrix did *not* possess. The rule, the secret rule, has been that only the Head Minister of the Council can know about this. I feel we are at an impasse regarding which decision—which path to proceed down. Thus, I have chosen to break the Minister of Council's secret oath and inform you of our magical potion knowledge. This is the path we must take. I will need to make this potion."

Trafagla spoke up. "I have already acquired the necessary items."

The entire group of Ministers and Allistair gave Trafagla a look of distrust.

"I do have a special gift." She took three vials out of her pocket and handed them to Minister Riveriron.

Taking the ingredients from Trafagla and ignoring the heated stares from the rest of the council, Minister Riveriron said, "You shall have your potion. How will you administer it?"

"We shall have a dinner as a farewell, and I will put the potion in his drink. After it has taken full effect, we will return Iggy to Fryscar so he can pass through the portal back to his land," Trafagla said.

"Good. That will be our plan," Minister Riveriron said. "This won't guarantee our timeline for survival though."

"No. It will only guarantee that the first timeline will not happen—the one where he stays, and this land is destroyed. Remember, there are two other possible timelines if he returns to his home: one good and one bad. We are only increasing our odds of survival with this potion." She stepped off the platform. "I will be back later today to pick up the potion." She strolled out of the chamber.

"Riveriron, this is not the last you have heard about this matter. Your privilege of secrecy will come to an end," Minister Sonham said.

"Yes, yes," Minister Riveriron said dismissively.

"Riveriron, you would be wise never to deceive or cross this council ever again," Minister Sonham said.

"That's 'Minister Riveriron' to you. And it would be wise for you to never threaten me again."

24

Darkness inundated Iggy as he turned around. Suddenly, flickering light from lit torches attached to the cave's walls was cast upon him. His shadow danced across the dirt floor. "You are not Tilead. You must die."

Voices resonated from all around him.

A shimmering vision wavered in and out of focus before him. He had two Nostaw swords encircling his neck. "I am Tilead, a Nostaw Warrior. Through this Blinak Ritual I pass my rights on to you. You are now Tilead. Become what I was and not what I am now." Then the vision faded.

All around him Nostaw swords came out of the darkness. This time the Nostaws holding them stepped forward into Iggy's view and stopped. One of them took an additional step forward.

"You have no right to have those swords. You are not Tilead. You will die."

Iggy reached behind his back, producing the swords and yelled, "I am Tilead, a Nostaw Warrior. Through the Blinak Ritual, Tilead's rights were passed on to me. I am Tilead. I have become what he is not and what I am now. If you want these swords, you must take them from me. I will not give them to you!"

"Prove you are Tilead!"

The shimmering vision of Tilead returned. "That is my song which is now our song. Keep it safely in your heart. You will know when to use it. It will keep you safe."

Instinctively, Iggy opened his mouth and out flowed a melodic song he'd never practiced and didn't know he knew. Halfway through it, the Nostaw Warriors surrounding him lowered their swords.

"This cannot be. You are not Nostaw. But we must honor this. You are Tilead. Go forth and be strong, Tilead." They faded into the dark.

Iggy sat upright in bed. It was the middle of the night. "How could I have been so stupid?" he asked aloud. "The song. My song. The Nostaw sang it to me. He said it was his song, which is now our song. Keep it safely in my heart. You will know when to use it. It will keep you safe. That is it. To bond my heart and soul with the Tipei, I have to share my song with them. Thus, bonding my heart with the Tipei, because the song is in my heart." Iggy climbed out of bed. "I have to go back to the training arena."

Iggy crept out of the inn and slipped through the night to the Tipei Training Arena. Cautiously, he made his way into the center of the arena and called out, "Come."

The lone resident Tipei left its nest and flew down to Iggy and flapping its wings up and down held itself steady in front of him.

Iggy took a moment to calm his nerves; his hands were trembling. Finally, he spoke to the bird in English. "I want you to tell me about Liquid Fire, where it is and how I can get to it."

The Tipei's eyes widened. It stared at Iggy. Iggy guessed its instinct was to open its mouth and unleash a devastating flame of fire. But it hesitated. In that moment of hesitation, Iggy opened his mouth and having never repeated or practiced his Nostaw song, he hummed. It started low and slow but came to Iggy naturally as if he had hummed it all his life. It was soothing to him and the Tipei, as the creature hovered at eye level to Iggy, its wings flapping.

When the song was finished, Iggy calmly asked, "Will you help me?"

At first what came from the Tipei sounded like chirps and squeaks. But the sound quickly morphed into words that Iggy understood.

"You are a person of honor and trust," the Tipei started. "You have opened and shared your heart and soul with us through your sacred song. I can see your strength, and it is good. Why do you want to know about our holy Liquid Fire?"

Iggy replied, unsure if he was speaking English or Tipei language—it all came naturally, "I am from a different world. I am told that the only way to return to my world is to finish my journey that has different quests along the way. My first quest was given to me by a Nostaw warrior." Iggy reached behind his back and produced his swords. "I must become a Nostaw warrior and to do that I must dip these swords into Liquid Fire. Only then will they obtain their true power and, in turn, elevate me to warrior status. With this quest completed, I will somehow find out what my next quest is on my journey to get home." Iggy looked into the eyes of the Tipei. "I only want to find my way home."

᠁

Allistair stood in the shadows, seething with anger as he stared at Iggy's Nostaw swords.

"So, young Iggy," he whispered, "you are a Nostaw Warrior. You are more dangerous than any of us realized."

He turned and left the training grounds.

᠁

The Tipei , still hovering in front of Iggy, said, "For us it is an easy flight. For you, though, you must find the only path to the pool of Liquid Fire. If you choose the wrong path, you will be lost forever."

"How do I find the correct path?"

"There is a mural carved in the living trunk in the center of the hollow Tree of Castles. You will find the home of the Tipei in that mural."

"How? It's a huge mural."

"There is a podium in the center of the floor of the tree. The morning sunlight shines through the doorway once a day. There are many crystals in that hall; one of those crystals will show you the way. You must place that special crystal on the podium. When the sunlight strikes the crystal, it will point a beam to your path. But be warned. If you use the wrong crystal, it will show you a wrong path, and you will be lost if you take it."

"Where do I get the correct crystal? There were hundreds of crystals stuck into the mural. How do I know which is the correct one?"

"That, young one, only you can answer. You must follow your heart. When the time is right, you will find the correct crystal in that hall." The Tipei lifted off and flew back to his nest.

"Wait!" Iggy stood there, then realized the Tipei would tell him no more, so he left with a new set of questions.

∾

A soft but firm knock rapped Trafagla's door. Sleep had been short for her for she had but recently gotten into bed. Upon opening the door to her room at the inn, she was surprised to see who was standing before her, cloaked in a dark robe and hood covering his head.

"Minister Riveriron," Trafagla said. "Come in."

After she closed the door behind him, Minister Riveriron said, "There is not much time. Allistair called a secret meeting concerning Iggy. At dawn's first light, Allistair will arrive with a security team to take Iggy into custody. He intends to have him killed."

"We cannot allow that to happen." There was no sense of urgency in her voice.

"You and Nyreada must leave with him now for Fryscar. Get him there before he is captured and get him through the portal." Minister Riveriron reached into his pocket and pulled out a small vial. "This is the potion to wipe Iggy's memory. You must give it to him before he passes back into his world." He placed his other hand on her shoulder and looked at her sternly. "He must never remember our land, and he must never return here. Do you understand?"

"I understand completely."

After a moment of silence, Minister Riveriron sighed. "You have to be careful. Barging in on the council meeting like that is not a way to endear yourself to them. After you left, they wanted me to have the guards arrest you. They are not very tolerant of affronts to their—"

"Their self-given intelligence?" Trafagla crossed her arms in disgust.

"Yes." Minister Riveriron touched her on her shoulder. "I do not understand why your people refuse to join our society and live with us."

"You mean live under your rules."

"What is so wrong with that?"

"We prefer to make our own rules. Our people, as you call us, tried that once, as you well know. And that did not go very well. Anyway, if they arrest me, you will not have a spy who travels to Skye and fills you in on what is going on there."

Minister Riveriron shook his head. "I must leave. Please get Iggy and Nyreada and leave immediately."

After shutting the door on him, Trafagla smiled as she stood alone. "Oh, I forgot to tell you, Father... Mother said hello."

When the sun's rays peeked over the horizon and Allistair and his team descended on the inn to arrest Iggy, Iggy, Nyreada, and Trafagla were many leagues away on their Rockhoppers. Iggy at first was defiant and he would not leave. But, with the reality of his painful death laid before him, he forwent his quest to find the Liquid Fire and save his life, instead. When his anger subsided, the decision came easy to him.

By evening, they entered Fryscar and dismounted. Iggy, Nyreada, and Trafagla stretched to get the kinks out of their backs.

"I am not sure we have much time. They may have sent a messenger bird ahead of us," Trafagla said. "Iggy and I will hide in the garden. You live here, Nyreada, so you know this place better than I. Take a quick look around. See if anything looks out of place. We have made it this far. I do not want to walk into a trap."

Nyreada nodded. "All right." Then she left.

"I need to ask you something," Iggy said, addressing Trafagla. "The other day in the square when you were on stage, it sounded like you were talking about me."

"Oh, I was."

"But how did you know all that? And why did you tell that particular story?"

"Iggy, there is so much you do not know about me. And it is better that way." She smiled at him. "I am thirsty. You stay here; I'll get us a drink from the fountain."

She walked to the fountain and picked up two of the empty cups from a shelf. Then, with her back to Iggy, she dropped in the potion of Memory Elimination. Without missing a beat, she returned and handed Iggy his drink.

She watched as Iggy drained his cup. There was a moment where he looked confused or as though he might speak, his eyes squinting, as though trying to remember something. Then a contented haze came over his eyes. Within moments, he was asleep.

Trafagla leaned toward Iggy. "Iggy, can you hear me?" There was no response as Iggy breathed gently. Trafagla looked around, and, confident that she was alone, she whispered in his ear.

⌇

Nyreada made her way back to the garden. When she rounded the stone arch corner, she stopped. She saw Iggy's head slumped over and Trafagla kneeling in front of him, talking to him.

"What's going on?" Nyreada called out. "Is he all right?"

Trafagla looked up, then quickly leaned close to Iggy's ear and said something. As Nyreada rushed over, Trafagla stood up. "Yes, everything's all right."

"Then why is he asleep?" She bent down to Iggy and shook him by the shoulders. "Iggy! Wake up!" Standing up, she confronted Trafagla. "What did you do to him?"

"I saved his life."

"I don't understand. Explain! Now!"

"I gave him a potion to make him sleep. It also allows me to erase whatever memory I tell him to forget."

"But why? Why would you do this?" Nyreada shouted enraged.

"It was the only way Minister Riveriron would help us and allow him to return to his own world. If Iggy remembered our world, Riveriron believed it was only a matter of time that others found out from him that we are here. The Ministers could not allow that. It was this or…"

"Or what?"

"Or what? Why do you think we have been racing to get here? Let it sink in: Allistair was going to kill him. I told you that. Did you think I was joking?"

"I thought we were just going to get him safely home."

"Oh, Nyreada, stop being so naive."

"Will he remember me?"

"No. He will remember nothing of this place. And that is important for you to remember. You will be brought before the council. And when you stand in the circle of truth you will be bound by Matreach laws to tell the truth. They must know that his memory of our land is gone."

"They will ask you also."

"I am a nomad, a wanderer. I roam the lands. I am bound by no laws." She smiled. "Now we need to get him back through the portal."

It was the dead of night as they half dragged and half carried Iggy, who was still sound asleep through the portal and onto the shore. They laid him on a bed of soft grass. Nyreada made sure his head was resting on something soft. With tears in her eyes, she leaned down and kissed him on the lips.

"Come, we must go now," Trafagla said.

As they entered the path to the waterfall, Nyreada turned and gave Iggy one last look, then she followed Trafagla back to the portal.

25

I t was late morning when Iggy woke up on a bed of leaves at the edge
of the lake. The day was warm, and the sun's rays shone through
the trees, casting gentle light around him. He rubbed the sleep out
of his eyes, stretched, and looked around. He had some thinking to do.

He remembered everything, especially Trafagla's last words she
whispered to him as he was falling asleep. "Iggy," she said. "You will
remember everything of Matreach. But you must be careful not to tell
anyone about it. Your life may depend upon it."

The days since Iggy disappeared had dragged on at a slow, agonizing
pace for Raraesa. There was no spring in her step. She had given up
all hope that Iggy would be found alive. Making her way through her
morning chores, she didn't notice when Lecque came in. He sat and ate
his breakfast of porridge, warmed bread, and tea in silence.

A rap on the door caused Raraesa to freeze. She spun around. Her
heart pounded. "Iggy," she muttered as she ran and pulled it open.
In an instant, her jubilance subsided, for before her stood Ansel the
blacksmith. Deflated, her emotions got the better of her as she broke
down in tears, turned, and ran to stand in front of the hearth, her face
buried in the palms of her hands.

Confused, Ansel followed her and saw Lecque at the table. He made eye contact with him. "What is this about?" Ansel asked.

"Come, sit, and I will explain." He poured Ansel some tea. "Iggy was very upset over the incident in town last week."

"Actually, that is why I am here. I saw what happened to Iggy and Raraesa and have been kicking myself for not stepping in sooner to stop it." Ansel took a mouthful of tea. "I came to see Iggy. After seeing his interaction with Frankie, I thought he needed some encouragement. I want to offer him a job. Nothing toughens one up more than working in a blacksmith shop and swinging a hammer hour on end. But unfortunately, it seems as though my journey was in vain."

"Yes," Lecque continued. "Soon after Raraesa and Iggy returned home, he ran away."

"Why didn't you let me know? We could have been searching for him. It is a shame. It has been almost a week; now he could be anywhere. But the first day he left, we could have found him." Ansel looked at Lecque then at Raraesa.

"That is just it." Raraesa teared up again. "We know where he is."

"I do not understand. Then why have you not retrieved him?" Ansel asked.

With a deep breath, Lecque launched into the story of what he'd seen at the lake. Ansel sat stoic for a few moments, processing the information. "Raraesa," Ansel said. "I am truly sorry. I wish it had been Iggy instead of me who had knocked on your door." He shook his head with regret. "You know, Raraesa, there was nothing Lecque could have done. No one has ever escaped the spell of a Liminade."

Raraesa shook her head. "It is ironic; the first time he does something brave, it kills him." She gave a mirthless chuckle tinged with sadness.

Without warning, the front door swung open, and Iggy crossed the threshold into the cottage. He was disheveled, head to toe covered in dried mud; he looked dazed.

"Iggy!" Raraesa yelled, jumping up from her chair. She ran to him, throwing her arms around him. "Are you well?" She stepped back and looked him up and down. "What happened to you? We were so worried."

"I'm not sure. I woke up in some bushes near the side of a lake, covered in mud."

Lecque stepped closer. "Do you remember helping a girl who was a prisoner of some soldiers and then running behind the waterfall with her?"

"Not really."

"What do you remember?" Raraesa asked.

"I don't remember anything much," he said, confused. "Have I been gone long?"

"Five days," Lecque interjected.

"Wow… five days." Iggy shook his head slowly.

"Are you hungry? I can get you something to eat," Raraesa said.

"Actually, I'm tired. If it's all right with you, I'd like to clean up and take a nap."

"I think that is a good idea," Raraesa said. "I will bring you a bucket of water and some cloth to wash with. Give me your dirty clothes. I will clean them while you sleep. You can use Lecque's bed." She gave Lecque a glare, warning him not to cross her as she led Iggy away.

"The Liminades have never let anyone get away. They protect their water kingdom fiercely, killing all who venture too close. That is why no one goes in that lake," Ansel said to Lecque.

"Yes," Lecque replied. "But I know what I saw."

Ansel looked at Lecque, considering. "There is more to that boy than we may understand."

"But look at him. Does he look like someone who can fight off a Liminade?"

"That is why my offer to toughen him up still stands."

Lecque pondered for a moment whether to tell Ansel about Iggy and the Nostaw but quickly decided against it. The fewer people who knew about that the better. "I will have him there the day after tomorrow. I think tomorrow I will let him rest and try to find out more as to what happened to him," Lecque said. "And let us keep this Liminade thing to ourselves."

"Agreed," Ansel said as he walked out the door.

⌁

The next day was warm with a slight breeze. Fair-weather clouds intermittently broke up the rays of the sun with shadows, keeping the countryside comfortable to move and work in.

Iggy had slept most of the previous day.

Lecque and Raraesa sat at the table alone. Iggy was still sleeping. They had let him sleep as long as he wanted. "So, Raraesa, what do you think? Do you feel safe around him? There is something strange going on here."

"I feel safe. That is not a problem. I do not think he poses a threat, truly. But what do we tell him about the Liminade, if he has no memory of them?"

"Honestly, I say we tell him nothing."

When Iggy finally awoke, he was groggy. He had fibbed to Lecque and Raraesa and told them he had no memory of what had transpired. It was a standoff, Raraesa not wanting to tell Iggy about the Liminade, and Iggy not wanting to tell Raraesa about Matreach.

"Your return home last night was like your initial arrival," Raraesa said. "Full of mystery. But we do have some good news. Ansel was here yesterday when you came home, and he told us he needed some help in his blacksmith shop."

"Both Raraesa and I thought it would be good for you," Lecque said. "You need something to do here since we do not know how to get you home yet. You should settle in and work and look like a member of the household. And, as of tonight, you are back to sleeping in the barn. I want my own bed back."

Iggy nodded.

"Then it is decided," Lecque said.

"When would I start?"

"How about tomorrow? You should rest today," Raraesa replied.

As the day rolled into early afternoon, Iggy wandered outside. He had a lot to think about. He needed to get back to Matreach. His quest was there. But he realized he was not emotionally or physically ready to return yet. He walked around the back of the farm, looking at the chicken coop and the two cows grazing in the field. His mood was somber, as if he were carrying the weight of the world on his shoulders.

With no thought, he reached behind his back and withdrew the Nostaw swords. Holding them in his hands felt natural, as if they belonged there. He looked at the blades, then at the engraved hilts. They had fine markings that weren't letters, nor were they pictures. He recognized them as runes; though, he had no clue what they stood for. He shrugged and held the swords in front of him, then swung them around with great clumsiness, pretending he was attacking someone and defending himself. As he did, he got too close to a tree, and one blade struck the tree trunk. The blade came to a jarring stop, and a shock wave of pain ran up his arm.

In disgust, he replaced the swords behind his back, where they melded into obscurity, and walked up to the tree. He touched it and reaffirmed that it was a hard tree trunk. "Yup, hard as stone."

Iggy caught a glimpse of Raraesa watching through the cottage window. She came out to him. "Well, Iggy, you need a lot of help and training."

They went into the cottage. "Do you know how to sword fight?" he asked her.

"Yes. I have had some training."

"I want you to teach me."

"When?"

"Now."

Raraesa led him to the clearing behind the barn. She had two wooden swords, one of which she gave to Iggy.

"These are practice swords. They are balanced like real swords. And the tips are cushioned so we can hit each other without getting hurt."

"Where did you get them?"

"Lecque bartered for them a few years ago. He got them for me. He said I needed to learn to defend myself in case he wasn't around to protect me. Here, take one."

Iggy took the sword in both hands, bent his knees, and leaned forward. Raraesa looked him up and down and did not correct him. Without warning, she swung her sword over her head, then brought it down toward Iggy. Iggy blocked it with his sword, but in that split second, Raraesa withdrew her sword off Iggy's and thrust the cushioned tip into Iggy's chest.

"And now you are dead." She stepped back and smiled.

"That wasn't fair. I wasn't ready!"

Raraesa laughed. "Combat is not fair. When your opponent is trying to kill you, do you think he will ask if you are ready?"

An hour later, Iggy was proficient at ducking, sidestepping, and stepping back to avoid getting hit.

"I think that is enough for the first day," Raraesa said as she lowered her sword.

That evening Iggy was filled with excitement. "I can't believe how much fun that was. You have no idea how much I've always wanted to learn swordsmanship like that."

"I must say, you are a fast learner." She smiled at him. "You really did well. You should be proud of yourself. I am."

Before he slept, he produced his Nostaw swords. He practiced swinging them in different patterns. Then he fell asleep.

Raraesa woke Iggy early and had a breakfast of porridge waiting for him. "Are you ready for today?"

"I am. What exactly will I be doing?" he asked as he sat and ate.

"I do not know."

A half hour later, they both were riding into town. By now Iggy was a proficient rider. Nonetheless, Raraesa accompanied him to town on her own horse. It made her feel better. Plus, she needed to take care of something.

After tying up the horses outside Ansel's blacksmith shop, Raraesa and Iggy walked through the door. "Hello, Ansel! It's Raraesa and Iggy," she called out.

Ansel entered from a back room. "Ah, Raraesa, and my new young apprentice, Iggy—right on time. Wonderful." Ansel spoke with a deep resonating voice. "I hope you got your rest. For today you start on your next adventure."

"You going to keep him all day?" Raraesa asked.

"Oh, I think for the first day; the morning will be long enough. Let us see if he survives that long for now." Ansel chuckled.

"Do you want me to sweep and clean up around here for you?" Iggy asked after she had left.

"Sweep and clean up? No, Iggy. You are here to start on your road to becoming a blacksmith, building the muscle and skill of a blacksmith. Put on one of those aprons and grab a hammer over there." Ansel pointed across the room.

Iggy took the smallest apron he could find—even then it hung down to his ankles—while Ansel disappeared into one of the back rooms, returning moments later with a round rock the size of a softball. Iggy grabbed one of the biggest hammers.

"Aggh, too heavy." He could barely lift it with both hands. He worked his way down the hammer sizes and weights until he could lift one, just barely, with two hands. "This one will do." But he still struggled with the weight of it, even though it was the smallest one he could find and carried it over to Ansel with two hands.

Ansel stared at the metal in his hand for a moment then at Iggy, his mind seemingly elsewhere. "Here, Iggy." He handed the metal ball to him. "First, you place it in this clamp, then rest it in the hearth in the corner. When it glows red, I want you to grab it with the tongs, bring it over to the anvil, and hit it five times with that hammer you have in your right hand, then switch the hammer to your left hand and hit it five times again. Keep switching hands, five blows at a time. When the rock starts to cool, you place it in that water bath and then into the fire again. That's your job for the day."

Raraesa came to a bend in the road on the outside of town and sat on a fallen tree off to the side. She sat quietly and waited. Half the morning passed, but Raraesa remained on the log. Finally, her patience was rewarded as she heard the scraping sound of boots walking down the road toward her. She stood, stretched, and stepped out into the middle of the dirt path.

"Hello, Frankie," she said.

Frankie stopped. "What do you want, another egg in the face?"

"No, I just wanted to see how brave you are when you don't have two of your whit-packer friends holding my hands behind my back."

Raraesa balled her hands into fists and let them fly.

26

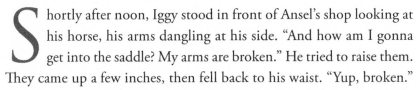

Shortly after noon, Iggy stood in front of Ansel's shop looking at his horse, his arms dangling at his side. "And how am I gonna get into the saddle? My arms are broken." He tried to raise them. They came up a few inches, then fell back to his waist. "Yup, broken."

From over Iggy's shoulder, he heard a deep, roaring laugh. He turned his head to see Ansel with his hands on his knees, bent over laughing. "Why, Iggy, you look like a puppet whose arm strings have broken. Let me help. I will toss you up."

Ansel hoisted Iggy with ease onto the saddle. Iggy sat there, head drooping, lifeless arms dangling at his sides. Ansel laughed again. "Stay home tomorrow. You will need a day to recover."

Barely holding the reins, Iggy walked the horse across the field and onto the path that led him to the cottage. Upon arriving there, he slid out of the saddle. Looking around, he saw Raraesa coming out of the side meadow.

"Hello," she called and waved. "I was just feeding the cows some extra hay. How was your first day?"

Iggy stood there and chuckled. "It was harder than I thought it would be."

"Oh my goodness! What happened to you? You look like you've been stomped on by a dozen horses."

Iggy's reply was slow and drawn out. "I feel like it. I-I think I need to rest." He handed the reins of his horse to Raraesa and walked into the barn without saying another word. Raraesa just laughed.

Midafternoon the following day, Iggy trudged out of his room in the barn after a long, hard sleep. "I feel like a truck ran me over."

"Iggy," Raraesa replied, "what's a truck?"

Iggy dropped his sagging frame into a chair at the table. "It's like a covered wagon that carries things. It's like the cars I told you about but bigger."

"Oh, it's one of those wagons that you sit in and press a stick on the floor to make it go. And it has a wheel that, when you turn it, makes the wagon go in that direction," Raraesa said, proud of herself.

"Yup."

"So, why would someone want to run you over with it? That could kill you."

"That's the point. It's a saying."

"Oh! Hmmm. Now I understand." Raraesa scooped some mac and cheese onto a plate for Iggy.

"You made mac and cheese." Iggy's eyes lit up. "Thank you!"

"Yes, I wanted to surprise you. I figured you needed a boost of energy and happiness after… getting run over by a truck yesterday." She smiled, and Iggy laughed as he dug into his food.

As the day went on, Iggy rested on the back porch and let his mind wander from his life in Pennsylvania to this different land he was in. He was still struggling to come to terms with how and why he ended up here. And how he would get home. Multiple times he had caught himself staring at Raraesa the same way he realized he would stare at Sandy while in school.

∽

The next day came around a little too fast for Iggy's liking. His muscles were still stiff and sore. Nonetheless, they rode into town on two horses, a little flutter in Iggy's chest going off every time he looked at Raraesa.

Over the next few days, Ansel went light on him. During down moments, they'd talk about swords and sword fighting. Iggy told Ansel about how Raraesa was attempting to teach him to sword fight, and they'd laugh at how badly some lessons went for him.

Iggy's days flowed into weeks. His routine remained much the same. He'd get up in the morning, eat some porridge, with Lecque occasionally joining them, and then he'd ride into town to Ansel's blacksmith shop. His days inside Ansel's shop were less than exciting; he'd heat up his rock until it was red hot, pull it out of the fire, and pound it with a hammer; five strikes with the hammer in his right hand, then five strikes with the hammer in his left hand, then he'd cool it in a water bath and return it to the fire. His muscles were becoming accustomed to the repetitive chore.

In the evenings, he spent time with Raraesa practicing sword fighting. He still always lost, though he was becoming more proficient. He needed to go back into Matreach, but first he had to get stronger. And he needed to learn how to defend himself much better.

By the sixth week, Iggy's frustration had bubbled to the top at the blacksmith shop. He would pound all day at the same rock repeatedly, but no matter how many times or how hard he'd hit it, the rock was still the same rock. Three or four times a day Ansel would walk over, inspect it, then he would shrug and walk away.

Finally, Iggy had had enough. He put his hammer down. "I am done with this rock."

Ansel turned around. "Is there a problem?"

"Yes, there is a problem. I have been banging that rock for I don't know how many days, and it's still a rock; it will always be nothing but a rock. Nothing is happening! It is still a rock!"

Ansel smiled. "Iggy, when you first walked into this shop you could barely lift that hammer with two hands. Now you swing it like you own it. Have you not noticed the muscles you are developing?"

Iggy lightened up. "Is that what this is all about? Why didn't you just tell me to exercise—you know, like in gym class." Iggy pointed to the dirt floor and imitated his gym coach. "Get down and give me ten push-ups!"

Ansel looked confused. "Gym class? Push-ups? Iggy, I have no idea what you are saying. The reason I have had you hitting that rock is that I want you to turn it into a sword."

"By the time I turn this piece of rock into a sword, gunpowder will have been invented!" Iggy's frustration had returned. "And don't ask what gunpowder is!"

"Do not get mad at me. You are the one incapable of turning that rock into something other than a rock."

Ansel obviously hit a raw nerve with Iggy. "Yeah. Well, look," Iggy picked up the hammer and smashed it down onto the rock. The vibration of the blow ran up his arm. "Oww!" Iggy dropped the hammer. "See! It's still a rock!"

"I do not think you are trying hard enough," Ansel said.

"Not trying hard enough! I'll show you who's not trying hard enough!" Iggy grabbed the hammer off the floor and with both hands tightly on the handle swung it high over his head. At that moment, he let out a loud battle scream. As his hands and the hammer arched down onto the rock, his amulet glowed, sending a warmth deep into his chest. Iggy smashed the hammer onto the rock. The hammer bounced out of Iggy's hand, and both Iggy and the hammer fell to the floor.

"Oh! Son of a bitch!" Iggy screamed as he lay on the floor in obvious pain. "There! Is that hard enough for you!"

Ansel's reply was only a smile.

"Stop mocking me. That's the best I can do. That's it—I'm fed up with hitting that rock." Iggy slowly got to his feet.

"Why, look. It is not just a rock anymore." Ansel continued grinning.

Iggy stared at the rock. The outer core had shattered away and what was left behind was a solid piece of shiny metal. "What the—?" He reached out to the rock, hovering his hand over it to see how much heat was still coming off it. A few moments ago the outer core was a glowing cherry red from sitting in the fire.

"Wow, there's no heat coming off of it," Iggy said, looking at Ansel. "Do you think it's safe to touch?"

Ansel stepped closer to the ball of shiny metal and looked at it. "Let us see." He dipped his hand into the bucket that rested next to them and scooped up a handful of water. He tossed it onto the metal. "Nothing. No hissing, no steam." He gently reached out and touched it. "That is peculiar. It is cold." He lifted it up and handed it to Iggy. "Here you go, young Iggy."

Iggy held it in his cupped hands and looked it over. "Why isn't it hot?"

"I do not know. It must have special properties to it that we do not know about. You should be proud of yourself. You did not think you had it in you. We should stop for the morning. I think it is time for lunch. Because of your great success we should eat something special today." Ansel grabbed several nails he'd crafted and handed them to Iggy. "Some days there is not much food being traded in town. Use these nails and see what food you can trade them for." He also reached into a pouch he always kept attached to his rope belt. He extracted a few coins and handed them to Iggy. "Try the nails first. If they will not bargain, use these. But please bargain first. When you return, we will sit in the back and eat fresh food today, and you can tell me more stories about that crazy land you say you are from."

"Sure," Iggy replied with a big grin. He grabbed the nails and coins, left the shop, and made his way down the main street toward the cheese shop. Halfway there, Frankie and his friends rounded one of the buildings, and Iggy was suddenly face-to-face with Frankie. Both stopped dead in their tracks and stared intently at each other.

Iggy stood with his eyes fixed on Frankie. He felt an inner calm as he stared him down. "Is there a problem?" he demanded more than asked.

Frankie looked at his friends. "Come on, let's go."

Frankie walked around Iggy, giving him a wide berth. His friends stared at him in disbelief but followed.

"Well," Iggy said to himself. "That was not what I expected." He looked at his right bicep and flexed it, staring at the small muscle. "This day is full of surprises."

After finding everything he needed Iggy headed back to Ansel's blacksmith shop, carrying a bundle. As he walked, he noted Frankie, without his friends, talking to an older man. The man seemed angry at Frankie and was lecturing him. "Well, that surely is the icing on the cake for me today."

Iggy didn't see Raraesa in the shadows listening in on the conversation Frankie was having with the old man.

Iggy and Ansel sat under the shade of a tree behind the shop and ate. Wiping his mouth on his sleeve, Ansel swallowed the last bite of his sandwich. "Iggy, that was tremendous. I have never thought to put ham and cheese between two pieces of bread. My goodness, you continue to surprise me. And you returned most of my coins to me. You are a marvelous trader."

"Yeah, and I continue to surprise myself. So, what are we going to do with that ball of metal now?"

"Not we—you. You are going to continue heating it and pounding it. Though, I must tell you that is a special rock I gave you. It will not be easy to flatten it."

"Why's that?"

"That rock was from up there." Ansel pointed to the sky.

"That was a meteorite?"

"I have no idea what a meteorite is. It just fell from the sky one day. It is very special, very rare. And it has different qualities from the rocks that we dig up. It's harder and lighter, and when we make into a sword, it is unbreakable."

"So, I'm making an indestructible sword?"

"That is correct. And, when you finish, that sword will be yours to carry with pride."

"Wow. Except I'm not doing too good with my training with Raraesa."

"You stay here. I will be right back," Ansel said as he got up from sitting under the tree and walked back to his shop. He returned moments later with two wooden swords and handed one of them to Iggy. "Let me see how you defend yourself."

"Hopefully, this will go better than with Raraesa."

Iggy looked at the wooden sword and gripped it tightly with both hands. He faced Ansel and took a stance with his left foot forward. He was wide-eyed with excitement and nerves. He stared at Ansel, waiting, not knowing what to do.

Ansel swung the sword over his shoulder, and as he brought it around in front he lunged at Iggy, who attempted to block it. The blow, though soft by Ansel's norm, struck Iggy's sword. Iggy hung tightly on to the wooden hilt as his sword was blown to his side and he was lifted off his feet and thrown to the ground. Only then did it come out of Iggy's grip and fall to the ground a few feet away from him, where he lay prone.

"Nope, not any better."

"Oh my," Ansel said. "We have our work cut out for us." And then he laughed.

"Here you two are," Raraesa said. "The shop was empty, and I thought the two of you may have taken off for the day."

Ansel let out a belly laugh. "No, we are enjoying a nice lunch. Iggy is introducing me to a ham and cheese sandwich. You should try it one day. And we are working on his sword fighting. So maybe one day he will beat you." Ansel laughed some more.

Iggy got slowly to his feet, rubbing his sore wrist, and retrieved his sword.

"It looked to me more like a slaughter than a lesson."

"We are doing fine. I think Iggy has done enough for today, so as far as I'm concerned he can leave now." Ansel took the wooden sword from Iggy's hand.

"You sure?" Iggy said somewhat excited. He would enjoy spending the day with Raraesa even if it was working on the farm with her.

"I am sure. Go, Iggy. See you tomorrow." Ansel gave him a pat on the shoulder and whispered in his ear, "I am glad she is teaching you. She is as good, if not better, than most men I know who can swing a sword."

Iggy turned and faced Ansel. "Really?"

"Yes, really. I did help a small amount in her training with a few technical moves."

Raraesa laughed. "You know I can hear you. And he taught me a lot more than a few moves."

"Go," Ansel said. "You two have fun and leave me to my work."

Once Iggy and Raraesa reached the front of Ansel's store, they stopped. Iggy shrugged. "So, I guess I'm helping you with farm chores today."

"I have them done until later in the day. So I have time to do whatever we want before we need to head back."

"What do you want to do?"

"Well, I hadn't thought about it." She paused for a moment. "It is a rather hot day. I have an idea. On the far side of town in the woods is a stream and a small pool. Let us go for a quick swim and cool off."

"Ah, the problem is I don't have a bathing suit." Iggy's eyes widened.

"A what?"

"A bathing suit."

"Iggy, when you bathe you are supposed to be naked." Raraesa scrunched her face, confused. "We are not going bathing; we are going swimming."

"Bathing suits are clothes you wear to cover you when you go swimming."

"Iggy. You are a strange one." Then she blurted out, "You have undergarments on? I hope?"

"Of course I do."

"Then you are all set for swimming. You take off your outer clothes and swim in your undergarments. I have no idea why you would put a different undergarment on to swim in when you are already wearing one."

Iggy found this sensible.

After a short walk, they entered the woods on the far side of town and proceeded down a dirt path. Eventually, Iggy heard running water in the distance. As they got closer, the air changed from the musty smell of the forest to a cool wetness with a sweet taste when he inhaled. He was hot and sweaty from work and then the walk. The air felt relaxing and calming. After rounding a bend, he was standing on the banks of a stream that flowed into a pool. He guessed the pool was about a hundred feet around. And on the far side the water lapped over a ridge and continued its journey downstream.

"This is fantastic," Iggy exclaimed.

"It is lovely," Raraesa replied. "Shall we?"

Before Iggy could say anything, Raraesa had hoisted her shirt up over her head and placed it on the ground. Next, she dropped her pants and stepped out of them. Her undergarments consisted of a white cotton top more like a T-shirt and cotton bottoms similar to men's boxer briefs.

Iggy took his shirt and pants off.

"Together on three?" he said.

"Three what?"

"We count to three. One, two, three. When I say three, we jump together."

"That is silly. Give me your hand." She reached out and grabbed his, and yelled, "Jump!"

The water was cool and refreshing. Iggy instantly felt rejuvenated. He and Raraesa surfaced together. They were inches apart, facing each other. Water rolled off her auburn hair that hung down her back, and the sun glistened off her moist skin. Their eyes locked on to each other; they stared deep into each other's eyes and froze. A twig snapped, and the moment was lost. Looking toward the far side of the pool, Iggy saw a deer staring at them, also frozen. Then it darted into the woods. *Damn, just my luck, Iggy thought.*

Suddenly Raraesa jumped up and grabbed Iggy's shoulders, then pushed him under the water. Iggy circled behind her underwater, popping up behind with his arms around her, then pulled her under. When they both surfaced, they splashed water at each other and laughed for the next few minutes.

Catching their breath, they both floated for a moment, when Iggy said, "So, you're an expert sword fighter. You did not tell me that."

"Not really." She laughed. "Lecque insisted I practice. He has always been there for me, protecting me. I guess he was concerned that there might come a day where he wasn't there."

"Well, that certainly explains why I can never beat you. Do you have your own sword?"

"We have swords. We just keep them hidden."

A short time later Iggy and Raraesa swam to shore, then they made their way back to town, to their horses, and home.

That evening, Lecque entered the kitchen, having finished the last of his chores. Iggy had gone to bed a short time earlier. He sat after pouring himself a mug of ale. Raraesa joined him.

"While I was in town, I saw Ankter talking to Frankie. And he was not happy. I listened from around the corner so they wouldn't see me," Raraesa said.

"Did you hear anything worth listening to?"

"He told Frankie he was not going to pay him anything until he finished the job of forcing Iggy to leave town."

Lecque perked up. "That is not going to happen."

"I know. I already took care of Frankie. He will not be bothering Iggy again." Raraesa balled her right hand into a fist and tapped it into the palm of her other hand.

"And I will take care of Ankter," Lecque said.

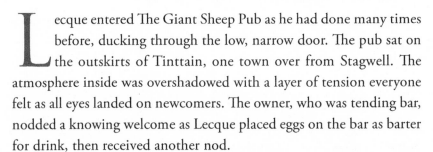

27

Lecque entered The Giant Sheep Pub as he had done many times before, ducking through the low, narrow door. The pub sat on the outskirts of Tinttain, one town over from Stagwell. The atmosphere inside was overshadowed with a layer of tension everyone felt as all eyes landed on newcomers. The owner, who was tending bar, nodded a knowing welcome as Lecque placed eggs on the bar as barter for drink, then received another nod.

"How are you holding up?" the owner asked, handing him a mug of ale.

"Surviving better than some."

"What brings you here today?"

Lecque responded only with a glance to the right, toward the small table for two, which was already occupied by one.

The owner understood and nodded. "I will leave you to your business." He turned and went back to greeting other patrons.

Lecque sat in the empty chair at the table. He settled in for a moment, remaining silent. Although he had not ordered, a barmaid approached and placed a mug of ale in front of him. He raised the mug and took a long, slow drink. Lecque looked across the table. "Ankter, I understand you hired a little dolt named Frankie to intimidate Iggy and drive him out of town."

"Apparently I either did not offer him enough or I hired the wrong person."

"Because Iggy is still here."

"Correct."

"Why are you so afraid of this boy?" Lecque asked, taking another swig of ale.

"Because I hear things. And what I hear concerns me. And it should concern you too."

"Tell me." Lecque returned Ankter's stare with one of his own.

"I hear of the death of a Nostaw and two individuals, one young and one older, standing over his dead body," Ankter started.

Annoyed, Lecque leaned in to Ankter. "That's because I told you about it. You know that was Iggy and me."

"I also hear of a Past Seer, sent by Mallak to look into the death of this Nostaw." Ankter took a drink from his mug, then continued, "And this Past Seer was unable to see what happened to the Nostaw or who these two were. And that was because some powerful spell blurred his vision so that he was only able to see that one was small and one was bigger."

"So what? Who knows who visited the body after we left?"

"I also hear that Mallak sent a group of soldiers to retrieve the Nostaw swords. And they were gone. But what is most interesting is that the Nostaw's hands were intact. Do you know what that means?" Ankter asked as his eyes stayed fixed on Lecque.

"It means a second Nostaw was around, and the dying Nostaw passed on his swords and elevated him to a Nostaw Warrior. Which makes sense, because when we arrived at the body, that Nostaw was already dead and his hands were intact. Wait! You think we got to the Nostaw before he died, and he gave the swords to me? You think I am a Nostaw Warrior?" Lecque gave a soft laugh. "You understand a Nostaw can only perform the Blinak Ritual with another Nostaw? Do I look like a Nostaw?" He stifled another laugh not to draw attention.

Ankter shook his head. "Not you."

"What? Iggy?" Lecque started to belly laugh. "You think that Nostaw broke all his traditions, traditions that guide their every waking moment, and made that scrawny kid a Nostaw Warrior?"

Ankter took a long drink from his mug. "I hear there was no other Nostaw in the area. So how would you explain the Past Seer's problem?"

"I do not know. And I do not care. You think if Iggy was so powerful he would let your little Frankie humiliate him and bully him? If he was such a powerful warrior, why didn't he stand up to Frankie?" Lecque stopped for a moment and stared down Ankter. "Iggy has been living with me just shy of eight weeks, and I tell you he is no warrior. Just the opposite. He is weak through and through. And if he is the one you're afraid of, then you are out and out crazy."

"You two better watch your backs," Ankter said in a low tone.

"No, it is you who better watch his back. I will tell you again, if anything happens to Iggy, it will be me you must deal with. I cannot believe with Mallak's powers increasing every day that instead of working with all of us to help bring him down, you are instead worried about a boy. This meeting is over. You had better hope I do not bring this to the others working with us. It would certainly be embarrassing for you."

Lecque stood and left the tavern.

The following day, and for the next few weeks, Iggy noticed a distinct increase in the intensity of Raraesa's sword training.

One morning, after an evening of training with Raraesa, Iggy was exceptionally quiet and kept to himself at Ansel's, pounding his shiny rock, deep in thought.

Ansel noted it. "Why are you so quiet today, Iggy?"

"Raraesa has been teaching me to sword fight. I've been learning and enjoying it."

"But?"

"But I'm tired of getting my ass kicked. Just once I'd like to trick her." He put his hammer down and looked at Ansel.

"Very well. Let us go in the back."

Moments later they stood with wooden swords in their hands. Ansel said, "Show me what she's taught you."

Iggy showed him the defensive moves and the attack moves he'd learned. Iggy showed him her trick moves that no matter how often he tried to stop, he always ended up dead. Ansel had helped train Raraesa, so he knew most of her tricks. He showed Iggy how to counter Raraesa's moves over the rest of the morning.

That evening behind the barn, Iggy and Raraesa squared off. "Let's begin where we left off yesterday," Iggy said.

Raraesa made her move, tricking Iggy into thrusting forward. As she blocked his sword and began her spin as in the previous nights, Iggy made his move, having perfected it with Ansel. Raraesa spun, expecting her sword to make an easy kill, but before she even completed the full circle, she felt the sharp sting of Iggy's sword smashing against her side.

"And now you are dead," Iggy said with a smile on his face and satisfaction in his voice.

Raraesa stared at him. "I am beyond impressed. You've figured it out, or you're just lucky. Let us go again."

Ansel had also shown Iggy three other moves, which he performed at different times—each time with devastating kills on Raraesa. Though she killed him ten times for every one he killed her, he did strike.

And with each strike Iggy made, he announced, "And now, you are dead."

After a good hour, they were both tired. Later, as they ate, Raraesa squeezed it out of Iggy that he'd been practicing with Ansel all day. As they laughed, Iggy said that it didn't matter, "A kill is still a kill."

Lecque would intermittently join their sword play over the next several days. Sometimes he would fight Iggy; other times he would fight Raraesa. Often he just sat there and watched, laughed, and encouraged Iggy. Lecque would pull him aside and give him advice. Iggy felt a bond forming with Lecque, very similar to the one he had with his brother John.

28

Iggy sat on his bed in the barn and slipped into the cottage to leave a note for Raraesa and Lecque. He wrote that he had to leave for a while. It was part of his quest and they shouldn't worry. He had to do it alone.

The sun had been down for almost an hour. The cottage was quiet, so he felt it was the best time for him to leave. What he didn't notice was Lecque followed him back to the barn. It was a long way to the lake, and he wanted to get there as fast as he could. He saddled the horse and started to walk it out. He was so focused on the task at hand he did not see Lecque standing in the opened barn door.

"Iggy, what are you doing?"

Iggy jumped back, startled. "Ou-out for a ride. I-I was having trouble sleeping."

"And you are having trouble lying. It is the middle of the night." Lecque walked up, took the reins from Iggy's hands, and tied the horse up. "Try again, but this time the truth." Lecque folded his arms and waited for a reply.

"Matreach. I have to get back to Matreach."

"What and where is Matreach?"

"I can't tell you."

"Then you are going nowhere."

"If I tell you, you cannot tell anyone. Lives may depend on it." This time Iggy stared Lecque down.

"You are serious?" Lecque was taken aback by Iggy's resolve.

"Completely."

A half hour later, Iggy led his horse out of the barn, Lecque following. Lecque had made it known in no uncertain terms he was accompanying Iggy to this land called Matreach and that decision was not open for discussion.

Silently, Iggy welcomed Lecque's company.

As they mounted their horses, Iggy turned to Lecque. "Thank you. I'm happy to have a brother-in-arms along."

"But I am not your brother."

Iggy just smiled, thinking of John, his other not-brother.

The ride to the lake took slightly more than an hour in daylight. So Lecque led the way, as the darkness hampered their travel. The trail was dark, and the night creatures announced their presence with calls, howls, and scampering. After a ninety-minute ride, they pulled up beside the lake—the same lake where his Matreach adventure had started. They walked along the water's edge to the waterfall and stopped. The air was filled with the sound of the cascading water, and the mist it kicked up filled Iggy's nostrils with moisture.

"How do you know we can get through that door?" Lecque asked.

"I'm not sure."

"Great."

Iggy walked behind the sheet of water, then turned to Lecque, and yelled, "Are you coming? We might only get one chance to pass through the portal. We need to stay close."

Lecque shook his head and muttered to himself that he must be crazy. But, in a moment, he was beside Iggy. Then they were behind the wall of water in a cavern carved into the rock. There was enough room for both to stand and walk three or four steps.

"Where is this opening?" Lecque yelled.

"I have no idea. I told you I hit my head and was knocked out."

Iggy pushed indiscriminately on the rock wall. Lecque took Iggy's lead and did the same.

Iggy knelt against the back wall. The moment he placed his hands against the rock his amulet glowed under his shirt and became intensely warm. Iggy's hand suddenly passed through the rock. The rock in front of him looked semitransparent, and the rock felt like bread dough. He turned and saw that Lecque had his back to him. Not knowing how long he had until the opening reverted back to solid rock, he reached out and grabbed Lecque by the back of his shirt and with a thrust of his legs pulled both of them through the portal that instantly closed behind them.

Lecque rolled onto the dry dirt and looked up at Iggy standing over him, calm and resolute. *My, how our roles have changed.*

"I guess we made it," Iggy said calmly.

"Yes. I would say we did." He took Iggy's extended hand and stood. "Where do we go now?"

Iggy had a pensive look on his face. "I really don't know. The two times I went through this portal I was unconscious." He shrugged. "We'll just have to go slow and careful." He turned and started toward the only opening out of the small cave.

Carefully and methodically, they made their way through the cave, into the cellar of a building and up a narrow set of steps. Passing through a hall at the end of the steps, Iggy felt fresh air streaming in. They came to an opening, and Iggy peered out. They were on the far end of the stone building he had woken up in during his first visit to Matreach. Off to the right were the gardens with the Rockhopper stables in the distance. Unfortunately, there was wide-open space between them and the stables. Even in the darkness there was enough light from the stars to highlight them in any direction they headed.

They made it unnoticed along the covered terrace that abutted the gardens on two sides, hugging the wall and keeping in the shadows. Iggy and Lecque snuck through the inner corridors of the stone building. They made their way up the main steps, creeping quietly, listening for any noise that would indicate someone was coming. Continuing down one of the corridors on the second floor, Iggy counted the doors on the right. He stopped at the seventh door.

"She said her room was on the second floor, seventh on the right."

"Who said?"

"Nyreada. The girl I told you about before we left."

Iggy rapped lightly on the door. He paused before rapping again. He heard what sounded like footsteps in the hallway. He turned to Lecque, eyes wide with concern. He quickly rapped on the door again. This time a little harder. The footsteps were getting louder. Finally, the door cracked open, and Nyreada peered out.

"Iggy!" she exclaimed. "What are you doing here?"

"Let us in; someone is coming!"

Nyreada opened the door and stuck her head out. "No, silly, that's the wall clock at the end of the hall." She stood there, staring at him with total surprise. "I do not understand. How are you here?"

"Can we please come in? Then I'll answer your questions."

With a confused but excited look on her face she threw the door open, and they rushed in. Nyreada looked Iggy up and down. He had changed. He was the same height, but he was more muscular and stood more confidently. After introductions between Nyreada and Lecque, Iggy told her his tale and his plans. She instantly agreed to help. But Iggy had a few rules for Nyreada's protection. She agreed to all of it and hurried out.

She came back a short time later. "Everything is arranged. There are two Rockhoppers waiting for you on the far side of the stables."

Nyreada walked them to the door. Before they walked out, she gave Iggy an enormous hug. "I am so glad to see you," she whispered in his ear. Iggy hugged her back.

"Me too. Thanks for all you're doing." He laid a hand on her check, and they gazed into each other's eyes, just for an instant. He turned and walked down the hall.

Iggy and Lecque made it to the stables without running into anyone. Two Rockhoppers stood behind the stables, as promised.

Lecque stopped in his tracks and eyed them up and down. "Wow. Your description was pretty exact."

Iggy walked up to the closest one. It knelt, and he climbed on. Lecque stood near his.

"Down, please," Iggy said in Tinte to Lecque's Rockhopper. It complied and knelt. "Just climb onto it."

Moments later they were moving across the field. Lecque was thrilled at the increasing speed of his Rockhopper, and when the wings swung out and they lifted off into a long glide, he whooped with delight, forgetting the danger they were in.

Iggy was relieved that they had gotten away with no confrontation, unaware that Oedsuer, Fryscar's town leader, was watching from the window in the high tower.

❧

Oedsuer looked through his single-tubed spy glass. His evening routine was a warm cup off Sekanjabin, then viewing the countryside with his spyglass for relaxation before he retired to bed. Tonight he'd seen some movement. When he focused his spyglass, he'd seen Iggy mounting a Rockhopper.

"What are you up to?" After two Rockhoppers rode off, he grabbed a piece of paper, wrote a note, and attached it to a messenger hawk.

"Fly to Minister…" He paused and thought for a moment. "Fly to Minister Sonham."

An instant later, the hawk was gone. Then he spoke to no one, saying, "Best to be on the right side of this shakeup if the rumors of Minister Riveriron's decreased influence on the council and Minister Sonham's rise are true."

❧

Nyreada jumped at the knock on her door. Upon opening it, a castle worker informed her that Oedsuer wanted her presence in his office immediately. She took a few moments to tamp down the anxiety rush that engulfed her.

After climbing the tower steps, she knocked on Oedsuer's door and entered. "I was informed you wanted to see me."

"I am incredibly angry and concerned. Please tell me you had nothing to do with what I just saw." Oedsuer stared her down.

"I have no idea what you are talking about. Are you mad at me for something?" she asked with great care in her voice.

"That boy! The one from Skye that you brought to our land. He is back! And he has brought another with him. Did you have anything to do with this?"

Feeling she was answering his question without lying, she said, sounding affronted, "Absolutely not. I had nothing to do with him coming back and am as surprised and shocked as you are. What should we do?"

"I have taken care of it already. I have sent a messenger hawk to the ruling council. That boy and his partner will be apprehended." He dismissed her with a wave.

Back in her room, Nyreada paced back and forth. Iggy and Lecque were most likely heading into a trap. She thought of how fast the hawk flew and how fast the Rockhoppers traveled. It would be close. She knew she would not catch them but, if she got there, she might find them before they were captured. Or, worse, killed.

She sneaked out of her room to get to the stable. She knew the blind spots that kept her out of sight of Oedsuer if he was looking out his window. In a short time, she was on her Rockhopper and charging across the open field in pursuit of Iggy and Lecque.

⁓

On the plains, Iggy and Lecque soared over the rolling countryside. Iggy was laser-focused, scanning the skies for Tipeis and the landscape for any danger that might confront them. Lecque vacillated between sheer exuberance of riding the Rockhoppers and snapping back to the reality they were putting themselves in mortal danger.

Iggy stared ahead with no idea that an hour behind them Nyreada was pushing her Rockhopper as fast as it would go to catch up to them.

✍

To Nyreada's dismay, when she arrived at the outskirts of Cranncairn, all she found were two Rockhoppers resting in the shade. Iggy and Lecque were nowhere to be found. Iggy had purposely kept her in the dark about his plans. There was only one person she knew she could turn to for help. She quickly headed off to where he lived.

✍

Iggy and Lecque snuck from building-to-building in the shadows until they were in the center of Cranncairn at the Castle in the Tree. Lecque stopped for a moment to take it in.

"It is a remarkable sight," Iggy said.

"I thought you were joking when you told me. But, as I have found up to now, you have not exaggerated one thing about this land."

Iggy looked off to the far side of town. There was a sliver of light appearing in the eastern sky. "We don't have much time before the sun rises. Let's go."

The two ran through the shadows, then crossed the open plaza as quickly as they could, swiveling their heads, looking for any guards. The archway door that led into the inner atrium was open, as always. The citizens were allowed free access. It was just the way things were done here.

Once in the atrium, Iggy walked to the center podium. Lecque looked around at the carved mural. "So what do we do now?"

"Somehow I have to pick the correct crystal off the mural and place it on the podium before the morning light shines through the archway," Iggy answered, bewildered by the hundreds of crystals inlaid into the wooden mural. He walked around the perimeter in dismay. "I have no idea what I'm looking for."

"Not even a clue?"

"No."

⁕

Nyreada arrived on the edge of the plaza in front of the Castle in the Tree. As she stepped out of the shadows to cross the plaza, she heard commotion and the sounds of footsteps running and getting closer. Unseen, she jumped back to a hiding spot. Moments later, ten armed guards with their swords in hand, along with Ministers Sonham, Leeforth, Tritdaw, and Hyluita, arrived and stopped outside the open door that led into the Castle in the Tree atrium. No Minister Riveriron.

Minister Sonham was obviously in charge. She heard him give the order, "When you get inside, slay them if they resist."

She was too late. Or was she? She turned and quickly ran in the opposite direction.

⁕

Lecque was the first to hear the commotion outside. "Iggy! We have to go!"

"What? No! I haven't figured out which crystal to use yet." Iggy was focused on his task and not tuned in to the danger at hand.

Lecque ran over and grabbed him by the arm. "Now! There are guards outside. We have to go!"

Iggy snapped to the present. He saw in that instant guards rushing in with swords in hand. "Up the stairs!"

The two bounded up the circular stairs that ran around the outer aspect of the atrium. Halfway up the first flight Iggy looked back. The guards had started up behind them. "Keep running! They're only half a turn behind us!"

"Kill them!" Minister Sonham yelled.

251

Lecque drew his sword when they reached the first landing.

"No! There are too many of them! Keep climbing the stairs to the next level!" Iggy said.

As they ran, Lecque demanded, "Do you have a plan on how to get us out of here? Or are we going to keep climbing until we reach the top where we will be trapped?"

"I'm thinking. Just keep running."

Iggy and Lecque went round and round up the circular stairs. Higher and higher, with the guards close behind. The higher they went, the more unlikely they'd find a way of escape. They stopped at the top floor.

"I am open to suggestions."

Lecque quickly jumped into action. "Help me!"

The two dragged a waist-high, six-foot-long cabinet over to the top of the stairs, and when the guards were only steps away, they pushed it down. It tumbled down the steps, causing the guards and the group of Ministers behind them to retreat or be crushed by the cabinet as it tumbled toward them.

"Now what?" Iggy asked.

Lecque looked around. There was only one hallway to go down. "This way."

Iggy followed Lecque, and they ran down the long, winding hallway past multiple doors that opened into stone castle rooms inlaid in the wooden tree limb.

Lecque stopped at the end. "We are trapped." Lecque turned the doorknob of the last door in the hallway. It opened. "In here. We will make our stand here."

They entered, shut, and locked the door. Quickly they moved furniture against the door.

◛

The guards made it to the opening of the hallway. They stopped.

"Why have you stopped?" Minister Sonham demanded.

"They are trapped," the sergeant of the guards said. "There are several rooms. They could be in any one of them. We will move forward methodically and carefully. Room by room. But we will capture them. There is no escape from this height."

~§

"I guess this is it," Iggy said with surprising calm.

He reached behind his back and produced his Nostaw swords. "The blades are not super sharp, but we know they can be effective when they need to be." He thought of the Baisd Bheulachs.

Lecque looked at Iggy with admiration. "You have done well. It is as you said, we are brothers-in-arms." Lecque held his sword in front of him and took a defensive stance.

"More than brothers-in-arms; we have become brothers."

Iggy readied his two swords in front of him.

And they waited.

~§

The guards stood outside the last door. The sergeant of the guards turned to Minister Sonham. "The door is locked."

Minister Sonham handed him a key. "This is the master key to all the locks."

The sergeant of the guards inserted it into the keyhole and turned it until they heard a loud click. Then he turned to his men. "Remember, show no mercy. They are dangerous. Dispatch them quickly."

They opened the door, pushed the furniture blocking the door aside, and rushed in.

They heard only silence. They entered the room and stopped. Other than the guards, the room was empty. The far window was open though.

"Where are they?" Minister Sonham demanded.

"Gone," said the sergeant of the guards.

"Did they climb out the window?" Minister Sonham asked as he rushed over to the window and looked out. He saw nothing. No rope, no handholds. No way down.

❧

Iggy, Lecque, Nyreada, and Minister Riveriron rushed down the hidden inner wall passageway, then quickly made their way down the hidden circular passageway carved between the outer atrium wall and the outer shell of the tree.

"We must be very quiet," Minister Riveriron said. "This corridor is only known to the head of the council. And I want to keep it that way."

When they reached the atrium floor level, they exited from behind a hidden panel. "You must leave quickly," Minister Riveriron said.

"No," Iggy responded as he charged into the center of the atrium. He looked in dismay at the center podium already ablaze in the morning sunlight. The shadows of the morning's sunbeams were quickly approaching the podium. He had only a few minutes at most to figure this out.

"I am not leaving until that beam of sun has left the podium. I didn't come all this way and place us in danger to run."

"You do not have long, then. Make it fast. Make your decision," Minister Riveriron said.

They could hear the guards coming down the stairs as their running footsteps echoed down the hollow tree.

Iggy shut his eyes. "Focus," he said aloud. "The Tipei said it had to be one of the crystals that were in the hall." He opened his eyes and looked at the hundreds of crystals inlaid into the mural. He shut his eyes again. What did Aunt Gwen always say? He took a deep breath in and said, "She would always say, when you are in a tough situation and need help, hold your hand over your mother's amulet. Press it to your chest. That will help guide your thoughts and show you the way." Iggy pressed his hand over the amulet and concentrated.

Suddenly he felt an intense warmth in his palm. His eyes shot open. "Of course. It is so obvious." He pulled off his amulet and looked at it. "This crystal *is in* the hall." Iggy placed it onto the podium. Instantly, the sunlight hit it, and an intense beam shot out and pointed to a spot on the mural. Iggy ran there and stared at the landscape carved out of wood. Two mountain peaks stood side by side that were taller than the other mountains carved in the mural. The beam pointed straight between the two peaks and stopped at the base of a mountain in the background.

"That's it!" Iggy ran back to the podium to retrieve his necklace.

"You must leave. Now!" Nyreada said.

Iggy took a quick second to make eye contact with her and mouthed, "Thank you." Then, in an instant, he and Lecque were gone.

∽

Nyreada and Minister Riveriron stood at the bottom of the stairway when the guards and the Ministers of the Council made their way down.

"Minister Riveriron," Minister Sonham said with indignation, "what are you doing here?"

"It seems I am protecting your rear flank. I have to thank Nyreada here for alerting me, or there would not have been anyone protecting the only exit from this mighty hall. So, were you able to apprehend our two intruders?" The sarcasm dripped off Minister Riveriron's words.

"We were not," Minister Sonham replied.

"So, twice you have let this dangerous young man escape from you. If you want to be head of council, as I have no doubt you are scheming to achieve, you must do better than this." Minister Riveriron turned to Nyreada. "Shall we take our leave? Would you like to join me for some early food?"

"Yes, uh, yes, I would," Nyreada replied.

Nyreada and Minister Riveriron left the atrium.

Minister Sonham said to the sergeant of the guards, "Send word to Allistair. He will have to gather his Tipeis, to locate and kill these intruders."

29

Iggy and Lecque rode their Rockhoppers hard. As they put widening distance between them and Cranncairn, they eased up on their rides, allowing them to go at their own pace. Iggy had scanned behind them so often his neck was sore.

Lecque rode beside him, occasionally glancing at Iggy. His newfound respect for Iggy had blossomed over the last day. All doubts of mistrust had been erased.

Their Rockhoppers ran and glided across the open plains, and before them, loomed mountains that matched those on the carved wooden mural. Lecque saw they were on a direct path heading toward the spot the beam from Iggy's crystal amulet had pointed them to.

The mountains got closer and closer with each running and gliding cycle. They glided around dense trees and faced an open field that brought them to the abrupt base of the mountain they'd seen in the mural. As soon as the Rockhoppers' hooves touched down, they pulled to a sudden stop. Agitated, they rocked back and forth on their hooves.

"What happened? Why did they stop?" Lecque asked.

"I don't know. They have never done this before. I think they sense danger."

Iggy looked across the field; it was covered with ankle-high scraggly weeds, and a good two hundred yards across at the base of cliffs was a passageway between two sheer walls.

The Rockhoppers knelt, allowing them to dismount. Once their feet touched the ground, the Rockhoppers jumped up and moved away from the field.

"I don't know what's spooked them. I guess we walk from here. I think we need to go into that pass between the cliff," Iggy said.

"Whatever spooked the Rockhoppers is hiding in that pass."

"Do you have a better suggestion?"

"No," Lecque said, resignation in his voice.

They started their walk across the field. Iggy led the way with an uneasy Lecque behind.

"This feels strange," Iggy said. Each time he took a step, the vegetation pushed back. "I feel as if I'm walking on springs."

They were halfway across the field when Lecque stopped. "Something's wrong here."

Iggy turned around to see Lecque leaning over and pulling off strings of vegetation that had wrapped around his ankles. In an instant, the vegetation had wound around Lecque's right hand and started to pull him over.

Iggy, who had also stopped, looked down; small vines had twisted themselves around both his ankles, too. He reached down with his right hand to free himself, only to have that hand covered with vines. He, too, was stuck.

"I cannot move," Lecque said. He attempted to reach for his sword, but his left hand was trapped tight with vines when he tried to pull his right hand free.

"It has me too!"

"Can you reach my sword?" asked Lecque, struggling to stay upright and bent forward at the waist with his ankles and wrist squeezed tight as the vines attempted to pull him over.

Iggy reached out and pulled Lecque's sword out of its sheath. He swung it against the vines around his feet, slicing them in half and freeing himself. To his surprise, a shrieking wail came from the vines when sliced. He swung the sword again, freeing Lecque.

The wails from the vegetation were intense, high-pitched, and loud. As unnerving as the screams were, Iggy looked down and saw each blade of vegetation had a single eye and a small mouth, open and wailing.

"These things are alive!" Iggy said as he swung Lecque's sword at them, running with Lecque close behind.

"And if they pull us to the ground, I promise you, *we* will not be. Keep swinging that sword."

Suddenly a different sound rolled over the field. Iggy and Lecque stopped for a moment. Even the vegetation stopped squealing. They heard "*click, click, click*" and the sound of a charging animal. Turning around, Iggy saw a hideous creature unlike anything he had ever seen before running across the field at them. It had the torso of a wild boar, although much wider, with the face of a spider monkey. Most frightening were two scorpion pincers coming off its front shoulders, each the size of one of Lecque's legs. The pincers stretched wide open with every stride the beast made toward them, stayed open for a moment, then snapped shut with such power it seemed they could crush bones to powder.

"Run!" poured out of Lecque's mouth. "Give me the sword!"

Iggy tossed the sword to Lecque, and they charged across the field with Lecque swinging his sword in front of them, cutting down the vegetation that now wailed at them with open mouths and a single eye per blade attempting to lasso their feet to stop them for the monster that stormed toward them.

They reached hard-packed dirt on the far end of the field devoid of vegetation at the same moment that the scorpion-like creature was on top of them. It plowed over Lecque, sending him flying to the ground with his sword catapulting from his grip as he smashed down.

"Shite! Shite! Shite!" he screamed.

The creature straddled Lecque with drool dripping from its mouth. It lifted its pincers above Lecque, opening them for a death snap. But one fell over Lecque's head and the other around his chest, stopping before they snapped shut, just inches from making contact with Lecque.

Iggy had taken his Nostaw swords and jammed them high into the monster's claws, keeping them pried open. In that split second, Lecque grabbed his sword and thrust it into the creature's belly, which reared up on its hind legs and let out a piercing scream. Blood ran down Lecque's sword, melting the blade down to the hilt.

Lecque scrambled aside just in time to avoid the monster's body pinning him to the ground. The vegetation let out a collective howl, then went silent. The vines' mouths and eyes suddenly disappeared as their blades swayed softly with the breeze. Suddenly another creature like the one now dead on the ground sprang out of the woods and charged across the field at them.

"We need to run!" Iggy said.

"We have no protection. My sword is gone."

"This way! Up into the ravine."

"We have no place to go! We cannot outrun it!"

"Not like we have another choice!" Iggy declared.

"Well, sard it!"

As they ran, the creature closed the distance between them, its pincer claws opening and snapping shut with clangs that echoed throughout the ravine walls.

As they ran, the passage narrowed, the rock walls on each side drawing closer together.

"Look up ahead. Stairs!" Iggy shouted as his legs pumped underneath him.

The walls were now inches to the right and left of Iggy's shoulders as he reached the first step. Lecque was so close Iggy felt the breeze from Lecque's pumping arms and his heavy breathing on the back of his neck. The creature's pincers opened and thrust toward Lecque's head. Lecque dove forward onto the steps, pushing Iggy forward, who fell forward up the steps. The pincers stopped inches from Lecque.

The two regained their purchase and scrabbled farther up the steps on hands and feet.

Iggy had the crazy thought: *See, Madam Trinity? This* is *how it's done.* Then there was silence.

Iggy and Lecque looked over their shoulders. Then both simultaneously rolled onto their backs. The creature was stuck. The walls of the cliffs had narrowed so much the monster was squeezed in, unable to move forward, unable to bring its pincers down and crush Lecque or Iggy. They watched as the creature backed up with great effort and freed itself. Unable to turn around, it continued to back down the ravine until it could spin around. Then the creature simply crawled away, leaving Iggy and Lecque safe on the narrow steps.

Lecque looked at Iggy. "Thank you. You saved my life back there."

"Are you hurt?"

"No. I do not think I am. You?"

Iggy shook his head. "No." He looked up. The steps extended up this tight ravine until they met the side of a mountain a good half mile away. "Shall we?" He stood.

They climbed in silence, Iggy deep in thought about what just happened and what could be ahead of them. They had no weapons other than two dull curved Nostaw swords to protect them. They did not have to say that aloud; they were both well aware of their predicament.

They stopped for a moment and sat on the steps to catch their breath. Lecque placed a hand on Iggy's shoulder. "Thanks again for… you know—what you did back there."

Iggy smiled. "Don't worry; I've got your back." He looked up. "The ravine ends soon. Where do you think we go then?"

"I do not know." Lecque extended his hand and helped Iggy up. "But I am sure we will find out."

A half hour later Iggy stopped as the ravine abruptly ended, flush against a sheer cliff. He turned to his right and saw another set of steps.

"This way," he said to Lecque.

Climbing thirty steps brought them out of the ravine and onto the base of a mountain that towered into the clouds. There was a path that led up.

"Up we go," Lecque said and started up the steep path.

As they climbed, Iggy stared to the right and left and could only see sharp, jagged mountains with steep falloffs to gorges below. Climbing on, he eventually spotted the top of their climb. Reaching the last step, they walked onto a landing with an archway of stone and a path that led through it. Once through the archway, they stopped.

A plateau stretched out before them, filled with thousands of Tipeis, and at the center a pool of liquid glowed with a pulsating blue-to-red hue.

The thousands of Tipeis went still and turned their attention to Iggy and Lecque.

"We are here. Now what?" Lecque asked.

Iggy stood motionless in the archway. "My first time here. I'm making this up as I go."

"Now you tell me." Lecque shook his head.

One of the Tipeis flew over and hovered in front of them. Iggy recognized it as the Tipei he had spoken to at the training arena.

In a slow voice that sounded like squeaks to Lecque but was an understandable language to Iggy, it said, "Welcome to our home. Your journey has been a long one and not an easy one. I watched as you defeated the Lioberis Grass and the Hilliod. Your bravery and ingenuity are impressive. No one has ever made it to the steps of Giestalatia."

"Giestalatia?" Iggy asked.

Lecque looked at Iggy as he spoke to the Tipei in a language he had never heard before. His face showed amazement when the Tipei spoke.

"Yes. Translated into your language it means The Shield of Sovereignty."

"You were watching us?"

"Oh, yes. I was high above you."

"Then why didn't you swoop down and help us?"

"This is your journey. It was not for me to interfere. Now that you are here, are you ready to finish your quest?"

"Yes. But what do I do?"

"This is the easiest part of your journey. Walk to the pool and dip your swords into the Liquid Fire."

Iggy looked at Lecque. "I think you should stay here."

He walked to the glowing pool of liquid and looked around at the thousands of Tipeis, on rocks, outcroppings, and trees, all intensely quiet. Their eyes all on him.

He reached behind his back and produced his swords. Kneeling, he hesitated, then he slowly dipped them up to their hilts in the liquid.

As he withdrew the blades, the swords vibrated and glowed red. The handles became warm but not intolerable to hold. After what felt like an eternity to Iggy, but was no doubt less than a minute, the glow of the blades stopped.

"It is done," the Tipei hovering behind him said.

Iggy stood and looked at the swords. They looked no different to him. He looked up at the Tipei. "Now what?"

"Now you are done. This journey is complete. What other journeys you have before you are for you to discover. You arrived here a young person. You leave a Nostaw Warrior. Mind those swords with your life."

The Tipei landed and bowed its head toward Iggy as did all other Tipeis as far as one could see.

Iggy held his head high as he walked back to Lecque. "Let's go. It's time to go home." Iggy walked through the arch and started down he steps. Lecque followed close behind him.

When they reached the bottom, they stopped, silent for a moment.

"I do not see that creature in the ravine," Lecque said.

They moved slowly forward. They scanned the ravine, listening intently for any sounds of a four-legged creature or the clicking of its pincers. Hearing nothing, they walked to the edge of the vegetation.

"Any suggestions?" Iggy asked.

"Not really."

Iggy produced his Nostaw swords and held them with confidence, one in each hand, determination on his face as he stared ahead. As he stepped forward, ready to do battle with the Lioberis Grass, he was surprised to see them open their eyes and bend the top part of each blade to bow to him. Instantly, a path through the field opened for them.

Iggy looked at Lecque. "Well, I guess they've had enough for one day. Shall we?"

Lecque nodded, and they calmly walked across the field. Upon reaching the other side, Iggy turned and bowed back at the Lioberis Grass. They found their Rockhoppers not too far away. They mounted them and headed back to Fryscar.

"I do not understand why those grasping vines did not attack," Lecque said.

"I think it was out of respect." Iggy turned to Lecque. "I am now a Nostaw Warrior. My quest is complete."

"How will this help you get back to your suck a hanna, pencil-vick place?"

"Honestly, I really don't know. But let's go back to Skye. That is my home for the moment. My home is with you and Raraesa for now."

This time, Iggy was relaxed and enjoyed the Rockhopper ride. As did Lecque. It seemed their problems were behind them. They simply needed to return to Fryscar and pass through the portal back to the Kingdom of Skye.

The sun was high, and there were no clouds in the sky as they journeyed across the open plains midway between the capital city of Cranncairn and Fryscar. It was a beautiful ride. Suddenly, darkness rolled over them. Iggy looked up expecting to see a massive thunderhead of clouds that would bring torrential rains, like back in Pennsylvania. Instead, he saw a black mass of Tipeis, undulating up and down as their wings flapped.

Lecque looked up too. "What is that?"

"Tipeis."

"What are they doing?"

"I don't know," Iggy shouted back as they continued their ride.

In an instant, the Tipeis had overflown them and gone over the horizon out of their vision. The sunlight had quickly returned, and Iggy and Lecque continued their flight to Fryscar; though Iggy was bothered by the Tipeis' appearance.

His fears were realized as they glided over a ridge: easily a thousand Tipeis were in front of them, hovering over the valley floor below them. Allistair stood in front of them, and next to him on either side were at least a hundred guards, half with swords in their hands, the other half archers with their arrows nocked at the ready, aimed at them.

"Do you think Rockhoppers can outrun arrows?" Lecque yelled to Iggy.

"Don't know. It doesn't matter; it ends here. Right now. We land." They glided to a stop in front of Allistair.

The Rockhoppers stood upright, not lowering themselves for Iggy or Lecque to dismount. The air was filled with the low vibration of flapping wings. Tipeis were stacked on top of one another, presenting a massive wall of black up into the sky.

"Well, Iggy," Allistair said, "you have become more powerful and dangerous than even I could have imagined."

"We just want to leave this land peacefully," Iggy called out.

"You know we cannot allow you to leave this time," Allistair shouted back.

The Tipei he had communicated with at the pool of Liquid Fire flew over to Iggy and stopped. Their eyes met. "Are you here to confront and stop me?"

"We were summoned. We must respond when summoned by our master," the Tipei explained.

"Will you hurt me or my brother?"

"Ah, he is your brother." The Tipei gave Lecque a once-over. "No, we will not hurt either of you. And we are forbidden to hurt our master either."

"Does he know that?"

"Yes. I am sure that is why he brought the guards. I assume we are here for intimidation."

"Will you protect us?"

"Yes, as we will also protect our master."

Without warning, one archer took aim, and his arrow flew toward Iggy. With blinding speed, the Tipei talking to Iggy snatched the arrow out of the air moments before it would have struck Iggy in the heart. The Tipei dropped the arrow, and by the time it had hit the ground, five Tipeis had descended upon the archer and ripped him to pieces with their talons and incinerated him with their fire breath.

The other guards sheathed their swords, and the archers withdrew their arrows from their bows in a split second.

Lecque openly gasped. "That was beyond frightening." He looked at Iggy. "You can control them?"

"Yes, I can." Iggy looked at Allistair. "I think we will be going now."

Allistair seethed with anger as Iggy and Lecque's Rockhoppers trotted by them and increased speed to a blinding run before they set off into a long glide.

The remainder of the ride was uneventful. They dismounted in Fryscar, gave their Rockhoppers a thankful pat on the base of their necks, and calmly walked to the portal. and exited through it to the cave behind the waterfall in Skye.

30

Iggy and Lecque walked away from the lake and up the bank to where they had tied their horses one day earlier. The first thing Lecque did was to check that his other sword was still in its sheath attached to the saddle. Satisfied, he turned to Iggy.

"Well, you more than proved your courage. I am starting to think that Nostaw knew what he was doing in picking you. Remember, though, you are not indestructible. You have a lot of training to do. You will not have any Tipeis here to protect you."

"We have each other, and Raraesa protects both of us."

Lecque laughed. "Yes, she does. Shall we head home, Brother?"

"Yes." Iggy mounted his horse as did Lecque, and they started off on the trail.

A half hour later they rode over a crest, rounded a bend, and pulled to an abrupt stop. Directly in front, blocking the path, were four dismounted soldiers, resting their horses.

"Just follow me and remain calm," Lecque said in a soft voice to Iggy.

Iggy gently tapped his heels into the side of his horse and followed behind Lecque. They started to go around the soldiers through the grass, when one called out, "You two, dismount now!"

"The boy and I are of no danger to you. We ask safe passage."

"I will not ask you again," the soldier barked as he drew his sword. "Dismount now!"

"Be calm, Iggy, and obey them," Lecque said. "We have done nothing wrong. Dismount, but stay alert. If I tell you to run, I want you to run."

"I'm done running. I am a Nostaw Warrior now."

"Iggy, you are not ready for battle. Sometimes the bravest thing to do is run. When you practiced last with Raraesa out of ten matches, how many did you win?"

"Three or four."

"Then you were killed six or seven times. And that was against one person. There are four of them. You could face two, and they will not be sticking you with wooden swords. Do you think you can kill someone?"

Iggy did not reply.

"If I tell you to run, you run."

"I told you both to dismount!" one of the solders yelled.

By now the other three soldiers had also drawn their swords. Iggy and Lecque complied and in moments were standing, surrounded by the soldiers.

The two groups stared at each other. Finally, one fixated on Iggy pointed his sword at him. "You! I remember you now. You were the one who freed our captive at the lake. Because of you I was demoted a rank. I saw that creature pull you into the water. I thought you were dead. Now you will be dead."

"Run, Iggy!" Lecque yelled as he drew his sword.

Iggy bolted between two of the soldiers before they could react and ran off the path into the tree cover. Lecque raised his sword and blocked a thrust from the closest soldier. As he stepped back, he blocked a parry from the second soldier, and then swung his sword to his right, catching the first soldier on the neck, instantly drawing blood. It was a death blow.

A whoosh of air passed by Lecque's right ear as an arrow flew by, piercing the neck of the third soldier. Momentarily distracted, the soldier closest to Lecque flinched, giving Lecque a clean thrust with his blade into the soldier's chest, dropping him instantly. Lecque turned to the remaining soldier and raised his sword. A second arrow flew by, striking the soldier in the chest. Lecque dropped to a knee and visually scoured the tree line. He saw no one.

"Iggy," he yelled as he jumped to his feet and ran in the direction Iggy had gone.

⁊

Iggy had run as fast as he could down an incline and around a bend where he stopped in an opening, walled off on three sides by steep rocks. He turned around to leave, but a soldier blocked his exit.

"And now you will die," the soldier said as he advanced.

Iggy's heart pounded through his chest, his breathing fast and chaotic. The soldier, now only four feet from Iggy, raised his sword and prepared to swing it in a death blow, when Iggy's back and chest became ablaze with searing heat. His back burned the most. In a reflexive manner, Iggy's hands reached behind him, toward the unbelievable pain. As the soldier swung his sword, Iggy pulled his hands from behind him to shield his face.

In his hands, though, were his curved swords, and with a swing he caught the soldier's sword mid-shaft. Iggy's blade glowed red hot and sliced the blade in half. Iggy swung the sword in his left hand and caught the soldier just below the elbow, slicing his arm off.

The soldier stood still in disbelief as blood poured from the open stump. Suddenly he stiffened and looked down at his chest as the tip of a blade pierced through. He fell to the ground, and Iggy saw Lecque standing there, withdrawing his sword.

Iggy stared at the curved blades in his hands, then at the dead soldier, at the stump where his arm had been, and at the blood pooling around the stump. Iggy opened his mouth as if to say something, but no words came out. Suddenly his stomach started to spasm, and he staggered off to the side, dropped to his knees, and vomited.

Lecque knelt by the dead soldier and picked up the shattered sword. The metal had been melted and cut cleanly through. He dropped it back to the ground and stood.

"We have to go. Now!" Lecque said.

Iggy, on his hands and knees, gasped for air, spitting bile out of his mouth.

"We have to go now!"

Lecque ran over and knelt beside Iggy. In a soft but firm voice said, "We have to go."

"He's dead, isn't he?"

"Yes," Lecque replied. "We are not safe here. We are not alone."

"Are there more soldiers?"

"I do not know. I only saw four and have no idea where the fifth soldier came from. And I fear there may be more nearby. That is why we must leave now!"

They ran back to their horses and were soon fast on their way to Nilewood.

~

At the site of the battle, a lone archer walked around, assessing the bodies. The archer bent down and examined the severed sword, looking closely at the melted edges. Dropping them back to the ground, the archer stood and grabbed her bow that she had laid next to the body moments before and said, "So the rumors are true. It has begun."

31

Three days had quietly come and gone for Iggy and Lecque. There was talk in Nilewood about soldiers that had been killed nearby, but, other than that, nothing much was said. They feared there would be repercussions for the soldiers' deaths.

The sun crossed over the high point in the sky and was making its way west. The shadow of Castle Maol cast its silhouette over the low-lying buildings below.

Mallak stood, arms folded, with a scowl on his face. Usually, the stale rotting odor that flowed off the lake below would lighten his mood. For him, it was like a breath of fresh air. But not today, for Mallak had spent the previous hours pacing and fuming with anger in the study behind the balcony.

Now he waited impatiently on the balcony, arms folded, his body rocking back and forth. His twisted, hooked nose twitched every now and then as it picked up different wafts of odors. No, they did not help.

"Emperor Mallak." A guard approached and stopped ten feet away, not daring to come any closer.

"Did you find him?" Mallak demanded.

"Yes." The guard answered straightaway without hesitation.

"Why did it take so long? Did I not give instructions that his carrier birds were to be followed? I want to know where he lives. I am tired of going through this charade of sending a bird with a note requesting he come here. When I want him, I want to send my soldiers to get him and drag him here." The veins in Mallak's neck bulged as his anger rose.

"Yes, Emperor Mallak. We have done as you requested. The bird always flew to the north, so we sent one hundred soldiers to the north to follow its path. But the next time you wanted him, the birds flew to the south. The next time you summoned him, we sent out a hundred soldiers to the north and the south, as far as it would take him to travel in one day. The next time the bird flew to the east. Then to the west. This last time, we sent out a thousand soldiers in every direction. The bird flew around and around the kingdom. And with each circle more birds joined it. There were hundreds of birds flying around the kingdom in a circle. We had no idea which one was the bird we needed to follow. Then, as if someone gave an order, they all flew in different directions."

The guard stood at attention, not making eye contact with Mallak.

Mallak stroked his chin with his hand, thinking for a moment. "And from what direction did he finally come from?"

The guard quickly answered, "He did not come in the front gate today. He was simply standing in the main courtyard. No one witnessed him arriving. And when we try to follow him when he leaves, he disappears into a crowd and is gone or walks around a blind corner and vanishes." The guard started to sweat, aware his answer was not pleasing.

"What are you waiting for? Bring him to me."

Breathing a sigh of relief, the guard turned and left the room, returning moments later with Gobus behind him. Mallak dismissed the guard with a wave of his hand.

"Well, Mallak, or Just Plain Emperor, or Emperor Mallak, whatever you want to be called today, what major kingdom malady have you called me to help solve for you this time?"

Gobus strolled around the room with a carefree attitude.

Mallak snapped, his face turning beet red. The veins on his forehead bulged and pulsed. When he opened his mouth, the words spewed forward in a high-pitched wail, "Do not ever mock me! I am your emperor!"

Gobus dismissed him with a wave of his hand. "Oh, stop the melodrama. You are who I train and teach you to be. Do not ever threaten me or think you can intimidate me. Remember, I am the teacher, and you are the student. There is nothing you can do to me. It would be wise for you to remember that."

Mallak snapped back, "That will not always be the case. It would be wise of you to remember that." His breathing was quick and spastic.

Gobus remained with a calm demeanor. "You will only become as powerful as I am willing to teach you. And that will never be more powerful than I am. Even if I wanted to let that happen, you simply do not have the capability of reaching that level. Let us dispense with this back-and-forth nonsense. Tell me why you asked me to come here today."

Mallak stared at Gobus for a moment and slowed his breathing. He turned and walked to the other side of the room to a table. "Over here," he said with no emotion in his voice. He pointed at the items that lay on it. "Tell me what could have done this."

Gobus picked up one item and examined it intently. It was the hilt of a soldier's sword. The end had been sheared off cleanly. The other half was lying on the table. He picked it up and examined it.

"How did this soldier die?" Gobus asked, examining the end of the sword without looking at Mallak.

Mallak replied angrily, "They were attacked by a group of insurrectionists."

Gobus snapped his head toward Mallak. "That's not what I asked. How was *this* soldier killed?"

"Guard!" Mallak screamed.

Instantly, the guard entered the room, sword in hand after hearing the scream from his emperor, no doubt fearful that he was being attacked and ready to defend him.

"Put your sword down," Mallak ordered. "How did the soldier who was carrying this sword die?" It was more of a command than a question.

"He was run through from behind by a sword, which killed him. Also, his right arm was severed off. Two of the other soldiers who were killed had arrows through their necks. But this one did not."

"Give me your sword." Gobus held out his hand to the guard.

The guard reacted by stepping back into a defense stance, his hand on the hilt of his sword, ready to draw it and defend his emperor.

Gobus smiled. "Guard, if I wanted to kill him, he would be dead. And that sword would not provide you or him any type of defense."

The guard looked at Mallak, who nodded. "Give it to him."

After Gobus had the sword, Mallak dismissed the guard.

Gobus looked at the sword in his hand. "Arrows through the neck, swords through the back. This person was not alone."

"He must have a small army," Mallak spat out.

"Or a small following."

Gobus twirled the guard's sword with his hand. "Do you have another sword here?"

"Yes."

"Get it." Gobus continued to twirl the sword.

When Mallak returned, Gobus held his sword in front of him with both hands. "Swing your sword with all your strength and sever this one into two pieces."

Mallak took a stance with his left foot forward. He swung his sword behind him, letting it rise above his head, and with a massive down thrust he slammed it against Gobus's sword. The two swords smashing together gave a resounding clang. The sword in Gobus's hand didn't budge. Mallak's ricocheted off and sent it, along with Mallak, to the dirty floor.

Mallak got up in a rage. "You used your powers to protect that sword and send me to the floor."

"Absolutely not," Gobus replied with indifference. "I used my powers only to hold the sword in one position, giving you a better chance of cutting it in two. Unfortunately"—Gobus examined the sword—"it did not even make a dent in the metal. That is disturbing."

Mallak rubbed his hands. The vibration and shock wave from the strike had sent painful aches up his arms.

"Put on your magic robe."

Moments later, Mallak returned with his robe draped over his shoulders, his arms pushing through the sleeves. The robe pulsated with dark-violet swirls that morphed into dark blue, green, and reds with silver sparks shooting across it.

"Now take up your sword again."

Gobus looked around the room, and his eyes settled on the coals of a recent fire that still glowed red in the fireplace hearth. He pointed to it. "I want you to focus as I have taught you. Draw the energy from the burning coals into your robe. Then transfer that energy into your sword when you are ready to strike again."

Mallak concentrated on the red-hot coals. His stare didn't waver as he fell into a slight trance. The robe pulsed deeper and deeper with changing colors that swirled around and around throughout it. Suddenly the sword he held in both hands also glowed. With a glint in his eyes, Mallak snapped his head up, focusing on the sword held outstretched in Gobus's hands. Mallak gave a guttural scream and swung his sword high over his head and then down onto Gobus's sword.

This time when the two blades made contact there was no resounding clang or backlash. Mallak's sword tore into Gobus's and stopped. It had penetrated, but it did not sheer it in half.

Mallak breathed heavily, sucking air in and out of his mouth as if he had just run from as far as one could see to where he was standing now. Mallak's vision cleared, and he looked at the two swords. He worked his sword back and forth to separate it from Gobus's.

Gobus glanced at the gouge in his sword. "I fear you have a big problem."

"Explain."

"Think of how long it took you to gather and transfer the energy from the coals to your robe, then into your sword. What would you do on a battlefield? Ask your opponent to stop and wait for you to energize your sword to smite them?" Gobus gave a laugh at the thought. "The person who did that"—Gobus pointed at the two halves of the sword that lay on the table—"had no idea of the extent of his powers."

"Why do you say that?" Mallak asked in an inquisitive voice.

"The soldier was run through with a sword from back to front. That is what killed him. If his powers were known, he would not have needed any help dispatching the soldier. But, more importantly, you needed time to muster the power into your sword to partially cut this sword in half. There is no time on the battlefield. There is also no specific source of energy to draw from. That"—again Gobus pointed to the two halves of the swords on the table—"was done instantly. A reaction. I assume the person who did this was consumed with fear. Fear is an immensely powerful energy. He was able to pull the energy he needed from inside of him without the need to draw it from an outside source. And that makes him an extremely dangerous and potentially powerful adversary."

"Why do you say potentially?" Mallak spit out the words.

"Because at this point it is clear he does not know, or understand, the depth of his power. But when he does, you, My Emperor, will have a major problem." Gobus had a sarcastic smile on his face.

"So, what do you recommend?" Mallak shot back at Gobus.

"You will need to work with me to increase your powers. And you need to find him and kill him."

3 2

A squad of Mallak's soldiers—ten swordsmen and ten archers—stood around the edge of Nilewood's town square. The captain of the squad waited quietly for a moment for the undivided attention from those in and around the square.

When he felt all eyes were on him, he spoke. "Let it be known that Emperor Mallak puts forth by decree today that anyone who comes forward with information that leads to the capture or death of those responsible for the death of his soldiers in the nearby woods will be rewarded by not having to pay their taxes to the emperor for one year.

"Let it also be known that anyone found harboring those responsible or of hiding knowledge of their whereabouts will forfeit their land to the emperor and will be jailed."

The captain looked around and saw that no one was making direct eye contact with him, except for one person who looked him directly in the eyes and gave a slight nod. Then that person looked to a side alleyway. The captain nodded back.

After the captain was done reading the decree, all those present moved on with their lives, heads down, not looking at anyone or anything lest it be construed that they knew something. In those moments, an elderly male with a frown etched on his face slipped down the alleyway and deep around the corner so as not to be seen by anyone passing by. Moments later, the captain joined him.

"I was told by one of my soldiers you had the information that we seek." the captain said.

⧼

The pounding on the wooden door was so intense, the dirt embedded between the planks shot into the air, filling it with a cloud of haziness. Iggy, Lecque, and Raraesa sitting at the table in quiet conversation, all jumped up.

Lecque cautiously opened the door with his hand on the hilt of his sword.

"Out here, *now!*" Ankter screamed. "We need to talk!"

Standing firm in the doorway, Lecque took his hand off his sword, letting it settle back into its sheath. "What do you want?"

Ankter stepped back fifteen feet away from the door. Lecque followed him, leaving the door wide open. "I will ask you one more time before I physically throw you off my land. What do you want?"

"I told you that boy would bring nothing but trouble to us! He needs to go!"

"The only one leaving is you." Lecque pointed down the path that led off his land.

Iggy moved closer to the door so he could hear. Raraesa joined him, standing behind him.

"Three days ago," Ankter continued with spittle spraying out with each word, "five soldiers were slaughtered. They had arrows through their throats, along with being run through by swords. One, they say, had his sword cleanly cut in half and his arm severed. They also say Mallak is enraged and has vowed brutal retaliation."

"And why do you think Iggy, or I, had anything to do with this?"

Ankter, now red in the face spat out, "He is dangerous, I tell you."

Iggy turned to Raraesa. "I'm tired of this." Iggy stormed out the

277

front door, screaming, "So you think I'm dangerous? Well, then, you should be afraid! Really afraid!"

Ankter drew his sword. "You come at me, you little runt, and I will cut you down."

Iggy's hands shot behind his back. Raraesa, two steps behind him saw the Swords of Nostaw were instantly in Iggy's hands.

"Iggy! No!" Raraesa caught up to him, placing her hands on his arms, stopping him from bringing them around to his front and revealing the swords. "Do not do it, Iggy," she whispered into his ear. "Put them away. If he sees them, you will never have any peace."

Iggy hesitated for a moment then opened his palms, and the swords disappeared.

"Sheath your sword!" Lecque demanded. "Or you will have me to face. Not some little boy."

Ankter placed his sword into its sheath. "This is not over, by any means."

"For your sake, it better be," Lecque shot back.

"You cannot be by his side and protect him every minute of the day." Ankter sneered.

Iggy replied with pure venom in his voice and a death stare at Ankter. "If you think I had anything to do with those soldiers' deaths, then you will be careful about threatening me. You should be incredibly careful."

Two dozen soldiers rushed out of the woods. Some with swords in hand, others with arrows in their bows, pulled taut, ready to fly toward their intended targets. Iggy, Lecque, and Raraesa stopped moving but for their heads turning from side to side.

"So, Ankter, you now declare which side you are on," Lecque said. "You will live to regret it."

"At least I will live."

Raraesa placed her hand on Iggy's shoulder. "Stay calm," she whispered. "This is not a battle we can win. If you show your swords, you will be struck down with a dozen arrows."

"No." Ankter walked up to Lecque. "It is you who has brought this on yourself. I will not have our towns burned to the ground just to protect that kid. I do not know if either of you had anything to do with those soldiers' deaths. I really do not care. He means nothing to me, but our towns and citizens do. If giving him to Mallak will protect us, then that is my decision."

Ankter turned to the soldiers. "Take them."

⤜

Iggy, Lecque, and Raraesa sat on the forest floor, their hands tied in front. A fire crackled nearby. They were close enough to the fire so the warmth of it kept the damp night air at bay but not close enough to be warm. The soldiers sat on the opposite side of the fire, talking, laughing, and eating the three wild rabbits they had caught, killed, and roasted.

Ankter approached Lecque. "I am sorry it had to come to this. I had to make a decision for the good of our village."

Lecque spat on the ground. "That is what I think of your decision. You have sold us out. How much did they pay you?"

Ankter chuckled. "You think I did this for money? You are indeed naive and foolish. I did this because since that boy arrived, bad things have been happening."

"So, you fear a little boy."

"Apparently Mallak does. And I fear *him*," Ankter said, then left them, returning to the opposite side of the camp.

"We will get out of this," Raraesa said to Iggy.

"I'm sorry I couldn't help. If I could have only gotten my swords out—"

Lecque shook his head. "The moment they saw those swords you would have been cut down by a dozen arrows. No, at that moment we had no options. Raraesa, can you loosen the rope binding you?"

"No. It is too tight."

"Mine too," Iggy said.

"Then I think we should get some sleep," Lecque said.

279

∽

Hours later, the fire had died to glowing red coals. Two soldiers guarded the campground while the rest of the group slept.

The quiet of the night forest was broken with a shout from one guard.

Iggy was the first to stir; he opened his eyes and studied the opposite side of the camp. A soldier stood with his sword in hand. An instant later, Iggy watched as the soldier lunged forward and drove his sword through a figure standing in the shadows. Instead of a groan or cry, Iggy heard a deep guttural laugh. The figure in the shadow grabbed the blade that stuck halfway into his abdomen and pulled it out. The soldier stepped back, only to be run through with his own sword. Before the soldier's body touched the ground, a hand reached out and touched him. Instantly, he turned to dust, which blew away on the slight breeze.

"Lecque, Raraesa, wake up!" Iggy stretched out his legs tied together at the ankles and kicked Lecque.

"What is it?" Lecque asked, quickly coming awake.

Iggy whispered, "Look!"

Raraesa, also awake, turned her attention, along with Lecque and Iggy, to the far side of the camp. Soldiers jumped out of their slumber and grabbed their swords. Others pulled back the strings of their bows and let arrows fly toward the intruder. Multiple arrows landed true, driving into their mark piercing the intruder closing in on them.

In response, it laughed, pulled the arrows out, and dispatched any soldier who dared get as close as the tip of his sword could reach. The deep laugh echoed throughout the camp and forest, instilling fear. Soldiers took up a defensive stance, allowing the creature to come to them. This the creature gladly did. With every approaching step another soldier turned to dust.

Iggy tried to push himself back into the darkness of the tree line that was a good ten feet behind him. But, with his ankles tightly bound and his wrists and hands wrapped into each other, all he could do was roll. That did not get him far, as he rolled into the side of a rock and stopped with his face pointing directly at the action.

"What do we do?" Iggy whispered to Lecque and Raraesa, who had made the same rolling maneuver.

"There is nothing we can do," Raraesa said, her own anxiety breaking through her normally calm demeanor.

The three watched helplessly as every solder disappeared.

The last man standing was Ankter, who stood frozen for a moment before turning and running into the forest and was gone. Ankter ran through the woods, his legs quivering with pain as he tried to will them to move faster and carry him farther away from the horror he had just witnessed. His breathing was hard as he struggled. His breath was hot, burning in his chest, finally forcing him to stop for a moment. He leaned one hand against a tree to keep him from falling to the forest floor. He bent over as his heart pounded in his chest. His anxiety rose higher because he was stopped and not moving away from the danger.

He stood up. "I have to keep going."

The moment he stood upright there was a whistle through the air and an arrow pierced his chest, its tip passing through him, impaling him onto the tree trunk. It was there he breathed his last breath.

With the last soldier gone, the creature looked up at the sky and let out a deafening howl of a laugh. Then, as quickly as he started to laugh, he stopped and turned to Iggy, Lecque, and Raraesa. It took a few steps toward them and stopped. Though it was dark, there was enough ambient light from the stars and moon to illuminate the face of the creature.

Iggy gasped—it was the Death Knight. Glowing black lifeless eyes scanned them as they lay helpless on the ground. Iggy gagged as the smell of rotting death permeated his nostrils. Flies buzzed around the moldy, decaying skin that hung off its skeletal face.

Dead silence fell around Iggy. "What do we do?" he whispered.

No reply came. The Death Knight took a few steps closer to them, sheathed his sword, turned, and walked to the opening in the woods he had entered from.

In the darkness, Iggy saw another shadow. The Death Knight stopped beside it.

❧

With its menacing, raspy voice, the Death Knight said, "I have kept my part of the bargain. You best keep yours." The Death Knight paused. "How do you know he is capable?"

"Because a father always knows what his son is capable of." Kylian looked at Iggy. "How do you know the sword will be used for its desired function?"

The Death Knight stared at Lecque. "Because as you say, a father knows what his son is capable of doing." The Death Knight turned and vanished into the woods.

❧

Lecque stared at the person still hidden in the darkness of the trees. "Who are you?"

The reply was haunting, the voice soft and weak. "I knew your father. He was a good man."

Again, Lecque called out. "Who are you?"

"I am Kylian. Your father did not deserve to die the way he did. He would be proud of the man you have become, and, Raraesa, the woman you have become. The three of you are safe for now. That may not last, though." He turned and melted into the darkness of the woods.

❧

Iggy, Lecque, and Raraesa lay on their sides on the forest floor. Lecque had stopped struggling against his rope-bound wrists for a moment. "My hands are bound so tight I cannot even wiggle my fingers. Raraesa, try wriggling over to me. You might be able to use your teeth to loosen the knots in my ropes."

There was a rustle in the woods. The three heard it and froze. A figure wearing a robe with a hood shadowing the face beneath stood in an opening between two trees, a bow slung over the shoulder and a quiver filled with arrows on the person's back. As the figure passed the fire, her hood fell back to reveal a beautiful woman with deep, mocha skin and intelligent eyes. She approached Iggy, Lecque, and Raraesa, with fluid grace in her walk, and pulled out a knife. She bent down, slid the knife between Lecque's wrists, and with one quick, upward pull cut through the ropes, setting Lecque's hands free. She then freed Raraesa and Iggy.

"Thank you," Raraesa said.

Iggy untangled the ropes on his hands and blurted out, "Who are you?"

"Scathach."

"You are the famous warrior Scathach?"

After the slightest of nods, Scathach turned to Lecque. "You can safely make it home. There are no other soldiers out this way. No one knows what happened here. I suggest you keep it that way unless you want Mallak and his soldiers on top of you again."

Lecque rubbed his forehead, a worried look on his face. "One did get away. He was the one who turned us over to the soldiers. He ran through the woods."

"He is now part of the woods. He will not be causing any more trouble. Walk with me, Lecque."

"How do you know my name?"

"I am Scathach. I know many things. Let us walk." She turned and strode to the opposite side of the camp, Lecque a half step behind.

Stopping, Scathach spoke in a low tone. "Keep Iggy close to you. Train him. When he is ready, he will need to find me for his final training."

"Scathach, we are up against a Death Knight. We need you, not Iggy."

"I cannot kill the Death Knight; you have Iggy. Train him."

"Are you saying Iggy can kill the Death Knight?"

"That remains to be seen. You must train him, though, and push him to the next levels."

"What do you mean, the next levels?"

Scathach smiled. "He is a Nostaw Warrior, is he not?"

Lecque looked at Iggy, who was rubbing his wrists and ankles where the ropes had been tied. "If he cannot kill the Death Knight, who then can?" When he turned back for an answer, Scathach was gone.

33

Mallak stood in the dungeon, astounded at what he saw. The bars of the cell that once held Kylian in confinement had been cleanly cut off, leaving an opening wide enough for anyone to walk through.

He bent forward and touched the end of one of the cut bars. It was smooth as he ran his fingers over it. The iron had been melted through.

"Just like the sword, cut in half," he whispered.

"Emperor Mallak—" the soldier started but was instantly stopped by Mallak, who raised his hand sharply into the air.

"Did anyone see who came down and when my brother left?" Mallak asked, rather calmly.

"No, My Emperor. The soldiers guarding the entrance to the dungeon are gone. As if they disappeared."

Mallak turned with no further words and left.

꩜

Kylian meandered around Ansel's blacksmith shop, which was illuminated by a smattering of lit candles.

Ansel entered with a satchel and placed it on one table. "I brought you some food for now to tide you over."

Kylian picked up the sandwich Ansel had taken out of the satchel for him and looked it over. His voice was a soft whisper and raspy as he asked, "What is this?"

"That is a ham and cheese sandwich. It is one of Iggy's creations."

After taking a bite, Kylian devoured the sandwich. "That was really excellent," he said as he wiped his mouth on his sleeve.

"I must say, Iggy has surprised us on many occasions."

"Thank you for keeping me informed of his progress since he returned."

"At times it was difficult getting information to you. I am sure you would have done the same for me."

"How is the sword coming along?"

Ansel got up and retrieved the partially flattened piece of metal Iggy had been working on for weeks. "As you can see, the outside shell is gone. You were correct. He had the capability to crack it. But getting him to succeed was trying at times," Ansel said. "Did you tell him that your wife was his mother?"

"No. Have you told him his mother is your sister? And that you are both Wiates?"

"No. I did not feel he was ready to know his true heritage yet," Ansel said. "Where will you go now?"

"I will go to LATO. They will protect me."

"The Lake Above the Ocean. No one knows where it is. How will you find it?"

"Ah, my friend. I have known where it is since I was a boy. I visited it many times."

"You are full of surprises. When will you leave?"

"Now. It is dark with a crescent moon. I will be able to travel there unnoticed in the darkness." Kylian let out a sad sigh. "I am sorry I cannot stay longer. We have so much to catch up on. But the longer I stay, the more danger I put you in."

Kylian placed his palm on Ansel's shoulder and gave it a friendly squeeze. "You know I need you to look after Iggy. Keep him safe and, most importantly, he must finish that sword. Much depends on it."

ABOUT THE AUTHOR

Photo credit: Le Petit Studio www.Petitpics.com

Being an Emergency Room physician for close to forty years, the pandemic brought forth new horrors in the ER. Writing this fantasy story about Ignatius became an enjoyable escape for Dr. Mucci from all that was happening in the real world.